THE WITCH'S REBELS BOOK SIX

D1603626

Rebel Reborn
Copyright © 2019 by Sarah Piper
SarahPiperBooks.com

ISBN-13: 978-1-948455-11-4

THE WITCH'S REBELS

Shadow Kissed

Darkness Bound

Demon Sworn

Blood Cursed

Death Untold

Rebel Reborn

THE WITCH'S MONSTERS

Blood and Midnight

VAMPIRE ROYALS OF NEW YORK

Dorian & Charlotte

Dark Deception

Dark Seduction

Dark Obsession

Gabriel & Jacinda

Heart of Thorns

Heart of Fury

Heart of Flames

TAROT ACADEMY

ONE

DARIUS

From the moment my fangs pierced her flesh, I knew only her blood on my lips, the warm and salty taste of it bursting across my tongue as it slowly filled my mouth. I swallowed once, twice, unable to stifle a groan of raw pleasure as I continued to suck.

A flame flickered to life inside my chest, then ignited.

I was burning. Raging.

All for her. My witch. My love. My eternal mate, in this lifetime and all that would follow.

I would die for you, Gray Desario…

The words escaped my lips unbidden as I finally broke our connection, forcing the orgasmic flames in my blood to smolder, ignoring the ache in my very being that so desperately wanted more. That would *always* want more when it came to Gray. But she hadn't yet turned; some part of me knew that if I took even a single swallow more, I would certainly kill her.

I lifted her off the ground and held her against my chest, burying my face in her hair, inhaling her scent. The gray mist of her soul had already slipped from between her lips, and now it floated freely, mesmerizing us all.

Jael whispered his fae magic, the very cadence of it so lovely it seemed to be weaving a spell around my heart as well. Slowly, peacefully, Gray's soul drifted toward the moonglass held reverently in the fae prince's hands.

"Holy shit," Asher whispered, and we continued to watch in awe as the essence of the woman we loved filled the glass sphere like smoke caught in a bottle, light pulsing from its misty depths.

Even the very winter's night seemed to be holding its breath until the last wisp of her soul was safely contained, and Jael sealed the glass and lifted his hands toward the moon, thanking her.

Tears streaked Liam's face, his wide, blue eyes like twin orbs in the dim. Gone was the omnipotent, ancient being we'd come to know as Death; he seemed in that moment quite young, and quite human.

His origins, his mysteries remained his and his alone. But there was one secret even the Great Transformation Himself could no longer hide:

He'd fallen in love with her.

I averted my gaze, feeling the need to give him privacy.

The woods surrounding our moonlit cemetery had gone silent during the spell. Before we'd begun, we'd sent the remainder of the group back to base camp under the protection of Elena, her shifter team, and one of Gray's hounds. The other paced a perimeter twenty feet out, keeping one ever-watchful eye on Gray, the other on the darkness beyond.

Snow continued to fall all around us, collecting in tiny drifts on the headstones, filling in our blood-soaked boot prints, erasing all evidence of our earlier battle. Gray's body began to tremble in my arms, but that was to be expected; the transition was never easy.

"It is done," Jael said softly, bringing the orb close against his chest. We locked eyes in that moment, mirror images, each one cradling a precious piece of the woman I loved.

I nodded, and he bowed his head in acknowledgment.

It was a moment of peace and understanding in an otherwise treacherous night, and everyone seemed to feel it at the same time, all of us releasing a collective sigh.

Then the others looked to me, to the woman lying limp in my arms.

"She *will* survive the change," I said, even as the tremor continued to snake through her body, even as the white mist of her breath ceased, her lungs no longer requiring air. "I can feel the life force inside of her. She's stronger than any of us ever realized."

"Stubborn as hell, too," Emilio said, and the rest of us let out a quick laugh. Stubborn as hell? Yes, that about summed it up. Who else could've talked us into under-taking such a risk but the fiercely beautiful, determined, impossibly stubborn witch we'd all fallen in love with?

Lowering my eyes to the moonglass in Jael's hands, I asked, "What of her soul?"

I was as desperate for the answer as I was afraid of it. Caught up in the intensity of Gray's plan, none of us had stopped to talk through the logistics of what would come after. By the time we'd agreed to support her plan, it had been enough to know that her soul would not be instantly damned.

But now?

"I must take her to my home realm," Jael said plainly. "It's the only safe place for her now. My family will protect the moonglass until it comes time for her to honor the contract with Sebastian."

"Your *family*?" Ronan's eyes turned demon black, his shoulders bunching with tension. "And what happens when the wind changes direction, and Queen Sheyah decides it's a fine day to stab us in the nuts?"

"My mother may be cold and calculating," Jael said, "but she's not cruel, nor is she a traitor to her blood. She will honor my wishes, Ronan. You have my word."

"Jael, there is *no* room for error on this," Emilio said firmly. "No room for petty squabbles, judgments, or old vendettas. This is Gray's *soul*. Should it fall into the wrong hands, even in your realm..."

The wolf trailed off, turning his face toward the moonlight, casting the new worry lines around his eyes into sharp relief.

I couldn't blame him. I didn't know which vendettas he referred to, but I didn't need specifics. The Seelie queen was a notoriously conniving woman; she never formed an alliance unless there was something in it for her, and like most bargains struck at an hour of desperation, her allegiance never came without cost.

I suspected she was one of the reasons—if not *the* reason —Jael and Kallayna had left their realm and made a new home in the Bay in the first place. Now Jael wanted to bring Gray's soul back there? Under the protection of the woman who—if the centuries-old rumors held even a whiff of truth —had once burned an entire village of humans and their livestock on the mere *suspicion* that they'd been harboring a runaway fae child?

"I have given you my *word*." Jael's yellow eyes glowed fiercely, his brow drawn tight. "Never mind that Gray has become important to me as a leader, a warrior, as well as a friend. Her soul will be well-protected. I shall give my life to that end, if it comes to it."

"You've been more than loyal, prince," Liam said.

"It's not his loyalty we're worried about," Asher said. "It's that whole 'if it comes to it' part."

"It *won't* come to it," Jael insisted, but I wasn't convinced. None of us were, and in the uncertain silence that followed, the fae prince finally exploded.

"Gentlemen," he began, his voice full of fire, "I have risked my sister's life and my own to bring you intelligence from the Bay. I have fought by your sides in battles I could just as well have left behind, narrowly escaping an army of hybrids intent on burning me alive and nearly succeeding. I have risked eternal banishment from all the realms by calling upon forbidden moon magic, all in service to the woman I've come to call a close friend. I did not take such actions only to betray her at the very last."

"Jael," I began, but he would not relent, his entire body tense but for his hands, in which he held the moonglass as gently as a soap bubble.

"I would not take her within a *galaxy* of my realm if I believed for one moment my family would bring her harm." Jael's voice shook with defiance. "I understand your concern for her, but I beseech you to take an accurate accounting of my proven fidelity before accusing me *or* my family of future treasons."

Emilio lifted his palms in a gesture of peace, but Ronan and Asher were still wound up.

That Jael believed he could protect her was obvious. But could we really trust Queen Sheyah, regardless of Jael's noble intentions? And what of her royal guard, her servants, her subjects? When had Jael last communicated with his family? How could he be certain he'd even find welcome in his realm, let alone protection for the soul of a human witch-turned-vampire he'd just risked his own eternal existence to save?

I closed my eyes and pulled Gray tight against my chest, my blood humming in recognition at the blood now flowing through her veins. We were beyond connected, beyond bound, beyond mated.

We were one.

Trust him…

The message was faint but clear, imprinted from one

vampire mind to another. The realization nearly made me weep.

She truly was assimilating.

Unconscious as her body was, Gray's mind was right here with us—right here with me. She trusted Jael. And as much as I hated the idea of letting her soul out of our sight, I knew what Gray had known from the very moment she'd made the decision to turn:

There were no other options.

Opening my eyes, I looked from Ronan to Emilio to Asher to Liam, nodding at each before my gaze finally came to rest on Jael's still-smoldering yellow eyes.

"Gray entrusted you with the extraction and guidance of her soul," I said, granting him the same small bow he'd offered me earlier. "We entrust you now to protect it in whatever way you deem best."

Ronan blew out a tense breath, but no one said a word to contradict me. We'd all come together to support Gray in her decision to change, and that—like so many things we'd done and shared together on this journey, whether I could remember the particulars or not—bonded us once again as brothers.

Jael wasted no more time.

"We must move quickly," he said, "while night still holds. I need to draw upon the moon's power once more, if she'll allow it, and weave a portal spell to open a doorway back to my realm."

"How long will it take?" I asked, eyeing the expanse above the snowy treetops. The sky was still inky black, but soon enough the sun would begin her ascent. I'd very much prefer Gray and I were back at basecamp with time to spare before the first rays touched the earth.

"Can you guarantee me complete silence and zero interruptions?" He headed off to find a clear spot beyond the headstones. He knelt upon the snow, nestling the moonglass into a downy drift at his side. "If so, it shouldn't take more than—"

The rest of his words cut off abruptly as a blinding pain split my skull.

It unfolded like a car crash—time slowing for an eternity before zooming forward, leaving my mind in a frenzied blur, uncertain where one moment ended and another began.

The agony and confusion brought me to my knees.

It was all I could do to shield Gray from the impact as we hit the ground, my head spinning.

"Beaumont!" Ronan shouted, but I couldn't see him, barely registering the motion of his body lunging for me. Someone else scooped up Gray, and I bent forward and pressed my forehead against the snow, desperate for something—anything—to numb the pain.

Useless.

My body shook, head to toe, the tremble so violent I bit my tongue. Blood filled my mouth, and the walls inside my mind burst like ancient dams, ushering in a flood of disconnected images and sounds and scents, each one unlocking another and another and another, slicing through me like hot blades. Arms and legs wild with spasms, I roared into the night, unable to contain the torment, certain my ears were bleeding.

"Darius? What's happening?" Someone was at my side, a warm hand on the back of my neck, another flat on my back. Ronan's? Liam's? I had no idea. There was only the torture unfolding behind my eyes. Only the haunting howl of a thousand ghosts inside my skull. Only the taste of Gray's blood welling up from within.

Only... only memories.

I managed to get to my knees again, and clamped my hands around my head, desperately trying to keep my skull from exploding. A flurry of images and sights and sounds poured unbidden into my mind, imprinting themselves all at once, disconnected and fragmented, but... but *mine*, I realized suddenly. Every last one of them was mine— flashes of the life I'd lived and lost, the lifetimes I'd rebuilt in the decades and centuries that followed.

Memories.

Memories of my wife and children, the family I'd mourned on so many long, lonely nights.

Memories of my brother, my turning, the anger that had burned like hot coals inside my chest when he'd stolen my mortal life.

Memories of friends come and gone, of careers, of homes.

Memories of everything I'd once loved.

And then—impossibly sweet, impossibly precious— memories of a brand new love, unfolding as gently as a spring bud, then rapidly growing into a flowering vine that had somehow crept in behind my walls and blossomed, wrapping itself so thoroughly around my heart I could scarcely remember a time when it hadn't been part of me, nor I part of it.

Gray. My witch. My little brawler. My vampire. My queen.

I remembered the night we'd spent in the cabin in the Shadowrealm, making love until we'd nearly no strength left in our bones, chasing away the cold with kisses and caresses. I remembered the heartbreak in her eyes as I told her how I'd been turned. I remembered the taste of her kiss, the promises inherent in each and every one.

I remembered the words she'd uttered so breathlessly at the mouth of the hell portal.

I love you, Darius...

I remembered my own words sliding into my consciousness, balancing on the tip of my tongue, desperate to be heard.

It seems I've fallen in...

The last had remained locked inside, stowed away as we came under attack from the demons that would steal my memories—memories that had just been returned to me.

Gray had saved me in all the ways that counted—then and now.

Her blood, our connection... she'd been right to trust it.

I would never doubt it.

My love for her knew no limits, no bounds, and deep inside me, that feeling expanded endlessly, chasing away the worst of the pain, steadying my hands. I was falling, experiencing each moment with her for the very first time, again and again and again.

"I'm in love with her," I announced, my tears turning to laughter as I felt the force of that love hit me full on. With Ronan's help, I got to my feet, swaying against his side. I was unsteady, but suddenly I felt unstoppable.

"For fuck's sake, Beaumont." Ronan gave me a shove. "We thought you were dying, asshole."

"Ah, but I was. And now I've been reborn!" Again I laughed, bordering on maniacal, and grabbed his shoulders, hauling him in for a fierce hug. "You don't understand, demon. I fell in *love* with her. I know I did."

"Yeah, you and me and everyone here." He pulled back and narrowed his eyes at me. "What's going on in that head of yours?"

"More than you know, friend," I said. "I *remember* it. All of it. All of you!"

Ronan glared at me a moment longer, then his eyes widened as the realization finally dawned. He gripped my arms, a smile cracking his stoic face. "You're shitting me. You fucking remember?"

"It must've been the—"

"Hate to break up the lovefest, but, uh…" Asher crouched down next to Sparkle and followed her line of sight to a dense copse of trees beyond the cemetery. The hound's haunches were raised, a menacing growl reverberating from her chest.

Asher got to his feet and rolled his neck, the bones cracking. "Fight or flight, assholes. We got company."

TWO

DARIUS

"Sellouts." Asher spat at the ground, leaving a smattering of blood in the snow. His jaw was red and swollen where he'd taken a hit, and his blue eyes blazed in the darkness, the adrenaline from the fight still zipping through his blood. "My guess? The inside team called for reinforcements, but these fucks wanted no part of it. They took their time getting here like a bunch of pussies, waiting until our numbers thinned out and the spellcasters left so they could get the drop on the rest of us."

"Agreed." I bent down to scoop up a handful of snow, using it to rinse the taste of hunter blood from my mouth. After the incident at the motel when I'd attacked two of them and overdosed—a brutal scene I now remembered with utmost clarity—I refused to swallow even a drop of their bitter poison.

There'd been about a dozen of them tonight, all human, hiding out in the dense trees and waiting to make their move. They'd underestimated us, though, as hunters with big egos and small pricks were wont to do. With Gray's loyal hound leading the charge and Emilio's wolf a close second, we'd left Liam to watch over Jael and Gray, bolted into the woods, and sliced through their ranks like a hot knife through butter.

Back on the other side of the cemetery, Jael continued to work on the portal spell, Liam doing his best to stand guard. He'd wrapped Gray in another cloak, and now he held her close, stroking her hair. The sight brought me comfort.

Liam was one of us now.

We're definitely *going to need a bigger bed…*

"You think we're in the clear?" Ronan asked, reclaiming my attention.

I turned to see him rubbing snow into his hands in an attempt to clean the blood. Moments earlier, when the last hunter standing had given us a rather detailed account of what he'd been planning to do to our witch, I'd watched with delight—and a good measure of awe—as Ronan tore out the bastard's throat with his bare hands.

I scanned the woods behind him, taking in as much sensory detail as I could. Save for our movements, the night had fallen silent once again. The air was tinged with the scent of human blood, but if any hunters had survived our attack, they'd scampered back the way they'd come.

"The last of the rats have either expired or fled back to their cages," I confirmed.

"For now," Asher said. "But we're still exposed out here.

14

Gray's immobilized, Liam's got no defensive powers, we can't risk anything happening to the moonglass, and we have *no* idea what other surprises are waiting for us in the woods."

"You think there are more fae out there?" Ronan asked.

Hunters were one thing; relatively easy to contain, they didn't stand a chance against a vampire, a wolf, a hellhound, and a pair of demons. But the dark fae could present a serious challenge—especially if there were a lot of them.

"Unlikely," Asher said. "The fae aren't fucking cowards. If they were anywhere in the vicinity, they'd already be on top of us. Nah, I'm more concerned about hunters playing games. We're stronger and faster, but that doesn't mean they can't fuck with us. Sun's not too far off now, and like I said, Gray and Liam are basically sitting ducks. They need to get the fuck back to the lodge. You too, Beaumont."

I nodded, conceding the point. All the vampire strength and speed in the world couldn't compete with a sunrise. "But we're not going anywhere until Jael—"

The force of the explosion knocked us to the ground, the light blinding.

"What the *fuck*?" Ronan shouted. We got to our feet and shook off the impact, trying to see through the thick blanket of smoke engulfing the entire cemetery.

Seconds later, Liam walked out of the smoke like an apparition, carrying the still-unconscious Gray.

A bolt of horror pierced my heart.

"Where is the moonglass?" I demanded.

But Liam seemed unfazed, his eyes cold and mysterious once again, just like his voice. "Jael has completed his mission."

"Successfully?" I asked.

"He and the moonglass have vanished, along with all signs of the portal."

"I'll count that as a win," Asher said.

"He could've been a bit more subtle about it," I snapped, brushing the snow from my backside. But with Gray's soul safely out of harm's way, and her body still whole, still assimilating, it was nearly impossible to hold onto my anger. By the time Liam placed her back in my arms, there wasn't even room inside me for mild annoyance. Her presence immediately calmed me, steadied me, and again I buried my face in her hair, taking in her scent.

She was still unconscious, which was a blessing. Yes, her mother had survived the turning. But Gray was the first witch I'd ever personally known to survive the change—to begin the assimilation process. I had no idea how her body would react once it completed the transition—I only knew that she'd be hungry. Ravenous.

We needed to get her secured and sedated before she became conscious of that.

Holding her tightly against my chest, I nodded toward a clearing in the distance—our way out. "We've still got a bit of a trek ahead of us, and it looks like the snow is picking up again." I stepped over the blood-soaked body of one of the hunters we'd dispatched. "Let's just hope this was the last and only ambush."

"Hope isn't a viable strategy, bloodsucker." Asher spit out another mouthful of blood, then rubbed his swollen jaw and sighed, exhausted but resolute. He looked to Ronan, as if asking permission.

"Do what you gotta do, brother." Ronan clapped him on the back, then whistled for the hound, who bounded out of the dense knot of trees, her fangs and muzzle dripping with hunter blood. Seemed Ronan had interrupted her midnight snack, but if she harbored any resentment, she wasn't showing it. She pressed her nose against Ronan's leg, and he reached down to scratch behind her ears.

"What is it you have to do?" I asked Asher.

"Tie up a few loose ends." Gesturing for the wolf, he said, "*El Lobo* and I will meet you guys back at the lodge in the morning. Don't wait up."

"Where in the bloody hell are you going?" I asked.

At this, Emilio cocked back his massive furry head and howled at the moon, his battle cry haunting and clear, a chilling warning to all who'd dare cross his path tonight.

Asher flashed a feral grin, teeth glinting in the moonlight. "We're going hunting, brother. Take care of our girl."

THREE

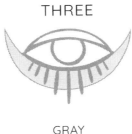

GRAY

So. Much. Blood.

The taste of it in my mouth, the smell of it in my nose, the viscous feel of it sliding deliciously across my tongue. My veins hummed with it, magic and power and strength, all of it crackling to life with a fierce intensity that made me feel like I could burn down the world with little more than a pointed glare.

I was born for this…

Flat on my back in nothing more than a T-shirt, underwear, and a thin sheet over my legs, I opened my eyes to complete darkness and tried to sit up. My body refused to obey. The blood inside me was buzzing and alive, my senses finely attuned, but my muscles felt slow and sluggish.

I sucked in a cool breath—the first I'd taken since I'd awoken—and realized at once we'd made it back to HQ. I could smell the familiar mix of salty ocean air and fresh-cut wood from the lodge's timber framing, and the scents of all the witches and men and shifters who'd occupied it, every one of them clear and distinct. Strongest of all was Darius's —that heady blend of leather and expensive whiskey that always made my blood sing.

Again, I tried to rise.

No luck.

My belly turned over with a terrible growl, empty. Craving. Demanding.

"You're hungry," announced a familiar voice, and slowly I turned my head to find my vampire standing near my bedside, still as the darkness itself. My eyes had already adjusted to the lack of light, and now I saw him as clearly as if he were bathed in afternoon sunlight. I blinked, not believing it, but the shape of him only sharpened—glossy dark hair, full lips that made my thighs clench with fresh, hot desire. His eyes narrowed as he took me in, his honey-brown gaze both tender and severe.

"Darius," I whispered, but there was no time to wonder about his breathtaking beauty or my enhanced vision. My stomach turned over again, bringing with it a wave of nausea so severe it made me gasp.

I needed to move, to feed, and again I tried to sit up, but the firm, comforting press of his palm against my chest steadied me. I hadn't seen the movement, but now he was standing right next to me, the scent of him nearly overpowering my senses.

I wanted him. Badly. My mouth watered for it, my core

suddenly burning with the unquenched flames of desire. Everything inside me craved his touch.

My hunger for him was even more desperate than my hunger for blood.

I'm going to die without it...

"What's.... happening to me?" I sputtered. "I feel like... like I'm..." I tried to reach for him, but my arms were locked in place, immobilized despite the fact that my skin felt like it was on fire.

No, not immobilized. Restrained, I saw now. Same with my legs and torso. I tugged hard against the binds—thick leather straps fastened tightly around my wrists, ankles, and across my lower rib cage.

They'd tied me to the bed. Under any other circumstances, I might've been turned on by the idea. Now, it just made me rage inside.

Still. I knew it had to be done. After all, I was a deadly predator now, recovering in a lodge full of warm bodies, every single one of them pulsing with thick, sweet blood.

A whimper escaped my lips.

"It's temporary," Darius assured me, his voice measured and tight. "Once we've regulated your blood intake and weened you off the hawthorn infusion, this arrangement won't be necessary."

"Infusion?"

He lifted the sheet covering my legs, revealing an IV taped to the top of my foot. I followed the tube to the bag dangling from the poster at the end of the bed, slowly meting out a clear liquid drip.

"It's on a time-release," he said.

Well, that explained the sluggishness I was feeling.

"After our return," he said, "I bathed you and helped you get settled in here. I've been with you ever since."

"Ever since when? How long was I out? Is everyone else okay? What about Jael? My sisters? Sparkle and Sunshine?"

"One question at a time, little brawler." Darius let out a low chuckle. "Let's see... Everyone is present and accounted for. Your sisters are well, chomping at the bit to see you, though we all agreed it would be best for the humans of the household to wait until you've fully stabilized before visiting. The hounds have scarcely left your side—I had to bribe them with raw steak just to get a few moments alone with you tonight. We've not heard from Jael, but he completed the portal spell and disappeared with your moonglass before we left the cemetery that night, and the queen has not declared war upon us, so we're assuming no news is good news on that front. All of the liberated prisoners are being treated for various medical issues and injuries, but everyone is expected to recover. As for you, you've been in and out of consciousness the better part of two days. This is the first time you've managed to stay with me for more than a few moments—speaking, besides."

My head was spinning. "Two *days*? I feel like I haven't eaten in months."

"Hours, actually." He rolled up his sleeve, revealing a muscled forearm and a wrist covered with punctures, dark bruises welling angrily beneath the skin.

The sight of it made me wince. For Darius to bruise and not immediately heal, I must've been pretty brutal, and I must've taken a lot from him.

"I'm sorry," I whispered.

"It's nothing, love. Few more hours, I'll be good as new. But my blood is a stopgap—not nearly enough to sustain you. You need non-vampire blood—preferably human. Quite a bit of it, at that."

My stomach growled again, and Darius replaced his palm on my chest, as if he'd sensed I needed his touch, needed him to keep me from slipping away. I closed my eyes and tried to ignore the parched feeling in my mouth, focusing instead on the rest of my body. My blood, singing and alive. My magic, crackling as always inside me, but more solid and sure than it'd ever felt before. I could hear laughter down on the first floor, the sounds of cooking in the kitchen, the splatter of wet snow against the window-panes. The curtains were open to let in the moonlight, but the night was dark and cloudy. When I inhaled, the wisdom of the sea filled my senses, sharp and ancient and as powerful as I felt inside.

My heart now beat more slowly than I remembered, but it was stronger, responding to Darius's touch with a deep familiarity.

"I survived," I said, the word itself bringing forth a rush of laughter. "I survived the turning."

"Yes, it appears your body has fully assimilated the change," he confirmed, his voice thick with a mixture of relief, surprise, and there, lurking just below the rest, a hint of sorrow.

I understood. This hadn't been his choice, after all, and I wasn't out of the woods just yet. Not until I could exist in the presence of others without trying to murder them.

A shudder wracked my body, but instead of passing as I'd expected, it intensified, rolling from head to toe and back up again. My teeth chattered, my fangs cutting through my gums, then sliding back in. Again and again. The taste of my own blood filled my mouth.

"D-D-Darius? What's happening now?"

"Shh, it's alright, love." Darius lifted the sheet and climbed into the bed next to me, his hand sliding under my T-shirt to trace a soft pattern on my belly. "This will pass."

"What is it? Why am I sh-shaking like this?"

"You're a vampire, little brawler," he said plainly. "A hungry one at that. Your instincts are telling you it's time to hunt."

Vampire...

Instincts...

Hunt...

The bed shook with my renewed efforts to escape— instinctual more than logical at this point—but the hawthorn had done its job. I couldn't break the binds.

"We can't grant you your freedom yet, Gray. You're too strong. If that primal part of you takes over, you could—"

"I get it, D," I snapped, but then I closed my eyes, forcing myself to count backward from ten, focusing on the feel of his touch until the tremble finally subsided.

None of this was Darius's fault—he was just doing what he had to do to keep everyone safe, including me. This was my choice, and I had to live with it. Besides, for the power and immortality of a vampire, hunger pangs and a few bouts of the shakes were a small price to pay.

I just hoped the transition period wouldn't last too long. Every hour I wasted in bed was another hour we were leaving Blackmoon Bay in the hands of Orendiel and the hunters.

And in the hands of my mother, a vampire-witch we now knew was the deadly, vulgar head of the world's most poisonous snake.

"My mother killed to feed herself," I said absently, my thoughts drifting back to the darkness of the crypt, the evidence we uncovered there.

"You will not be reduced to such savagery. Elena has reached out to her connection at the local hospital to procure what we need, and at present, our demons and the wolf are braving the weather to retrieve it. You'll have a fresh, humanely-harvested supply very soon."

"What about after? What happens when that runs out?"

"Then we'll find more."

"Darius, you need to eat, too. As will the vampires we rescued, including Fiona. We can't just drain the city's donor supply."

"No, I suppose we can't."

"And until we can figure out how to deal with this winter apocalypse," I said, glancing out the window as a fresh bout of wet snow slapped against the pane, "I'm pretty sure imported goods are in short supply."

"All true," he said, though he seemed completely unconcerned about our predicament.

"At some point, we'll need to—"

"At some point, at one point, another day, tomorrow, next week, next year, next century… All pointless frames of reference for us now."

"How do you figure?"

"Gray, you're an immortal. If you start worrying about everything that can go wrong, everything that can throw a wrench into your day…. Well, there are a hell of a lot more days to worry about now."

I closed my eyes as the brutal wind whipped another wave of slush against the lodge. Darius was right. I had to take things day by day or I'd drive us all mad.

"All things considered," he said, forcing a note of cheer into his voice, "you're handling this extremely well. Much better than most."

I nodded, forcing the desperate gnawing inside me to settle. I knew from the stories I'd heard—not to mention the things Darius had shared about his own turning—that things could've been so much worse for me.

"I guess that means I didn't slaughter anyone in the night, right?" I asked, only half-kidding.

"Well, let's see…" He tapped his lips, his tone light and teasing. "As of our last accounting, the casualties stood at four shredded bath towels, one shattered windowpane, an upended china cabinet full of porcelain shards formerly known as priceless antiques, two splintered dining chairs, and a fruitcake Verona was particularly proud of, but the rest of us secretly cheered for *that* loss. Oh, you also punched Asher in the mouth."

"Holy shit, Darius! Are you serious?"

Darius shrugged as if this was all par for the course. "To be fair, he had it coming. Your incubus gets rather mouthy when—"

"But how did I manage to do so much damage? I don't even remember coming home. I don't remember anything after the bite. And I'm tied up, besides!"

"Initially, we thought we could forgo the restraints, relying only on the hawthorn. But you're too strong, Gray. The few times you surfaced into consciousness were brief, but wild. You needed to feed, but my blood left you... Well, it left you a bit mad, to be honest. Asher insisted on trying to reason with you, convinced he could sweet-talk his way past thousands of years of predatory evolution." Darius shook his head, holding back a laugh. "The moment he unfastened one of your restraints, you clocked him."

Now I was laughing, too. The whole scene sounded pretty ridiculous—and one hundred percent Asher. "What did he do then?"

"Complimented your right hook, cursed up a storm, then retreated to a dark corner of the lodge with a bottle of tequila and a bag of frozen peas while I secured your restraints and got you calmed down. He hasn't gotten close since."

"I suppose I'll have to make it up to him at some point."

"I suppose." Darius nuzzled the skin behind my ear with a string of kisses I felt all the way to my toes. "But it seems you're through the worst of it, anyway."

"I hope so."

Most newborn vampires went absolutely wild with bloodlust. Without a present sire to tame them, to guide them through the early part of the change, to feed them and help them see the difference between instinct and choice...

I forced away the thoughts, unwilling to follow them any further. That wasn't going to happen to me. I *did* have a sire. One I trusted with my life.

With my heart.

"So I guess I have to call you *sire* now," I said, another laugh bubbling up as I turned to meet his eyes.

Darius flashed me a sexy smile, tracing his thumb across my bottom lip. "I wouldn't refuse a nickname like that, if you insisted, of course."

"You mean you like it better than D?"

"Hmm. That one *has* grown on me since our halcyon days in the Bay, but only because it's from you." He leaned forward, pressing a chaste kiss to my lips that only left me wanting more. Apparently, it left him wanting more, too. The hot, hard press of his cock against my thigh told me everything I needed to know about that.

I shifted closer to him, as much as I could with the binds, the movement inspiring a low groan from my vampire.

"So what now, *sire*?" I teased.

Darius laughed again, his breath tickling my cheeks. His

honey eyes sparkled with a thousand new facets, flecks of otherworldly colors and bottomless depths I was seeing with all new vision.

"Oh, little brawler," he breathed, the length of him growing harder. "First my delivery girl, then my witch, and now my vampire... You really *are* going to be the death of me, in this form or the next."

This form...

It hit me all over again—the magnitude of what we'd done. The magic of it. Sure, I was hungry, but I'd survived the change. I was a fucking *vampire*. A bloodsucker. An immortal supernatural. A fearsome, apex predator.

I must've said all of that out loud, because Darius suddenly laughed and said, "Yes, all of those things and more. So much more."

"Right," I said. "So, *how* is it that I'm not freaking out right now?"

At this, Darius could only shrug. "Because you're *you*, love." He kissed my eyebrow. "Completely baffling." The tip of my nose. "Wholly unusual." Then, just as softly as before, my lips. "An utter mystery, the likes of which none of us will ever fully solve."

I rolled my eyes. "In other words, a total weirdo."

"Yes," he teased, his lips still dangerously close to my mouth. "But you're *our* total weirdo, and that's the important bit."

I longed to touch his face, his hair, his lips. The tremor had returned, but this time it wasn't a side effect of the change. It was a side effect of the sexy, dangerous, seductive vampire in my bed, and the fact that my desire to feel him inside of me had sparked to life once again, smoldering between my thighs.

Why are you next to me instead of on top of me, vampire?

"What is it love?" he asked softly, his voice holding a note of playfulness. He knew damn well what it was, and he was enjoying every minute of tormenting me.

"I feel... hot," I said, my body already beginning to writhe under his intense gaze. "Under my skin. Inside me. Everywhere."

"Is that so?" He ran his finger down the front of my T-shirt to the top edge of my underwear, sliding it back and forth beneath the lace, his touch kindling the embers inside me into a blaze.

"Darius," I whispered, my eyes fluttering closed. "I'm dying."

"And I'm not unsympathetic to your plight." His fingers dipped lower, but not low enough. I arched closer, but he only pulled back, starting the whole torturous process again. He trailed those teasing fingers slowly down my T-shirt, back to the lace, sliding lazily down, down, down... then back out again.

Holy hell, bloodsucker.

"Could've fooled me," I snapped.

"Mmm. I remember the first thirst of a newborn vampire," he said, every word laced with seduction. "The need. Bone-deep, all-consuming, a blinding fire that rages unchecked. It's not just the blood you burn for now, is it?"

I shook my head, my mind and body both unraveling.

Vampire influence had no power over another vampire, but Darius's words were having the same effect, winding me tighter, leaving me wet and aching for his mouth between my thighs.

"I cannot feed you," he said, his voice a liquid whisper against my mouth, "but perhaps we might sate a *different* sort of hunger tonight."

FOUR

GRAY

"Tell me," Darius said, his nose grazing my jawline, making me shiver. "Tell me what you need, love."

I needed to touch him. To taste him. To feel him inside me, on top of me, all over me. Straining hard against the straps, I said, "Untie me and I'll *show* you what I need."

"Untie you? I think not." Darius arched an elegant brow, a smirk sliding across his mouth. His fingers ghosted across my wrist, caressing the thin swath of skin exposed along the edge of the leather strap, then feathered down the inside of my arm to the crook of my elbow. "Even if you *weren't* a dangerous newborn predator, I rather like this look."

Swallowing the thickness in my throat, I whispered, "Helpless and hungry?"

"Hmm." His eyes ignited and he leaned in close again, soft lips buzzing my own, his erection pressing urgently against my hip. "*Bound.*"

I strained against the straps, desperate to uncover both the promises and the demands inherent in that single word. The leather creaked at my effort, but the hawthorn had dulled my strength just enough to prevent me from breaking free.

"Don't struggle, love," he said. "No point in it, really."

"Touch me," I begged. "Please, Darius."

"Do you trust me?"

"You know I do."

"Then let me take care of you." Without waiting for a response, he glanced around the room, then opened a dresser drawer, fishing through it until he found what he was looking for.

"You want to... blindfold me?" I asked, dragging my gaze down from the wicked gleam in his eyes to the black bandana in his hand.

He folded it into a long strip of fabric, tugging it tight, the snap making me flinch.

"If I may?" he asked.

I nodded, struck mute by the sudden force of my arousal. I'd never been tied up or blindfolded before—rendered nearly powerless, putting a man in complete control of my body, my desires, my pleasure. The idea sent a thrill down my spine, and my slow-but-steady vampire heart kicked up into a quick staccato beat.

"Close your eyes, little vampire," he ordered, and I did as he asked, my body laced tight with anticipation as he fastened the blindfold around my head and tied it tight.

"Darius, are you—"

He cut me off with a violently passionate kiss, fangs scraping across my bottom lip, drawing blood.

"You will not speak again unless I command it," he said, licking the blood from my lip. "For the next hour, I will decide what you feel, when you feel, and most important-ly…" He shifted away from my mouth, and seconds later, his hot breath misted at the apex of my thighs. "…*where* you feel. Is that perfectly clear?"

I opened my mouth to respond, but then shut it, nodding instead. The domineering alpha side of Darius's personality had always been there, simmering just beneath the surface, but he'd never unleashed it on me in the bedroom. Not like this.

And oh holy *hell*, was I on *fire* for him right now. My body had erupted in goosebumps, my nipples tight beneath the T-shirt, begging to be sucked.

Darius pressed a hot, wet kiss between my thighs, his tongue lingering, heat emanating through the silk of my underwear. The teasing pressure of his lips hinted at the devastating kisses to come.

Groaning softly, he bit the fabric and tugged it down, exposing my bare flesh to the cool air and the all-too-brief brush of his mouth. His silky hair tickled my inner thighs, and my hips arched closer, demanding more. But the restraints left little room for maneuvering, and the harder I fought for control, the quicker it eluded me.

Darius pulled back and released the fabric from his teeth.

"Naughty little vamp," he teased, clearly enjoying the game. "I believe you need a lesson in manners."

I groaned in delicious frustration, but didn't dare speak out, didn't dare break his rules. My senses had never been so sharp, so attuned to every little movement, every current of air, every stroke of his tongue, and he'd never teased me so relentlessly before. He was going to bring me to pure ecstasy, but first, he was going to torment me to within an inch of my life.

And I was going to love every impossible, crazy-making, panty-melting second of it.

"Would you like to watch me, love?" he asked. "Watch me taste you, touch you?"

I nodded emphatically, but this only made him laugh.

"Sorry, not a chance. Tonight is all about… Yes. Feeling." A soft kiss alighted on my hip bone like a butterfly, then vanished, only to reappear on my knee. "Tasting," Darius said, his tongue dragging seductively down my calf, swirling over my ankle bone. Then, fingers fluttering between my thighs, "Anticipating."

He let the word linger on the air as he increased the pressure, grazing my clit with teasing strokes that quickly turned hot and fiery—and then stopped.

I am going to die. And then I'm going to come back from the grave and kill him, too.

Pressing my lips together to hold back a desperate moan, I waited breathlessly for his next kiss, his next teasing touch.

It didn't come.

Minutes passed, then slowed, then stretched into an eternity. Scenting the air, I noticed his whiskey-and-leather scent had faded. Save for the storm raging against the window and the muted sounds filtering from the rest of the lodge, the room had fallen into complete silence.

Did he actually leave *me like this?*

Rules be damned. I opened my mouth to call out for him. No man *or* vampire got me all worked up, only to leave me helpless, unable to even take care of myself.

But before his cursed name reached my lips, my sexy, sneaky, commanding vampire was on his hands and knees on top of me.

Naked.

Hard.

And still not close enough. Never close enough.

"You seem flustered, little vampire," he teased, grazing my throat with his fangs, his tongue. The tip of his cock brushed my clit, still shielded by the underwear I was quickly growing to hate. "Are you not enjoying the game?"

"No, I'm not," I huffed.

"Liar. I could scent your desire clear across the room." Without warning, he tore my T-shirt down the middle, as far as it would go with the straps locked around my lower ribs.

My nipples pulled tight, and he took one into his hot, wet mouth, sliding his palm across the other. He sucked and licked, teasing me with his fangs, buzzing his lips over my flesh until I ached, my hips undulating beneath him.

I arched my back, ever so slightly, and Darius bit down,

then soothed me with his tongue. The pleasure was so concentrated, so intense, so…

Oh, fuck… How is this happening already?

"Darius!" I cried out as the orgasm suddenly claimed me. I clenched the sheets at my sides, straining once again to break my binds. He hadn't even fully touched me yet—not where I needed it most—but somehow, he'd brought me all the way to the edge and pushed me right over.

Darius moaned softly, but he didn't relent. His hair spilled forward over my flesh as he tongued me, and I longed to run my fingers through it, to hold him against me and ride out these insane waves, but I'd surrendered my body to him completely, and it was clear my vampire wasn't going to relinquish even an inch of that control.

I'd just started to regain my balance from the retreating orgasm when his touch evaporated once again, only to be replaced by the weight of his full body pressing down on top of me. In no more than a heartbeat, he tore off my underwear and slid inside me, steely and hot, his own control quickly unraveling.

The rules of the game continued to blur as we lost ourselves in each other, Darius no longer pretending to have even a *modicum* of restraint. He wanted this as badly as I did, and as much as he'd enjoyed teasing me, raw desire had finally claimed us both.

He was wild, kissing and biting, lips and teeth and hands exploring every accessible inch of skin. He gripped my ass, and without warning, slid a finger between my cheeks, delicately teasing. At my soft groan, he slipped a finger inside, and I gasped, the shock immediately replaced with pure pleasure.

"You like being touched like this," he said. Not a question.

I nodded, mute. Lost to the new sensations he was unlocking inside of me.

"Have you ever…?"

I shook my head, knowing what he was asking. No one had ever touched me or done anything else to me there, not like that, and the feel of it as he stroked me in time with the thrusts of his cock had me bracing for the next wave. The pressure was already building, winding me tighter.

"Perhaps," he said, pushing in deeper, slowly, "we'll try something a bit larger next time."

Fresh heat flooded my core.

"With so many of us desperate to touch you," he said softly, seductively, "we may need to start getting more creative. One from behind, another in front…"

God, he was making me even wetter. How was that possible?

Darius claimed my mouth, his tongue sliding between my lips as his cock thickened inside me, and I couldn't help but imagine what it would feel like to have him take me like that, sliding into me from behind while Asher took me from the front, Emilio sucking my nipple, Liam running his tongue along the side of my neck, Ronan touching himself before me…

The image of all of my rebels together, naked, surrounding me and filling me up… I couldn't hold out another minute. My body began to tremble with the force of the explosion building inside me.

"Darius," I breathed. "I can't wait. I'm too close... I..."

"Come for me, love," he said. "Let yourself go."

His liquid voice undid me, and I shattered, heat surging through my core, racing down my limbs, lighting up every nerve ending with an intensity I'd never felt before. It was so wild, so impossibly intense, I thought my blood would literally boil. My body began thrashing, and Darius pressed his full weight against me, shuddering as he came, both of us making the bed shake so hard I worried it would splinter and send us both crashing to the ground.

It was several long moments before I regained the power of speech, and when I finally did, my voice came out hoarse. "Is it always going to feel like that now?"

"Mostly," Darius said. "Vampires are quite sensual, and we feel things *very* acutely, especially for the first few years." He laughed softly, nuzzling my ear. "As I recall, there were moments when even walking outside during a stiff breeze posed a distinct challenge. Emphasis on the word *stiff*."

"So you're saying being a vampire comes with a constant, insatiable horniness?"

Darius laughed again. "That's one way to put it, yes. But like all hunger, we learn to mediate it—when to indulge, when to refrain, when to spend several hours in an ice-cold bath."

"How many hours of your life have *you* spent in cold baths?"

"Since I met you? More than I care to count, love."

Goosebumps slid across my entire body at the thought. Being with him... Everything had felt sharper, deeper, more connected—the slide of his hot length inside me, the touch of his fingers, the mist of his breath on my nipples, the scent of him filling my senses, threatening to overwhelm me in the best possible way. I was already revving up again, a low throb pulsing between my thighs like a warning.

"I suppose you should consider yourself very lucky," he said, trailing kisses across my jaw and lightly brushing my lips. "You've got five men practically banging down the door, waiting for a chance to touch you. All you need to do is ask."

"Darius?" I breathed, the ache in my core deepening as he slid a hand across my belly. "You're not helping."

"Hmm. What would help?"

I strained against the straps again, the leather stretching, but not quite snapping. "Untie me. Please."

"I'm sorry. I can't do that just yet. But I think we can get rid of this for now..."

Darius finally removed my blindfold. I still couldn't run my fingers through his hair or pull him into an embrace, but as he leaned close, I stared into his golden eyes, once again mesmerized by the kaleidoscope of colors glittering before me. He was so beautiful it almost hurt to look at him now.

Darius flashed his sexiest grin. "To answer your next question? Yes. I have *always* been this devastatingly handsome."

I rolled my eyes. "That's not what I was going to say."

"You were thinking it, though."

"Maybe." I tried to laugh, but it quickly turned into a yawn. The hawthorn was kicking in again, and my body was tired, desperate for rest and the blood that hadn't yet arrived. As hard as I tried to stay conscious for this—for all of it—I was losing the battle.

I'd just about drifted under again when a sudden bolt of realization slammed into my skull, forcing my eyes open.

"Darius!" I gasped.

"Ahh, and there it is," he said, touching the tip of my nose. His grin stretched wider now, his eyes dancing with pure joy. "The realization has finally dawned."

"You said something about when you'd first turned! The whole stiff breeze thing?"

"Indeed, I did."

"And earlier, you told me you remembered the thirst of a newborn vampire." I reviewed our entire conversation in my mind, his words hitting me now as if he'd just spoken them. "And our time in the Bay, when I was still delivering imports to Black Ruby!"

"All of those moments, and so many more."

"Does this mean...?" I held my breath, my heart hammering wildly.

Dare I hope?

He'd had flashes of memory before, but never enough to call it restored. This was the first time he'd remembered something so far back in his past—so many different details. It *had* to mean something.

"It means exactly what you think it means," he said, still smiling.

Tears blurred my vision. "But... How? When?"

"Turning you, taking in so much of your blood... It unlocked something for me, Gray. You were right all along. The connection was there. Whether your blood held my memories and returned them to me, or simply unlocked them from some dormant place deep inside my own mind, it matters not."

"How did it happen?"

"All I know for certain is that within moments of drinking from you, I was struck by a pain inside my skull so blinding, it drove me to my knees. It was like something literally cracked open, and everything just... It all came flooding back."

"Just like that? In one big rush?"

"Everything was a bit topsy-turvy at first, but eventually the memories sorted themselves into the right order. I remembered everything I'd ever lived through, all the things I'd done, falling in love with you." He cupped my face, tracing my jawline with his thumb. His eyes were filled with love for me, blazing bright, but soon the smile began to diminish, and the look in his eyes turned to regret. "I remembered becoming a vampire, all the choices I made since that day. The people I hurt along the way. I—"

"Don't do that to yourself." I shook my head, my eyes pleading with him to stop before he went any further down that dark path. "We've all done things we're completely ashamed of. Things we'd die before even *thinking* about doing now, consciously, in our so-called right minds."

"Yes, but I've had much longer to do such things—and much longer to regret them. Lifetimes upon lifetimes of bad decisions and—"

"And lifetimes of good ones." I wriggled my fingers until he grasped my hand, and I squeezed it tight, needing him to understand. "Do you remember what you said to me that night in the Shadowrealm, after I told you how sorry I was for what you'd gone through?"

He lowered his head, his hair falling into his eyes. "That all of it had brought me to you."

"And you wouldn't wish for another outcome."

"That's still true, love. Don't ever think otherwise." He brushed his knuckles along my cheek, smiling faintly, then frowning again. "I suppose I'd simply gotten used to carrying my regrets—after so many decades, they'd simply become background noise. But losing those memories, only to have them return full force... It's as if I'd committed some of those most terrible mistakes only yesterday."

"But you didn't. You're a different man now, Darius. And a hundred years from now, you'll be a different man yet again." I squeezed his hand again. "The difference is, now you'll have an immortal witch-vamp by your side, keeping you out of trouble."

This, finally, got a small laugh. "Causing it, more likely. Especially if you let me tie you up again."

"Again? That implies you actually untied me, which

you haven't." I squirmed again, but Darius only shook his head.

"Not a chance, little vampire. You're just lucky I haven't been able to figure out the camera on my phone."

"Guess you'll just have to hold on to this memory extra hard."

"Oh, you can count on it."

He leaned down and kissed me, tender and sweet.

"Thank you," I whispered when he pulled back. "For that night in the cemetery. It's the greatest gift you could ever give me."

"Turning you into a bloodsucker?"

I shook my head. "Honoring my choice, and helping me see it through."

Darius nodded, but suddenly, he seemed lost. Regret flooded his eyes. "Gray, I... I know how badly you wanted this. And logically, I understand your reasoning, just as I understood it the other night in the cemetery."

"Then why do you look so conflicted?"

"I feel like a bit of a fraud."

"How so?"

"You're thanking me for this so-called gift, but I have to confess... If I'd been myself when you'd asked, I wouldn't have changed you—not for all the pleading and logic in the world, no matter how badly I wanted to support you."

"Irrelevant. If you hadn't changed me, you wouldn't be yourself."

He flashed a smile, but it faded before it even reached

his eyes. "Being a vampire… Yes, you're stronger. Faster. Immortal. But this fate isn't—"

"This has nothing to do with fate, Darius Beaumont." Now I was getting pissed. "This was a choice. *My* choice. And your choice was to support me, just like you've always done."

Darius nodded, but said nothing.

"How much have we lost?" I asked. "How much has been completely outside of our control? From the moment Sophie died, we've taken hit after hit. For every win, we've got more losses and setbacks than I can count."

"Like I said, Gray. I get your reasons. I just wish there'd been another way that didn't involve risking your soul."

"We're about to turn the tide. All of us. The odds we're facing? That doesn't happen without big risks."

"I know all of this, love. There's no need to rehash. You're a vampire now—there's no going back." He closed his eyes and shook his head, and I feared this would turn into a bigger argument. But when he opened his eyes and looked at me again, his gaze was warm and clear, full of love and appreciation. "But your mine, love. And *that's* something I would never change, no matter which form you've taken."

He pressed a kiss to my forehead, and the last of my anger evaporated.

"Finally, something we agree on," I said.

"I'm so sorry. I don't want to argue with you. Not about this or anything else."

"Hmm," I teased. "So what *do* you want to do with me?"

"For starters…" He rolled on top of me, hard and ready, his eyes darkening with pure desire. "This feels about right."

"More than right," I whispered, and he sank inside of me, deeper and deeper as my body welcomed his touch. I wasn't as sensitive as I'd been earlier, but despite the hawthorn, I could still feel every inch of him.

But just before he whipped me into another white-hot frenzy, a heard of beasts crashed through the front door and up the stairs, carrying with them the scent of two demons, a wolf shifter, and—most importantly—my dinner.

"It's them," I announced, unable to keep the excitement from my voice. My stomach tumbled with fresh hunger, my mouth watering.

"Bloody hell," Darius grumbled. Then, loud enough so they'd hear him, "Brilliant timing, you gits."

"We've got maybe thirty seconds before they get all their boots off and come crashing through the bedroom door," I said.

Darius shot me a wicked grin, sliding inside me again, faster this time. "Then I guess we'd better hurry."

FIVE

GRAY

I was still seeing stars from the insane rapid-fire orgasm Darius had just delivered when the guys barged in, spilling through the door in a wild tumble of arms and legs and takeout bags, Sparkle and Sunshine right on their heels.

Asher took one look at the vampire lying on top of me and laughed. "Did I call it, or did I call it?"

"*Dios mio.*" Emilio shook his head, a grin lighting up his face. "We told you to *check* on her, not *climb* on her."

"Huh. I could've *sworn* you said climb." Darius, who still hadn't bothered to extricate himself from between my thighs, shook his head, feigning confusion. "Must be your accent."

Asher was still cracking up. "Must be you're an insatiable sandbagger who offered to keep watch tonight just so you could get our girl alone and steal her vampire virginity."

"I assure you, Mr. O'Keefe," Darius said, finally

SARAH PIPER

climbing off the bed and covering me with the sheet, giving me a covert wink as he did. My vampire was completely naked, totally unfazed as he turned to face the firing squad. "Nothing was stolen in this room tonight, save for our privacy."

"Privacy, huh?" Asher scanned him head to toe. "I can see you're pretty concerned about that."

"Victim-blaming will get you nowhere." Darius gave Asher a playful smack on the cheek, then finally located his pants, taking his time picking them up off the floor while I enjoyed the view.

"So that's how it's gonna be, Cupcake?" Asher turned his playful blue gaze on me. "You haven't seen the rest of us in days, and suddenly you've only got eyes for the bloodsucker?"

"He's the only one who's naked," I said matter-of-factly.

Asher grabbed the hem of his T-shirt, lifting it to give me a mouthwatering peek. "We can fix that right now."

The briefest glimpse of his tattooed, rock-hard abs had me damn near drooling.

But Darius grabbed Asher's wrist, stopping the show just before it got good. "She needs to eat, and then I'm taking her for a shower. So whatever thoughts are tumbling through that lecherous mind of yours, incubus, put them on ice."

"A shower, huh?" Asher rubbed his jaw, slowly approaching my bedside as Darius ducked into the bathroom to wash up. "Better give her an extra shot of hawthorn this time. Girl's got quite an arm on her."

50

The teasing smile hadn't left his face since he'd first walked in, and now I returned it with one of my own.

"Consider it payback for the time you took me down at the safe house," I said.

"That was for your own good. And anyway, you're way stronger than me now." Asher swept the curls from my forehead and pressed a kiss between my brows, his eyes twinkling with a mixture of happiness and that seductive, bad-boy edge he'd never quite lost. "You feeling a little less psychotic now, bruiser?"

"Why don't you kiss me for real and find out," I teased.

"You fight dirty, Cupcake."

"I learned from the best."

Never one to turn down a dare, Asher planted one right on me.

"You're looking good, Desario," Ronan said when Ash finally pulled away, the relief in his eyes belying his light-hearted tone. "Color is back to normal."

"What do you mean?" I asked.

"For a while there, your skin was the shade of warm milk," he said.

I winced. That didn't sound like a good look.

"Three guesses as to what put *that* fresh shade of pink on her cheeks," Asher said.

"You're welcome, love," Darius said, returning from the bathroom, freshly showered and fully dressed.

"Yeah, you're welcome for my contribution, too," Asher said.

I laughed. "What contrib—"

He cut me off with another kiss, this one so deep and delicious I couldn't help the moan that escaped my mouth.

"Okay, kids," Ronan grumbled. "Knock it off before this shit turns into a health code violation. I've got dinner here, remember."

He set two large paper bags on the dresser and emptied out the contents, consisting of several take-out containers from Marcella's Diner and a twelve-pack of beer, along with what I could smell were a few large hunks of raw meat for the hounds, wrapped up in butcher's paper.

"So Marcella's is still up and running, even with the storm?" I asked, keeping my eyes peeled for the only meal I cared about in that moment, which would arrive neither in take-out containers nor butcher's paper.

Ronan nodded. "Pretty sure it's the only restaurant in town still open. Place was crowded as hell."

The smell of all that hot food drifted toward me—burgers, fries, fried chicken, pancakes, pie. Ronan crumpled up the empty bags, then said, "Okay, remind me who ordered what."

Panic gripped my limbs. Was that all they'd brought back? "What about the—"

"I've got you covered, *querida*." Emilio held up a small cooler I hadn't noticed, then popped it open and pulled out two opaque bags of blood. "Still cold though. Should I warm it up?"

My body reacted on instinct, arms and legs straining hard against the straps, my stomach growling like a wild animal. I felt the slide of my fangs, the sharp points piercing my lips.

It seemed like I wasn't in control of any of it.

"Relax, Gray," Emilio said, his voice gentle. "You're okay. We'll take care of this right now." He passed one of the bags to Darius, then cut the corner off the other one with his pocketknife and tilted it toward my lips.

My body settled instantly, the moment I tasted the first drop.

Relief. It was the only word in my mind as the tangy liquid flooded my mouth. Drinking cold blood felt a bit like drinking warm beer, but at the moment, I didn't care. It was food—the only kind that would truly sate me—and for that reason alone, it was practically a gourmet feast.

Besides, I didn't want so much as a *smear* of warm blood touching my lips. Better to not know what I was missing than to ever develop a real taste for it.

The guys watched me closely, a mixture of wonder and curiosity on their faces as I downed the entire bag. Even Darius seemed mesmerized, despite the fact that we were sharing the same meal.

When I'd literally sucked it dry, I let out a small burp, then smiled, feeling much more like myself. "Okay, you guys are starting to freak me out. Why are you staring at me? It's like you've never seen a bloodsucker before."

"We've seen plenty," Emilio said. "Just... Just not you."

"Am I that revolting?" Suddenly self-conscious, I licked my lips, hoping I hadn't spilled anything.

"Revolting?" Asher laughed. "That's a negative, Cupcake."

"I think we're all still a bit awestruck, love," Darius said. "You're quite different now."

"Different how?" I asked.

"You're kind of radiating," Asher said. "Like, you've always been super-hot, right? That hasn't changed. But now you're... well, you're just more."

"More hot?" I rolled my eyes.

"More everything. Not just how you look, but your vibe. Your energy. We can just... feel it." He shifted uncomfortably from one foot to the other, and I glanced down, finally noticing the massive bulge in his jeans.

"Yeah," he confirmed, before I could even ask. "That's exactly what I'm talking about."

"Seriously?" I couldn't help but laugh. "Are *all* of you getting hard watching me eat, or is that just another special incubus thing? Because I realize some guys have food fetishes, but if you're sprouting boners every time I take a snack break, we're going to have a serious problem."

"One person's problem is another person's opportunity," Ash said.

"Your power affects us, Gray," Emilio said. "Each in different ways, maybe, but there's no denying it."

The more I thought about it, the more it made sense. Darius had always had an effect on me—even before we'd become blood bound.

I looked from Emilio to Asher, to Ronan, to Darius, and my chest tightened with a fresh wave of emotion. The last time we'd all been together, I was convincing them to let Darius turn me.

And they'd stood by my side through all of it.

"It's so good to see you guys," I said, tears flooding my eyes.

"You have *no* idea," Ronan said. The relief in his voice was plain.

Emilio squeezed my foot, and Ash ran his fingers through my hair, while Darius held my hand.

They were all here with me save for Liam, who now fell under the "no humans allowed" restriction. I really wanted to see him, as well as my sisters and the others, but it was better to wait. Tied up, bloody mouth, still a little wobbly inside from the hawthorn... Yeah, I wasn't exactly a welcome sight.

As everyone dug into their takeout, they updated me on everything that had happened since my turning, including Jael's decision to take my moonglass back to his home realm—a move the guys didn't seem too thrilled about.

"But Jael... he's okay, right?" I asked.

"All evidence suggests he made it back to his home realm with your soul intact," Emilio said, sharing a few more details about Jael's portal and the hunters they'd taken out in the woods, as well as the ones he and Asher had chased down after the ambush.

"Lucky for us, they weren't very careful about covering their tracks," Emilio continued. "We followed the path they'd made back to an abandoned park service lodge a little deeper into the woods. By our estimate, the whole group had been holing up there, roughing it for the past few weeks at least. Seems most of them were dispatched up to the cemetery during our attack, but two hunters hung back."

"What happened to them?" I asked, though I already knew the answer.

"Let's just say the glamoured cemetery is no longer the only burial ground up there," Asher said. "After we took out those two, we tracked in a little deeper, then circled back up to the spot where they'd tried to jump us. No one was left. *El Lobo* and I made damn sure of that."

I didn't doubt it.

"So it seems we made it out of the whole mess in pretty much one piece," I said, blowing out a breath. I was still getting used to the whole not-needing-air thing, and the gesture felt a little forced. Darius had always seemed so natural.

Years of practice, I supposed.

"The issue now," Darius said, "is that we've got no communication with Blackmoon Bay. Kallayna—via her brother—was our only link."

"We've still got Reva," I said. "I say we stick to our original plan—keep practicing with her until she's ready, and then let her do her thing. I know she can get in there remotely—she's a strong kid, and just as dedicated to this as the rest of us."

"Her dedication isn't an issue," Emilio said, raking a hand through his dark hair. "I hate putting her at risk like that, but I'm afraid it may be our best shot at getting any

56

sort of intel. Otherwise, we're heading in blind—and that's if we can get in at all."

"She's just a kid," Ronan said. "If they find her snooping around like that… No. There has to be another way."

"There isn't," Emilio said. "We've been over it from every angle. Between the fae spells, the unpredictable weather, the Council's treachery, and the beating we've taken at nearly every turn… We're up against a wall here, Ronan."

Ronan shook his head. "Liam's been working with her for days, and she still hasn't made any progress. We can't just turn her loose like that. What if she get's caught? What if—"

"Guys. Seriously?" I looked around from one gloomy face to the next. The air was suddenly so thick with their collective hopelessness, if I actually *had* to breathe it, I'd probably choke. "We saved all those lives the other night—witches, shifters, and vampires alike. We destroyed an army of insane hybrids. Wiped out another pack of hunters. We got more intel from the inside—okay, maybe not as much as we'd hoped, but a hell of a lot more than we had when we started. Haley and I found our sister. And hey, guess what? I'm a scary immortal vampire now—bonus!"

I bared my fangs and hissed, hoping to make them laugh, but only Asher cracked a smile.

"Hey!" I said. "Where's the sense of accomplishment here? The hopeful optimism?"

"Now you're starting to sound like your sister," Ash said. "Always trying to find the bright side."

I smiled, taking it as a compliment. From the moment Haley and I had started getting closer back in the Bay, she'd been a bright spot in my life. Not that she never felt down or scared or pissed off, but even in her darkest moments, she still had a way of bringing out the best in everyone.

"Maybe my sister has a point," I said, channeling a little bit of Haley's eternal optimism. "If Haley were standing right here, she'd make each of us share one thing we're grateful for."

Ash groaned. "Thank fuck she's not standing right here, because that exercise sounds completely—"

"Okay, Ash, you go first." I grinned at him, big and bright, letting him know there was no way out of this.

"You want gratitude? Fine." He huffed and puffed, then finally found his answer. "After we took out those hunters, we looted the park service lodge. Brought home a few more fae blades, some tactical gear, shit like that."

"See, that wasn't so hard," I teased. "Emilio?"

He squeezed my foot again. "You survived the change. That's enough to get me through whatever shitstorm comes next."

I smiled. I was grateful for that, too.

"Darius, what about you?" I asked.

Without missing a beat, he said, "I just got laid by the hottest vampire-witch in existence. That's my final answer."

The crass declaration from the otherwise proper vampire shocked us all into a bout of laughter.

"I should probably smack you for that," I said, "but I'm tied up."

"As if I could forget," he said with a wink. Then, to Ronan, "Alright, hellspawn. You're not getting out of this, either. What's your answer?"

Ronan locked me in his fierce autumn gaze, his eyes burning with some new urgency.

"Everybody out," he demanded. "I need to talk to Gray alone. *That's* my answer."

SIX

RONAN

The guys gave me a world of shit, but eventually, they took the hounds and cleared out, leaving me alone with Gray for the first time since she'd changed.

I couldn't stop staring at her.

"I must be a total mess." Gray lowered her eyes, her smile suddenly shy.

"A beautiful mess, though," I said. So beautiful it broke my fucking heart. She was immortal now. In a matter of one short night, the number of things that could kill her had been slashed from infinite to two. Only two.

Incineration and beheading.

But that built-in safety feature had come at a cost, and she'd given up a part of herself to get it. And no matter what she believed—no matter what Jael had promised about her soul—I wasn't convinced she'd ever get it back.

Still, she'd survived. That was the important part.

And her eyes glittered with new facets, the depths of

which I'd only just begun to explore. Staring into her eyes, losing myself there, it was almost enough to make me forget about the fact that I still couldn't touch her.

"You've got a little…" I swiped my thumb across my lower lip, indicating the blood smeared across hers. I wasn't sure I'd ever get used to the sight of that, but as long as she was healthy, it didn't matter.

She licked the blood clean, then offered another faint smile. "Sorry. I'm still a little—"

"I love you," I said, my voice breaking on the words. I knelt at her bedside, leaning as close as I dared, wishing I could take her face into my hands. "I loved you as a witch, I love you as a vampire, and I'll never fucking stop. I need you to know that. To truly know it. My heart has and will always be yours, even when I'm acting like a fucking asshole."

She closed her eyes, a tear streaking down her cheek. "I do know it," she whispered. "I always have."

"All that shit I said to you back at Inferno, when you'd first returned from hell… I thought I was doing the right thing. I was so twisted up about Sebastian cashing in on your contract, so fucked up about not being allowed to touch you… I guess I just lost my shit. All I could picture was you locked up in one of his dungeons, and him sending me to retrieve you each time he had some bullshit job for you, and you just looking at me with this… this broken look in your eyes, wondering how the fuck the man you loved so much could ever do something so low." I pinched the bridge of my nose, trying to keep my own tears in check. It was a losing battle. "I thought it would be better if you just... If you forgot you'd ever loved me."

"Yeah?" She opened her eyes and glared at me with new fire. "That makes you a fucking asshole *and* a fucking idiot, Ronan. I could *never* forget how I feel about you. All that stuff about letting me go, about things being over between us... Did you honestly think I'd believe you?"

I shook my head. "Deep down, I guess I knew you wouldn't. Hell, I *hoped* you fucking wouldn't. I was out of my mind, Gray, and I didn't know how to handle it. So I fucked up, and I hurt you, and I've spent every night since then haunted by the look in your eyes and silently begging you for the forgiveness I know I don't deserve."

She lowered her eyes, and silence wrapped us up completely, save for the constant roar of the wind and the ocean. She didn't move or speak for so long, I wondered if she'd drifted off to sleep. I was about to stand up and head out when she finally met my gaze again, pinning me in place.

"I forgave you the moment those stupid words fell out of your stupid mouth. I forgave you because I knew you didn't mean them, and I knew you were only trying to protect me from some future heartbreak. I love you, Ronan, even if you never touch me again. Even if you're marching down to my dungeon every single night for the rest of eternity to do Sebastian's bidding. So the next time you get the bright idea to break up with me, go ahead and stick it right up your ass, because I'm not going anywhere."

Her eyes were full-on blazing now, swirling with a mix of anger and love and desire and yes, forgiveness too.

My heart damn near pounded out of my chest, and I had to shove my hands into my pockets to keep from reaching out to her. Touching her. Making up for all my shit with one devouring kiss at a time.

"You're my best friend, Desario," I whispered. "And the love of my life. I will never break your trust again. So you want to know what I'm grateful for? What's my one piece of good news in all of this?" I shrugged. "It's the simple fact that you haven't given up on me. On us."

"I never will."

I blew out a breath, the weight of my guilt lessoning a fraction. Her faith in me, however undeserved it may have been, was a precious gift. One I wouldn't risk losing again.

"Your soul is under the protection of the Seelie Queen," I said, shifting gears. This was a conversation we couldn't avoid, no matter how much I wished we could sweep it all under the rug. "It's likely your situation with Sebastian has changed."

"You think we finally found that loophole?" she asked.

"I don't know. He's got no jurisdiction in the fae realm, and I doubt the Queen would make a deal with the prince of hell. But depending on the exact language in your contract, he could see this as deception on your part."

"Who cares what he thinks? If he can't get his hands on my soul, he has no claim over me."

"I'm not sure he'll see it that way, Gray. Sebastian is nothing if not resourceful. Once he finds out that you're a bloodsucker, he's probably gonna come at you. I just think we need to be prepared for it."

She nodded, the space between her eyebrows creasing with new worries.

"I'm not telling you this to freak you out," I said. "More than anyone else in my existence, you seem to have some influence over him. You just need to figure out how you want to spin this."

Gray flashed her fangs—a look that terrified me as much as it turned me on. "Can't I just bite him and be done with it?"

"He's a demon—the most powerful one in existence. I'm afraid you'll have to get a little more creative than that." I leaned in close again, inhaling her sweet scent, now mixed with the faint tang of blood. "Hey. We've got this. Don't ask me how, but we've got this. You and me? We always figure shit out, and this is no different. Okay?"

She smiled up at me, her eyes sparkling. "Ronan Vacarro. Is that a note of optimism I detect?"

I grinned, my lips just a hair's breadth from hers, and whispered softly, "Don't tell a soul."

"I wish you could kiss me," she said, and I nodded.

"You and me both, Desario."

A wicked smile slid across her face.

"What kind of trouble are you brewing up now?" I asked.

"No trouble. I was just thinking… Apparently, I've got vampire influence now."

"Comes with the territory, I suppose."

"I thought you might want to help me test it out."

"You don't really need my permission," I said. "That's kind of the thing with influence, right?"

"Probably not, but I'm still going to ask. So?"

"Fine." I got back on my feet and stretched, stifling a yawn. "But don't make me see anything too crazy. It's been a long few nights already and I still need to take the pooches out for a—holy *fuck*, Gray."

I stumbled a step backward as the images invaded my mind. Gray, breaking her straps and pulling me on top of her. Kissing me. Grinding up against me and begging me to take her, right there…

I blinked rapidly, and the scene evaporated.

Back here on planet reality, my dick hard as stone and my witch still strapped tight in her bed, I shook my head. "Well, that was… interesting."

She smiled up at me like a little imp. "See anything you like?"

"Not sure I quite got all the details," I said. "Maybe we should try another—oh, okay, that's… fucking… nice…" My eyes drifted closed as I let the hallucination wash over me, Gray on her knees before me, freeing me from my jeans, taking me into her mouth, one luscious lick at a time. It was all I could do not to grab myself right there and finish the job, but that would kill the vision. Right now, hallucination or not, I only wanted it to be her, not my own damn fist.

She moaned as she took me in deeper, and I had no fucking idea whether it was the real Gray or the hallucination making that noise, but I didn't care. Both of them had the same effect.

And both of them were about fifteen seconds away from making me come.

"Don't stop," I said. Whatever she was doing to me with her mind, it felt fucking amazing, her mouth hot and hungry, her soft little sighs sending jolts of white-hot electricity skittering across my skin…

I felt the sudden tingling in my balls, my heart hammering, my body about T-minus five seconds from exploding—

"Everything alright in there?" The fucking vampire asshole knocked on the door, shattering the vision, breaking my concentration, and earning himself a permanent spot on my shit list.

"Awesome, asshole," I grumbled. My dick went instantly limp, and I opened my eyes, blinking away the last remnants of that beautiful dream. "Give us a few more minutes."

"Very well," he said. "Tell Gray I've drawn her a bath and will be back to help her post-haste."

"Post-haste?" I whispered to Gray. "Who the fuck says that?"

"I heard you, hellspawn. You've now got one minute to say your goodbyes."

I flipped him off.

"I heard that, too," he said.

Gingerly I got to my feet, the ache in my balls throbbing. Yeah, that was gonna be a situation.

"Sorry about that," Gray said, biting her lower lip. "I was really hoping we could see that through."

"Another time," I said. "Definitely another time."

"At least we know my power works, right?" She beamed at me, and I couldn't help but laugh.

"That's an understatement."

"What are you doing the rest of the night?" she asked.

"Cold shower," I said, limping toward the door. Shit was brutal. Wouldn't trade it, though. Until I could finally touch her, this was the next best thing—something she'd chosen to share with me and me alone.

"Ronan," she said, and I turned back to catch her wicked smile.

Seconds later, another image flooded my mind, Gray in the shower with me, suds sliding down between her breasts...

I braced myself against the door, cursing under my breath. "Not helping, Desario. Not fucking helping."

"You know you love it."

Hell, she was right.

"Yeah, I do love it. And you. Now please put your new toy away and let me go put this little situation on ice." I opened the door, grabbed my stiff dick, and hobbled out into the hallway with a smile on my face. Sure, I felt like I'd just gotten kicked in the nuts by a four-hundred-pound gorilla, and Beaumont was out there smirking at me like a total prick, but my girl was alive. She was safe. She was immortal. She had a dirty-as-fuck mind, and she was more than happy to give me a peek.

And the best part? After everything, she still loved me.

For the first time in months, it seemed the universe was finally on our side.

"Wait, Ronan? Serious question this time. I promise."

I turned back to see her wriggling against her straps.

"When do you think I'll finally get sprung from here?" she asked.

"Soon. We just need a couple more days to make sure everything's cool once we stop the hawthorn."

"*Days?*" She pressed her lips together, and I knew she was biting back another argument. But ultimately, she relented. We all knew she'd never put the people she loved in danger—particularly her sisters and Liam, who wouldn't be able to fully defend against her vampire instincts if it came to that.

"Fine," she finally said. "What happens after I'm cleared for takeoff? We rally the troops and ship out for Blackmoon Bay? The longer we wait on making a move, the—"

"Slow down, Desario. There's one *very* important thing we need to do first, *post-haste*," I said for Beaumont's benefit.

"What thing?" she asked.

I grinned at her, raking my eyes over her body from head to toe and letting out an appreciative sigh. "First day you get your official hall pass? The boys and I are taking our hot new vampire-witch out for a test drive."

SEVEN

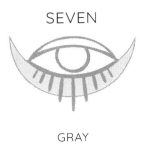

GRAY

Two nights later, I found myself standing next to Darius in a narrow ditch at the bottom of an icy hill, excitedly bouncing on my toes. He'd run me up and down the steep incline so many times, we'd melted a path through the thick layer of ice and snow clear down to the mud beneath.

And still, I wasn't even winded. I had energy to burn, and after being on house-arrest for the last few days, I was more than ready to light it all up.

"I think we've established that I'm faster than you, D," I teased. I'd beaten him nine out of the last ten runs, and the ones we'd done before that were all ties.

Doing his best to hide his frustration, Darius nodded toward the top of the rise, where Asher, Ronan, and Liam stood waiting for us. Liam was holding a stopwatch and clipboard, while the demons took turns cheering us on and keeping Sparkle entertained with an old tennis ball she'd dug up. Emilio was around somewhere, too—he'd shifted into wolf form, and he and Sunshine were keeping an eye on our perimeter, making sure we didn't have any unexpected drop-ins.

The guys still thought it best that I steer clear of the humans for another night or two, at least until they could run me around out here and assess my strength and control. But Liam, who was so used to disappearing and appearing at will, was having no part of it. While the guys had attempted to whisk me away under cover of darkness, he'd snuck into the back of the SUV and hid under a tarp without anyone even noticing, surprising us all by leaping out of the back when we finally arrived at the trailhead.

There was a lengthy argument about whether to drive him back, but in the end, Darius's logic proved no match to Liam's philosophical counterpoints, and he was finally given permission to stay and make himself useful— provided he and I didn't make any physical contact.

About half-a-mile down the dark forest trail, while the others had drifted ahead with the hounds, I grabbed Liam and dragged him behind a tree, stealing a long-overdue kiss.

He gladly returned it, wasting no time deepening the kiss, sliding his hands into my hair and backing me up against the tree, his every touch making my whole body shiver.

"I missed you," I whispered, breaking away just long enough to let him catch his breath before stealing another kiss. We didn't stop again until his cheeks were bright red, he was panting for air, and Darius was shouting from the trail ahead for us to keep up.

"According to Liam," Darius said now, "we've not yet achieved statistical significance. Until we do, the fact that you're so-called *faster* than me remains unproven, from a scientific perspective."

"It's okay," I teased, turning and stretching up on my toes to plant a kiss on his cheek. "I know you're just letting me win to boost my confidence. I'm sure it won't happen on the next run."

He grumbled something unintelligible, even for my vampire super-hearing, then pulled away. "Pay attention, Gray. This is important."

I nodded, biting back another retort. Despite his grumpiness, Darius was a great coach, and this was the best night I'd had in a long time. Together with my rebels, running around in the snow, stretching my new legs... For a little while, it was easy to pretend we were just out for a fun romp in the woods on a chilly winter's night. The winds had died down, and the snow that managed to reach us through the thick canopy of evergreens was light and fluffy, the kind made for catching on your tongue.

It was all kind of romantic, actually.

Or it would be, if they weren't assessing and training me for the attack sitting on the horizon.

Stealing myself for another run, I held up my hand to let the guys know we were ready, then Darius counted down from three.

We were off, racing up the steep hill at a clip so fast, the trees around us were no more than an inky smudge across the snow-white canvas. When I reached the top and spun around, I caught Darius just cresting the rise.

This time, I couldn't help myself. "Have I kicked your ass enough times for it to be statistically significant yet?"

"I concede, little vampire. You are faster than me. But your instincts could use some work." Without warning, he darted close and grabbed me, his body a blur. It happened so fast, I didn't even realize what he'd done until I felt the sudden, icy bite of snow between my boobs.

I squealed, desperately shaking the snow from inside my shirt as I chased him back down the hill, then up again, scooping up snow along the way. I slowed down and waited until he thought he'd bested me, then charged again, pelting him with a wet snowball right between the eyes.

"Nice shot!" Asher shouted as I blurred past them again. I was so puffed up about my snow-fighting skills that I didn't see my enemy lurking behind the trees. Too late, he leaped out from the shadows and tackled me, both of us rolling back down the hill, my lungs aching from laughing so hard.

When we finally reached the bottom, tangled up in each other's arms and legs, tears of laughter were already freezing on my cheeks.

"Concede my victory yet?" Darius nudged my nose with his, a grin stretched across his lush mouth. "Or do you need another lesson?"

He lifted a hand from behind his back, threatening me with a full-on snowball to the face.

Still cracking up, I squirmed in his arms, begging for mercy. "You win, you win! You're the best snowball fighter there is."

"And the most handsome."

"And the most handsome. As well as charming, intelligent, and sexy."

"That's more like it." Darius brushed a quick kiss across my lips, then stood up, hauling me to my feet and dusting the snow off my ass.

I turned and flashed him a mischievous grin. "But I'm still faster than you."

I raced back up the hill, leaving him to chase after me once again.

"And that's another win for Gray," Liam announced, marking the time on the sheet. "We can safely say that her superior speed has been scientifically proven."

"That one doesn't count!" Darius finally made it back to the top, his hair crusted with snow, his eyes bright and happy. To me he said, "Asher was right, love. You fight dirty."

"Not as dirty as we do," Ash said, and I turned just in time to duck before he and Ronan launched a volley of hard-packed snowballs right at Darius's head.

Darius charged, tackling both demons in one swoop, all three of them rolling around in the snow like puppies. Liam tried to take a step back to avoid the chaos, but he was too slow; someone's hand—not sure whose—reached up and snagged his boot, dragging him down and into the brawl.

I was laughing my ass off, no idea who to even cheer for as the four of them pummeled one another with snow, Sparkle yelping as she ran circles around them. Seconds later, Emilio and Sunshine appeared, tails wagging, both of them jumping right into the fray.

"Boys!" I shouted, still trying to get my laughter under control. "We're supposed to be working!"

"Oh, you're going down, Desario!" Ronan shouted, beaming me in the chest with a well-aimed snowball.

"That was wholly unwise, hellspawn." Keen to defend my questionable honor, Liam pounced on Ronan from behind, taking him down and shoving his face into the snow.

We spent the next hour chasing one another through the woods in an epic winter battle, making alliances and breaking them, pushing faces into the snow, shoving snow down shirts and pants and anywhere we could find an easy opening. By the end of it, all of us were laughing so hard I wasn't sure we'd ever be able to talk again.

Poor Liam was shivering his human ass off, but the smile hadn't left his face. Through chattering teeth, he finally said, "I'm fairly certain my vessel has never seen snow in his life, let alone gotten up close and personal with it."

"I'd say the perpetually wind-tossed surfer hair and the pineapple tattoo on your hip are pretty solid indicators," I teased.

"Dude… what?" Asher cracked up. "You have a *pineapple* tattoo? On your *hip*? Did you lose a bet or something?"

"I'm not sure what gambling has to do with my vessel's choice in body art," Liam said, pulling down the waistband of his pants and boxers to reveal the tattoo in question. "Are pineapple tattoos offensive on the material plane?"

I tried not to stare, but couldn't help it. It'd been a long time since I'd seen any part of Liam's unclothed skin, and seeing the flash of well-defined abs transported me right back to our time on the beach in the Shadowrealm. To the moment of our first kiss, so passionate and intense, all those sparks…

"Gray, you okay?" Asher's hand on my shoulder snapped me out of the memory, and I looked up to find Liam staring at me, his eyes twinkling with mischief. Something told me he and I had been thinking about the same thing.

"The snow has been an interesting experience," Liam said, refusing to break our gaze, "but I prefer the beach."

A smile twitched at his lips, and I returned it, feeling the heat rise inside me.

But the moment passed, and it wasn't long before the guys were back in coach-mode once again.

Ronan grinned at me now, shaking his head like he still couldn't believe any of this was actually happening.

I knew the feeling.

"She's fucking fast, Beaumont," Ronan said to Darius. "Faster than any vamp I've come across."

"Don't remind me," Darius said, but he was smiling, too. "Gray, you're a natural. Truly. And you've assimilated the change better than any newborn I've ever encountered—your magic seems to be neutralizing the worst of the side effects."

"I feel great," I told him. "Better than ever."

"Yes, and I can't tell you how relieved we are at that. But don't let it go to your head just yet. Speed, strength, and fortitude are just a few aspects of your new form. You've got a lot more to learn if you want to be able to fully leverage all of your strengths and skills."

I nodded, more eager than ever for the next lesson. "Hit me with your best shot, boys."

EIGHT

GRAY

"Use every advantage you've got," Darius shouted, his voice an echo from the dark woods behind me, one I couldn't pin down no matter how hard I tried.

After running through numerous exercises testing my strength and agility, all of which I'd passed with flying colors, the guys decided it was time to test my instincts. They'd blindfolded me and led me deeper into the forest, none of them speaking as we marched for what felt like an hour.

If it wasn't for the feel of Darius's firm grip on my arm and the sound of Liam's chattering teeth, I wouldn't have known they were still with me.

Eventually, the trees thinned out, the snow thickening at our feet an inch at a time until I was pushing hard through hip-deep snowpack. The wind was chillier out here, too—compete with wet, heavy snow that splattered against my cheeks.

They'd brought me to the middle of what I could only guess was a wide clearing, leaving me with no warning of what was to come. All I had to go on was Darius's final instruction: *Don't let anything touch you.*

"I'm fresh out of advantages!" I called out now. "I can't see, and everything smells like ice—my nose is useless." Hearing was also a challenge; the wind was picking up again, howling through the treetops behind me, making them shiver and creak. My instincts were screaming at me to take off the blindfold, but I promised Darius I'd leave it on. That I'd see this through, no matter how frustrating.

But frustrating didn't even begin to cover it. After doing so well with all the physical tests, I felt like a total failure out there.

I lost my sense of time, waiting for what felt like hours for something to happen, only to feel everything speed up again at the first sound of footsteps breaking through the icy snow-pack. I had no way of knowing whether it was one of the guys or something else, but I wasn't taking any chances. I spun around, arms out, bracing for an attack that never came.

Seconds later, something brushed along my arm, and I yelped like a scared puppy. So much for instincts.

"Try harder, Gray," Darius called, his voice still far away. Clearly he wasn't the one touching me, but no matter how hard I tried to get a sense for *something*—the fiery scent of one of the demons, the feel of Emilio's thick wolf coat, the sound of Sparkle or Sunshine panting—I just kept coming up empty.

I took a deep, unnecessary breath, the familiar gesture calming me, helping me to refocus. I'd just gotten my bearings when something shoved me from behind, knocking me face-first into the snow.

"Fucker!" I shot to my feet, spun around, and lunged, but again, there was only air. Only snow. Spinning back around, I tried my best to scan my surroundings with my available senses, but all was silent and still.

It reminded me of the night we'd invaded Norah's house to rescue Asher—the cloaking spell inside that had rendered all scents and sounds invisible.

"Guys, this isn't working. Let's try something—"

Impact.

I was flat on my back, snow falling wet and heavy on my face as I tried my best to keep the tears locked down. Emilio could see right through it, though, even in his wolf form, which was currently pinning me down in the snow.

He let out a soft whine, then licked my face, refusing to stop until he finally got a laugh out of me.

"If that turns into frostbite, you're in big trouble." I reached up and sunk my fingers into the coarse fur at his neck, taking comfort in his warmth, in the familiar touch, in his presence.

I gave myself about two minutes to enjoy it.

And then I gave him a good shove, launching him clear off my body.

"Vampire strength for the win," I said, but when I got to my feet and turned around, he was already gone.

Footsteps approached in the snow behind me, and again I whirled around, only to feel a tug on my hair from behind.

They were totally screwing with me.

I wanted to scream. I was literally fighting blind.

"Alright. I'm done!" I called out, reaching for the blind-fold. There was no point in continuing this particular test. Clearly, I'd already failed.

"You're *not* done," Darius said firmly. No longer an echo in the distance, he was standing right in front of me. His hands came to rest on my shoulders, and I relaxed as his familiar scent finally broke through the cold. "You've simply forgotten, little vampire, and you're letting it upset you."

"Forgotten what? How to fight invisible monsters in three feet of snow?"

"Your newly acquired senses are not your only assets, Gray. That's what you've forgotten."

"What do you mean?"

"You're a witch, are you not? A Silversbane at that. If your vampire senses are incapacitated for any reason, draw on your magic to guide you."

I wanted to argue back, to lash out from the place of wounded pride I'd found myself in. But Darius was absolutely right. The answer was so obvious, so ridiculous, I could only laugh. "Wow. I'm kind of an idiot."

"Don't even think it," he said, tilting my chin up, then stealing a quick kiss. "This is all brand new for you, love. You can't expect to master everything there is to know on your first night of training."

"But we don't have much time, D. We don't have the luxury of weeks or months to explore the finer points of being a vampire-witch. People are dying."

"No, we don't have weeks or months. But a few nights? We have to take that, at least. We can't risk going in unprepared. Doing so could make everything worse— not just for you, but for the very people we're trying to save."

"Alright," I said, deciding to leave the blindfold in place for now. "One more try. Let's see if I can connect with my realm out here. I need—"

"I would advise against it," Liam said. I had no idea whether he'd been by my side through all of this, or had just crept up, but he clearly didn't like my plan. "Your realm isn't safe, Gray. Not with Jonathan's whereabouts still unknown."

"It's the source of my magic," I said.

"No, Gray. *You* are the source." He placed his hand against my chest. "In here. Your realm helped you connect with it more deeply, but it has and will always be within you."

"But half my power comes from the Shadowrealm, and it's connected to my realm through the rune gate," I said. "Accessing that power is my best shot at defending myself."

"Your Shadowborn powers flow through *you*," Liam said. "Always. You do not need to access them from the realm any more than you need to breathe air. Gray, listen to me, please. I wasn't able to locate Jonathan in your realm.

We have to assume he's still there, waiting for you to return."

"I took care of him last time. The only reason he got away from me was that I'd found you and Emilio, and that was the priority."

"You can't assume the situation will be the same. For all you know, Jonathan has gotten even stronger."

I shook my head, not wanting to accept this. I'd ignored my realm for so many years I'd almost forgotten what it even looked like. But since I'd started connecting with it again, reclaiming my magic, it'd become a part of me. Important.

Maybe I didn't *need* it, but I wasn't ready to say goodbye to it, either. And I damn well wasn't about to let a cockroach like Jonathan Reese lock me out.

If and when I let it go, I would do it on my own terms.

I told the guys just that, but Liam was adamant.

"There will likely come a time when you have to face Jonathan again," Liam said, the tone in his voice imploring. "That is the nature of such conflicts. But that time does not need to be tonight."

"Spooky's right," Asher said, squeezing my shoulder. Apparently, they were all there now. "No unnecessary risks, remember?"

I steamed for another minute, then finally relented.

"No unnecessary risks," I said. They were right. There was no need for me to go to the realm tonight, no need to waste energy fighting an enemy hiding in the shadows. There would be plenty of time for that later.

Besides, I was a leader now, not some rogue witch playing dress-up with her powers and hiding out in the shadows of Blackmoon Bay. Those days were long gone. The witches were depending on me to see this through. And the guys had stood by me when I'd made the decision to become a vampire, despite their own personal feelings on the matter. I owed it to them to do this thing right. To learn my new strengths and weaknesses, figure out how they meshed with my old ones, and leverage all of that to become the most powerful vampire-witch I could.

"I'm good," I said, finally shaking off the funk of all my failed attempts. A new burst of energy shot through my limbs—I was so ready to do this. "Let's see how much mojo I can access without tapping into my realm."

Still blindfolded, I waited a few minutes to give the guys time to scatter, then I stretched my arms wide, reaching for the energy around me, beneath me, inside me. It took a few minutes, but then I felt it again—the familiar tug, the warmth, the buzz of my magic as it connected with the earth and sky.

The sensations felt the same as they always had when I tapped into external magic, but tonight, with my vampire senses on high alert and my mind newly focused, everything was so much clearer.

I could sense the cold kiss of every snowflake alighting on my skin, feel the cool air whispering across the hairs on my neck, taste winter's breath. If I concentrated hard enough, I could hear the snow falling, feel the earth shifting beneath it to accommodate its weight.

I am part of this. All of it.

Power surged inside. I felt amazing, like there was literally nothing I couldn't do, no foe I couldn't best, no battle I couldn't survive.

"Come at me!" I shouted, a giggle bubbling up to the surface.

And come at me they did. Rather, come at me they *tried*.

For the next hour, they played the same game as before. But this time, no one even got close. I could feel the shift in the energy around me as they approached, sense the change in the air when they moved to grab me. I could scent each one of them, my mind seeing their moves a millisecond before they made them.

I danced and sidestepped every attempt easily, as smooth as water flowing over stones.

"You were right," I said, when Darius finally called an end to the exercise. "The key was my magic. I felt like it unlocked something inside me—all that vamp potential. I feel incredible."

I couldn't help the smile that stretched across my face, but I could tell from the tight feeling inside that Darius wasn't smiling back. I could sense him more clearly now, too—not just his presence, but his emotions. More than any of the other guys, I felt like I had a direct link to him now.

"What?" I asked him. "What's wrong?"

"You definitely have an advantage over the rest of us mere single-entity beings," Darius said. "Many advantages, actually. But you're not wholly indestructible, Gray, and neither are any of us. We all have to fight hard, and we have to fight smart. You've still got a long way to go. I'm not ready to give you a medal just yet."

"I think I'm doing pretty damn great for my first time out," I said, a little defensively. Hadn't I just proven that? Hadn't I spent the last few *hours* proving that?

"For your first time out, absolutely," he replied. "But that's exactly what this is—your first time out. Liam's right about statistical significance. We need more time to train, more time to know this isn't just a fluke."

"A fluke? Are you—"

"Sunrise isn't for a few hours yet," he said, leaving no room for argument. "I think we should run through that exercise one more time. After that, I've got some mental tests I'd like to…"

His words trailed off as I headed back the way we'd come, ditching my blindfold on the way.

"We're not done yet!" he shouted, his voice echoing across the meadow. "You can't possibly tell me you're tired."

I wasn't tired—the opposite, actually. My body was buzzing with energy, glad for the exercise and the fun night out, despite the few hiccups and Darius's apparent inability to dish out a compliment.

But I was also eager to get back to the lodge, to rest up before tomorrow night. I'd proven myself stable enough for public exposure—that much was certain. After a day's rest, I'd finally be able to spend some time with my sisters.

I hadn't even spoken to either of them since we'd gotten

Adele out of that cell. The three of us had so much catching up to do.

"You guys can stay if you want," I called over my shoulder, "but I'm ready for some hot chocolate and a nice roaring fire with—"

The howl of the wolf pierced my eardrums, and I spun around just in time to see Emilio charge at Liam, knocking him to the ground.

Liam struggled in vain to fight back.

And then Emilio, the man I loved, the one I trusted with my life and the lives of everyone I'd ever cared for, tore out Liam's throat.

NINE

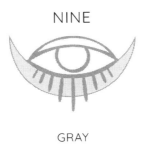

GRAY

"Liam!" I shot back across the meadow, launching myself at Emilio, desperate to put an end to the carnage…

I face-planted into the snow.

Emilio vanished. Liam vanished. The crimson pool of snow… All of it was gone.

What the fuck is going on?

I got to my knees, blinking away the lingering images, shocked as Liam came back into view.

He stood between Ash and Ronan, shivering in the cold but otherwise unharmed. All of them were watching me like I'd totally gone off the rails, which I basically had.

"Gray?" Liam's brow furrowed as he knelt before me, reaching up to touch my face with a gloved hand. "What's wrong?"

"I don't…" I closed my eyes, then opened them, certain I was losing my mind.

"You're trembling," he said.

"But... You're alive!" I blurted out, hauling him against my chest in a crushing hug. Seconds later, Emilio bounded toward me, still in his wolf form, and pressed his nose against my thigh.

There was no blood. No vicious snarl. Only my beautiful, gentle wolf. I reached out and stroked behind his ear.

I'd imagined the whole thing.

"I heard Emilio howling," I said, trying to piece it together. "Then I saw him... He attacked Liam. He... he killed him."

Liam pulled out of my embrace and narrowed his eyes at me. "Gray, are you feeling alright?" Then, to Darius, "Perhaps we should get her home. The drop in external temperature seems to be adversely affecting her, or maybe the stress of all the activity after her lengthy bedrest."

Darius shook his head. "I can assure you, Liam. Neither of those things is affecting her."

"Then what the fuck was that?" I demanded, my limbs still vibrating, my heart heavy. Even with Liam in my arms, the grip of loss and grief had yet to fully retreat. "I saw him lying in a pool of his own blood."

"That," Darius said, hauling me to my feet, "was a lesson in the power of influence."

"That... That was *you*?" I glared at him, my mouth dropping open. He'd actually made me hallucinate—made me believe—that one of the men I loved had just brutally murdered another.

How could he have been so cruel?

"I'm sorry for springing that on you," Darius said, softer

now. He took my face into his hands, swiping my tears with his thumbs. "It was the only way to make you truly see."

"See what?" I asked. "You made me think Emilio... That he.... I watched him tear out Liam's throat!"

"Dude, seriously?" Asher turned a fiery gaze on Darius. "That's a little fucked up, even for you."

"What you call 'a little fucked up', hellspawn, I call making a very important point." Turning his attention back to me, Darius said, "It was the first thing that came to mind —something I knew would blind you to all personal risk and send you charging in without a second thought. And you took the bait without question. You bolted straight for them, didn't you?"

"I thought he was *dead*, asshole!" I shoved him in the chest, expecting to meet a solid wall of muscle, but sending him sprawling on his ass instead.

Right. Vampire strength.

The realization offered little consolation.

Darius got to his feet and brushed the snow off his backside, unfazed.

"You are physically stronger now, Gray," he said. "Your speed and agility are almost limitless, your raw power like nothing I've ever encountered in a newborn, and your instincts—once you learned to start trusting them—are spot on. Your magic enhances all of those qualities, and we've only just begun to tap into that potential."

"So what's the problem?" I snapped, turning away from him. I wanted to keep my eyes on Liam and Emilio, to make sure they were still here. Really here.

"Despite all of that," Darius continued, "you're still not immune to the powers of a sadistic vampire bent on getting inside your head. If we run into rogues in the Bay—which we almost certainly will—they're going to exploit you the first chance they get."

"Then you're basically saying we don't stand a chance," I said. "If anyone can make me hallucinate images like that, I'm toast." I bent down and put my hands on my knees, still trying to catch my—well, breath wasn't the right word anymore. More like my equilibrium.

That little mind trip had left me absolutely reeling.

"They can *try* to make you," he said. "But they won't succeed. Not if you learn to shield your mind."

"That takes a lot of concentration, Darius. Not to mention energy. Not the most reliable tactic in a full-on combat situation, when I might have five other assailants coming at me, not to mention trying to keep track of the witches and you guys and everything else going on."

"For a witch, yes, it would be a lot of energy," he said. "But for a fellow vampire? It's just a matter of learning the right technique. Then it becomes second nature."

I let out a bitter laugh. "That simple, huh?"

"I never said anything about simple, love. Just possible." He folded his arms across his chest and glared at me, driving home the point. "You're the one ready to call it a night, so sure you've learned all you can. Perhaps next time you won't be so hasty to dismiss the idea of additional training time."

I stepped into his space, glaring at him right back. "Perhaps next time, *bloodsucker*, you won't break into my head with a vision guaranteed to scar me for the rest of my damn life."

Darius exploded, fisting the front of my jacket and hauling me close, nose to nose. Through gritted teeth, he said, "And how long do you expect that life to last if you refuse to learn even the most rudimentary—"

"Darius." Ronan stepped in, a firm grip around Darius's arm. "Can I have a word, please?"

His eyes had gone completely black.

Darius finally released me, and I turned my back on him, grateful as Ronan practically dragged him to the other side of the meadow. When I turned back to look at them, I saw Darius standing firm, arms crossed over his chest while Ronan paced in front of him, arms gesturing wildly.

Good. I hope he's tearing you a new one.

"You okay?" Asher asked, offering a warm smile. It felt like the first I'd seen in a year, and when he opened his arms for a hug, I gladly accepted the offer, waving for Liam to join in.

A few minutes later, Ronan and Darius returned, Ronan sparing me a sympathetic glance before marching ahead, back toward the woods.

His eyes had returned to normal.

The others headed for the path, too, and I turned to follow them. But a soft touch on my shoulder stopped me in my tracks.

"I don't want to talk right now, D," I said.

"Then just listen. Please, Gray."

Folding my arms across my chest, I nodded and turned around.

"I'm so, so sorry for putting you through that," Darius said, his eyes glazing with unexpected emotion. "I wouldn't have gone to such extremes if I thought I could make the point any other way."

"So you're sorry, but you're standing by it?"

"I don't know what else to say. I'm trying to protect you."

"Darius. You have to know that if any one of you went down like that, not even a freight train could stop me from getting to you."

"I understand. Which is why I needed you to see just how easy it would be to get inside your mind. If that happens when we're fighting in the Bay, even for an instant, there's nothing you'll be able to do to regain the upper hand. You may not even realize you've lost it."

"So we just have to make sure that doesn't happen," I said. He'd been right about that part, anyway. I still had a lot more to learn, and not a lot of time to learn it. "I get it, Darius. You made your point. Mission accomplished."

"Hey." Darius hooked a finger beneath my chin and tilted my face up, but I refused to meet his gaze. "Look at me, love. Please."

I finally gave in.

"I meant what I said," he continued. "I'm deeply sorry. I never meant to hurt you, only to shock you. Understand, Gray... I'm your sire. Yes, becoming a vampire was your decision, but ultimately, you would not have undergone the transformation if I hadn't agreed, regardless of the state of my memories at the time."

"What does that have to do with anything?"

"I made you. It's my responsibility to guide you through this. To ensure, to the absolute best of my ability, that you can come into this new power fully, to explore every facet of it, to know your strengths as well as your weaknesses. If I overlooked something, and you got hurt as a result, or worse..." His voice broke on the word, and he closed his eyes, shaking his head. "It was a bad call on my part. I should've found another way."

"I... I accept your apology." I wrapped my hands around his wrists, and he opened his eyes, his hands still cupping my face. His gaze softened as he looked at me, sweeping down to linger on my lips.

I swallowed, my mouth already watering for the taste of his kiss, sweet and tender and full of the love I knew he felt for me, sealing the momentary gap that'd come between us.

But I couldn't kiss him. Not right now.

Offering a small but brief smile, I pulled out of his touch. "I said I accept your apology, and I do. And I promise I'll do whatever it takes to learn the shielding techniques, and any additional training you want to put me through. But I just..." I closed my eyes, the image of Liam's bleeding corpse still flashing through my mind. "I need a little space, okay?"

When I opened my eyes again, Darius was still standing before me, his lips pressed together, his face tight with guilt. With pain.

He hadn't moved, hadn't granted me the space I'd requested.

But I didn't need to wait for it anymore. I was faster than him now, and without another thought, I blurred out of sight. The guys were still clomping through the snow along the trail, the hounds keeping guard at the rear, and I sped past the whole lot of them, not stopping until I reached the car.

By the time they all got back, I was already tucked safely into the back seat, wrapped up in a blanket, pretending to be fast asleep. Only Liam dared to sit near me. Dared to take my hand.

I squeezed it tight, holding it close for the drive home, taking comfort in the warm and solid reality of it.

The weight of Darius's guilt felt like another person in the front seat. I didn't want him to feel that way, but I couldn't find the words to make it better for him just then. He didn't understand—I wasn't even particularly angry with him anymore. Yes, his choice of imagery had been shocking and cruel, but I understood why he'd taken such an extreme measure.

It wasn't that I'd needed space from *him,* or from what he'd done.

It was that I'd watched Liam's blood soak into the snow until he had none left to lose.

In that brief moment, it had been real to me.

And for the first time since the Lord of Shadows visited my bedroom with talk of necromancy and the rare powers of the Shadowborn witch, for the first time since our journey through the Shadowrealm and hell, since he'd kissed me, since he'd confessed his betrayals, since he'd given me a rock carved with his signature raven feather, since he'd helped me bring Emilio back from the dead, since he'd sacrificed his eternal soul for us, since I'd fallen in love with him... For the first time in our long and winding relationship, I finally and truly understood that Liam—the Great Transformation, Older than the Seas, formerly known as Death Himself—could die.

TEN

GRAY

I spent the early morning sleeping in my own bed, bliss-fully alone and free from the restraints, blinds drawn tight against the daylight, door locked and guarded by both hounds to keep any would-be visitors away.

By the time I woke up, the sun had just set, and the lodge was buzzing with activity. I crept downstairs on quiet feet, hoping to catch my sisters alone. I found them in the kitchen; Verona had them working hard, pulverizing dried herbs and portioning them into glass jars while several other witches fluttered around them, collecting and labeling the full jars, looking over ingredient lists, taking stock of the herbs in the pantry.

They didn't notice me at first, and I lingered in the door-way, taking a moment to soak it all in.

Haley was practically buzzing, talking a mile-a-minute, her smile bright and warm. If she was still dwelling on the blood oath she'd sworn in the crypt, she didn't show it one bit. Her curves were coming back, as was her hair—the fuzz I'd gotten used to was now a cute pixie cut that made her green eyes pop.

Adele looked a hundred times better than when I'd last seen her in the cemetery, which was a huge relief. Her face was still gaunt, tattooed with the bruises and scrapes her captors had given her, but those marks were already beginning to fade. Her color had completely returned, those beautiful brown eyes sparkling. They were kind eyes, open and trusting despite the fear lingering there.

Despite our different eye color, she looked a lot like me. Same cheekbones, same blonde hair, though hers was a bit longer. Apparently, her captors hadn't cut it, and now it curled over her shoulder in a low side ponytail.

I blinked back tears. I still couldn't believe I had sisters, that they were here, that three out of the four of us had finally been reunited after more than two decades apart.

And we'll find Georgie, too. Whatever it takes.

"Gray! You're up!"

Haley's squeal of delight snapped me out of my thoughts, and I stepped in through the doorway, beaming at her as she darted across the kitchen and launched herself into my arms.

"You look fucking amazing, girl." She laughed as she pulled back and took me in, head to toe. "I missed you so much! I've been trying to get in to see you for days, but your supreme protectors were having none of it."

"That was for *your* protection, not mine." I pulled her in for another quick hug. It was so good to see her, to feel her, whole and alive. Despite all the obstacles we'd yet to face, I felt stronger just knowing we'd be doing it together.

"How… how are you feeling? I mean, is it… Am I… Do you…?" Haley trailed off, but I read the questions in her eyes.

Giving her a reassuring smile, I said, "I'm feeling better than I've ever felt in my life. It's super weird. And no, you're not in any danger from me."

Haley laughed. "Good to know, because now that I've got you back, I'm not leaving your side. Well, other than when you need to pee, or you're having 'special' time with—"

"*Special* time?" I rolled my eyes, cracking up. "That's not… Hay, you *really* need to get some 'special time' of your own. Sooner rather than later."

"I keep asking if the guys have any hot brothers, but no luck." Haley linked her arm in mine. "Come on. Come meet Addie—officially, this time. She's dying to talk to you."

She led me to the counter at the center of the kitchen, where Adele and McKenna, the boisterous witch who'd helped Asher and Haley take care of the witches in the cave prison, were pouring some kind of herbal powder into bottles through a paper cone. The cone tipped, and I grabbed it, catching it just before it spilled all over the counter.

"Thank—" Adele looked up, her eyes going wide when she saw it was me. McKenna winked at me, then slipped out of sight, leaving me alone with my sisters.

"Addie, meet Gray," Haley said softly. "Gray, meet our sister, Addie."

Adele—Addie—smiled, her eyes glazing as she took me in. "Gray, I… I just…"

She was suddenly overcome with emotion, unable to get the rest of the words out, and seeing her tears broke the dam on mine. Righting the cone, I walked around to the other side of the counter, then pulled her in for a hug. She stiffened at first, and I worried I'd done the wrong thing—maybe she didn't like touching, or wasn't ready for that kind of intimacy with me yet.

But just before I released her, she softened in my arms, her shoulders shaking as she finally let loose the sobs she'd been holding in.

My own tears falling freely, I held her close, rubbing her back, letting her get it all out. She'd just been through a torturous hell I could only imagine, and whether she'd known about us before or not, finding out you had a built-in family was beyond intense. The poor woman was on an emotional roller coaster—I had no idea how long she'd been on this ride, and no idea when she'd be able to get off.

When her breathing finally evened out, she pulled out of my embrace and met my eyes.

"Gray," she said again, this time with a steady smile. Then, in a clear, determined voice completely at odds with her red nose and glassy eyes, she said, "Thank you for saving my life. For everything you're doing here. For all the… I mean, Haley told me about the prophecy and the covens, and everything that's happened, and the stuff in

Blackmoon Bay, and your friend Sophie, and… Shit. I'm sorry. I didn't mean… *God*." She let out a nervous laugh, swiping away the tears from her bruised face. "How am I fucking this up so badly already? Five minutes into meeting you—that might be a new personal record."

"You're not fucking *anything* up," I assured her, then smiled. "The first time I met Haley, she practically decked me."

"Hey!" Haley said. "You're conveniently leaving out the part about you acting like a complete bitch."

"Okay, first of all, I wasn't acting. And second of all, my best friend had just died. I should've gotten a free bitch-pass." I winked at her to let her know I was teasing. I would never joke about losing Sophie, but somehow, making light of my own feelings felt okay—almost as if Sophie herself were watching, egging us on. As painful as that day at Norah's house had been for me, it was also the moment Haley had come crashing into my life, slipping a note into my pocket that would lead me to Jael and Sophie's book of shadows, and to everything that had come after.

Everything that had brought us closer. As close as sisters.

I wouldn't trade it for the world.

Haley tossed a dried rosebud at me, pegging me between the eyes. "If I'd known I was your big sister back then, I probably would've skipped the *practically* part and gone straight to kicking your ass, so consider that your free pass."

"Oh, you want some of this?" I teased, spreading my arms. "Take your best shot, girl."

"Hmm. Hard pass. You weren't a super-powered blood-sucker back then." She grabbed a clean cutting board and knife from the drying rack next to the sink, then handed them to me, her eyes twinkling with laughter. "Now wash up and get to work. Bloodsucker or not, there's no such thing as a free lunch around here, Desario, and you've been laying around for days."

"Yes ma'am." I knotted my hair in a loose bun and washed my hands, excited to roll up my sleeves and dig in. It felt good to be doing something tangible, something other than practicing violence, or worse—executing it. After everything that had happened with the guys last night, a few hours of peaceful herbcraft with my sisters sounded like just what the doctor ordered.

"So, what are we working on today?" I asked brightly, joining them at the counter. "Healing potions? Protective charms? Dinner?"

Addie held up a vial marked *hemlock*. "The fine art of poison-making."

I laughed. So much for a day of peaceful herbcraft.

"Sounds like a party." I rubbed my hands together and grinned. "Where do I start?"

ELEVEN

GRAY

"Crafting the perfect poison is both an art and a science." Verona, who'd been supervising all the activity in the kitchen, set an armload of clean vials and jars on the counter before us, then handed me a sheet of instructions.

I scanned it carefully, memorizing the ingredients, measurements, and specific incantations necessary for crafting the deadly poisons our witches would be carrying into battle, just in case.

Not everyone had built-in offensive powers. But we'd make damn sure they weren't left defenseless, either.

I closed my eyes, took a moment to set my intention for this deadly work, then grabbed the kitchen knife and a bottle of what looked like tiny twigs, ready to chop.

Everyone in the lodge was working on something—poisons, spells, protective charms, healing potions, combat training, weapons inspection and inventory, meal planning, cleaning, mending, weatherizing the windows and doors against the insane winter. Half the guys were on guard duty with Elena's men on the beach and in the woods, Liam was working with Reva on her shadow traveling practice, and the rest had gone out with Elena on another grocery run which, according to Haley, was starting to become a real challenge. A handful of local stores were doing their best to stay open and stocked through the storms, but they were having trouble getting supplies delivered. Most of the major roadways into the Cape and surrounding communities had been intermittently shut down, leaving the National Guard and emergency services to pick up the slack.

If things had gotten that bad here in the Cape, I could only imagine what they were experiencing in Blackmoon Bay—ground zero for the entire disaster.

It took me a few minutes to get into the groove, but once I did, the work became easy, almost meditative. My sisters and I got our own little assembly line going, with me chopping, Haley measuring and mixing, and Addie portioning everything into bottles.

Everywhere I looked, people were in motion. Bodies moved. Hearts beat. Blood flowed, warm and sweet and seductive.

I couldn't say the presence of so many people didn't faze me, but I meant what I'd told Haley: no one in this house was in any danger from me. The times I felt the hunger welling up, I just stepped outside for some air, or took the hounds for a romp in the snow, or grabbed some blood from the stash Emilio had brought back for me.

It got the job done, just enough to take the edge off. But it wasn't satisfying. Not in the least. Drinking donor blood was a choice I made *every* time, and I was only a few days in.

Darius had been doing this for centuries.

Darius…

I hadn't spoken with him since our argument last night. I'd gone straight to bed after we'd arrived at the lodge, and last I heard, he was out patrolling the beach tonight.

I missed him. I needed to see him, to let him know I was okay. That I understood what he'd done and why, even if the image of Liam still haunted me…

Desperate for a distraction, I turned to Addie and blurted out, "So what's your superpower, sis?"

Haley cracked up. "Nice, Gray. Way to ease into it."

"Well, we're all witches, right? Magic isn't exactly a four-letter word around here."

Haley shot me a smug glare, and even though my magic didn't come with mind-reading powers, in that moment I could read her thoughts like a book.

I'd come a long way since that first day at Norah's, when I was willing to do just about anything to keep my magic on permanent lockdown. Back then, I really believed I could outrun my destiny.

Anyway, Addie was our sister. I wanted to know her, just like I wanted to know Haley. And I wanted them to know *me*, too. Maybe it wouldn't happen overnight. Maybe we'd fight and keep secrets and avoid any subjects that cut a little too close to the bone.

But magic? That was neutral territory. It was something we all had in common, and a good place to start.

"I guess you'd call it foresight," Addie replied, and I nodded. Deirdre had mentioned as much.

"But not in the usual ways you hear about," she went on. "I don't literally *see* the future so much as sense it. Like, they're not visions exactly, but I get these impressions— feelings and smells, mostly. Sometimes I'll hear things, like a song or a voice or some other noise that helps me home in on whatever it is I'm sensing."

"Sounds like Sophie's gift," I said. "She'd pick up on emotional impressions whenever she touched something. Like, a piece of furniture or jewelry or clothes. People too. I used to call her the human lie detector."

"Haley told me about that." Addie smiled. "But it's not so much about touching objects for me. It's more like... like there's something out there, right? A force, divine intervention, an invisible time-traveling multi-dimensional being, something. It taps into my intuition, and then stuff just sort of... appears. From there, it's up to me to put the puzzle together."

"What do you mean?" I ask. "How does that even work?"

"Let's say I pull a Tarot card, and the message I get from it has to do with children. Six of Cups, maybe." She tapped a small bottle against the counter, settling the powder inside before sticking a rubber stopper in it. "Once I accept that message or keyword or whatever, that's when I open up. Suddenly I'll smell crayons and paste, or hear kids playing outside, or taste school lunch. That tells me something is going to happen at an elementary school. So I might draw another card to try to pull in more clues—is this an emergency situation, or just something I need to know about? Does this affect someone I care about? These are really simplistic examples, though—usually I'll get a lot more intuitive hits, all at once. I just try to stay open to whatever messages are trying to come through, and from there, I can usually piece together a prediction."

"That's fucking cool," I said. "Just that you can do that. I feel like I'd get totally overwhelmed."

"Sometimes I do. I mean, it *is* cool. But it's also maddening, especially when I *know* there's something important trying to come through, and I can't quite figure it out." She reached for an empty bottle and set it up with a fresh paper cone. "Like you guys, for instance. Looking back now, I can see that I've been getting bits and pieces about this moment for years, but I had no context for it. I didn't know what the hell the universe was trying to tell me.

"I grew up in North Carolina—about as far as you can get from Washington, at least in the states. I'd always assumed I'd been there. I didn't learn about my adoption until two years ago—my mother finally told me, but she left out a lot of details. I thought my real parents had died."

"That's what we all thought," I said. "I take it you don't have any memories from before?"

"Just flashes, but nothing that ever made sense. Haley told me about our mother, about what she did to us…" Her hands stilled around the bottle, and her eyes went far away, narrowing as if she were trying to pull the memories out of the mists of time. But then she blinked and shook her head, blowing out a breath. "I don't know if I blocked it all out, or someone altered our memories, or what."

"Maybe a little of both." I scraped the latest batch of chopped twigs into the big bowl in front of Haley, then dumped another batch onto my cutting board.

Altered memories. That was the theory Haley and I had come up with. Ultimately, I'd remembered that day at the creek when our mother had tried to drown us, but Haley never did, and she was the oldest—she would've been about four when it happened. Deirdre had told me she'd altered our mother's memories to make her believe she'd succeeded in murdering us, so it wasn't much of a stretch to assume our grandmother had "adjusted" our memories as well.

After all, she was trying to keep us apart. To keep the prophecy from coming true.

"Anyway," Addie continued, "A couple of years ago, I started getting this massive influx of impressions—way more than at any other time in my life—and they all had to do with the west coast. Like, the wind would rustle the trees outside my house, but I'd hear the sound of the ocean instead. Or I'd be eating barbecued chicken at Mom's Sunday dinner, but it would taste and feel like fresh crab. In bed at night, I'd feel like I was on a boat—you know, that rocking sensation, the wind in my hair, the smell of the sea. Or I'd be watching the sunset over the hills, and suddenly I'd see it setting on whitecaps instead. One morning I just woke up with this urge—a need, really—to go west. Washington, specifically. Don't ask me why—I'd never even been here."

"You sensed us," I said. "Deirdre said that would happen. We were all born in the Bay—she said we'd all be drawn back to it."

"That's what Haley told me." Addie sighed. "I was always a little on the impulsive side, so when it got to the point where I couldn't sleep anymore because all I could think about was making my way west, I did it. I gave notice at work, broke my apartment lease, packed my belongings into my car and took off. My parents thought I was nuts, but they'd always encouraged me to have a sense of adventure. Mom was a witch, of course, so she knew all about intuition and feelings and signs. Well, and obviously she must've known that my origins were here, but she never said anything. It's only now that I realize it."

She got that faraway look in her eyes again, and lowered her head, her hands fidgeting with the bottle.

After a beat, I put my hand on her arm. "Addie, have you been back in touch with them since you got out of…?" I trailed off. I couldn't bring myself to say the word prison, or cell, or crypt or torture chamber of nightmare hell, but she knew what I was asking.

Addie shook her head as a tear slid down her cheek. "The hunters… It was one of the main ways they kept us all in line. They'd show us pictures or video of our families every few days—they said they had people watching them at all times. If we disobeyed, if we tried to escape, if we tried to get in touch with anyone on the outside, they'd...."

I glanced at Haley, wondering if anyone had tried to reach out to Addie's parents, but Haley only shook her head.

"Addie, listen to me," I said firmly. "We left *no* one alive in that compound—not hunter, not hybrid, not fae, not a soul. Even if they *did* have someone watching, the hunters have much bigger problems now."

"I know." She sniffed, dashing away the tears. "That's exactly what I've been telling myself. But I'm not going to risk calling them—not until we're out of the woods. At this point, it's almost better that they think I'm..." Addie shook her head, blowing out another breath.

"Addie," Haley asked, putting her hand on our sister's back, "how did you get mixed up with the hunters in the first place?"

"They nabbed me in Port Franklin about ten months ago. I was their prisoner, plaything, and medical experiment every day from that moment until you guys came busting into that crypt."

"Holy shit," I whispered. Haley coughed, doing her best to hide her own gasp of shock.

Swallowing the lump in my throat, I said gently, "How did they get to you?"

"I'd been living there just over a year by then—it was the first place I'd landed after leaving North Carolina, and I'd fallen in love with it immediately. It had the small-town, artsy vibe I'd always wanted, and the people were so friendly and open. I found work right away, waitressing in a place that catered mostly to witches. I'd recently started dating, and saving for my own place. I thought I wanted to set down roots, you know? I still wasn't sure why I'd felt called to move there, but at that point I was happy to roll with it, trusting that when the time was right, all would be revealed. But then things started getting weird."

"Weird how?" I asked

"A few of my regulars—they'd started acting kind of paranoid. At least, that's how I saw it at the time. Whispering about old hunter conspiracies, and witches being murdered in their beds... I... Sorry, Gray. I didn't mean..." Her cheeks darkened, and when she met my eyes again, her own were full of compassion. "I know they weren't rumors after all, but at the time, no one had heard from the hunters in decades. It all seemed a little far-fetched—like everyone had heard it from a friend of a cousin of an ex-husband, but no one had any firsthand info.

"The vamps and shifters," she continued, "who normally stayed pretty sequestered in their own territories, started getting into skirmishes. One night a family of lynx shifters was slaughtered in their home, little kids and everything, and their whole community blamed the vampires. After that, things started going downhill fast. My restaurant shut down, and I was laid off. I was in shock, literally wandering the streets with my head hung, wondering what my next move was going to be. I swear—the second the question was in my mind, I felt it."

"Felt what?" I asked. I'd long since given up on chopping. Haley and I, along with the other witches in the kitchen, were all riveted by the story.

Sadly, I was pretty sure a lot of them had similar tales to tell.

"That foreboding. Like when every hair on your body stands on end, and your heart just starts banging away for no reason. I reached in my bag for my mace, but by then, someone was already on top of me, jamming in the needle." She closed her eyes, a full-on shiver working its way through her body. I could sense the uptick of her heartbeat, the adrenaline spiking through her blood as remembered panic set in. "I woke up in a cell. You can pretty much figure out what happened next."

It was a good thing I'd already set down the bottle of herbs I'd been working with, because I was pretty sure anything in my hands would've shattered in that moment.

"Addie," I said softly, forcing myself to keep my voice calm. Gentle. For my sister's sake. For the sake of every witch in the room who'd gone through the same impossible hell. "You're safe here. All of you are safe here. And I promise you, we're going to kill every last one of those motherfuckers if I have to tear their throats out myself."

I was shaking with rage, so consumed by it that I didn't even notice Haley standing in front of me until she reached out and grabbed my arm. "Gray? Take this. Please."

I blinked back to reality, taking the steaming mug from her outstretched hand. Closing my eyes, I took a second to dial it down, then managed a tight smile. "I appreciate the effort, but I don't think Merry Mint is going to do the trick this time."

"This brew is." She winked at me. "My own special blend. I call it Vampire's Delight."

I brought it to my nose, inhaling the scent. I smelled the mint first, then a subtle pinch of dried hawthorn—nothing that would knock me out, just strong enough to blunt my sharp edges—finished with a spoonful of O-positive. I sipped it slowly, forcing myself to relax.

"Thank you," I said. "That's actually... really good."

"Told you." She handed a mug to Addie. "This is straight-up honey lavender. No blood, unless you're into that sort of thing."

Addie laughed, happily wrapping her hands around the mug. "I think I'll stick with the honey-lavender, thanks."

We sipped our tea and got back to work, giving Addie a few moments to gather her thoughts. Whatever she'd gone through, it was clear this was the first time she was talking about it out loud, and I knew this was only the very first crack. Eventually, that crack would turn into a fissure, and all hell would break loose.

The difference now was that she wouldn't have to go through it alone. Not anymore.

After a few moments of companionable silence, Haley turned the conversation toward our other sister. "How do you guys think Georgie got tangled up with Trinity when the rest of us managed to stay under her radar?"

"I don't know," I said. "I'm guessing Trinity found her somehow. Maybe that's how this whole thing got started.

Now that we know she's involved with the Fae Council, we can connect her to Orendiel and the hunters. So it's possible that Trinity found out that we were still alive, and set the wheels of her plan in motion."

"But why would she track down Georgie and not the rest of us?" Addie asked.

"Maybe she's still looking for us," Haley said.

That thought sent a shiver down my spine, but there was no room for fear. I grabbed Verona's instruction list, scanning for the next batch of poisons. If and when Trinity came for us, we'd be ready for her.

"You guys said that we were all called to the Bay," Addie said. "That we sensed each other somehow."

"That's what Deirdre thinks," I said.

Addie capped off another one of her bottles. "Do you think Georgie senses us, too? What if she's trying to get back to us, and Trinity's holding her hostage?"

"We can't assume Georgie is a hostage," I said. "For all we know, she and Trinity are working together." I hated myself for saying it, but someone had to. The girl we'd seen in our vision during the blood spell hadn't looked like a hostage to me.

Haley looked up from her bowl of herbs, glaring at me across the counter. "Do you actually think our sister is evil?"

"I'm not saying she's evil, Hay. But we can't know her motivations. She might not realize what's going on. Our mother may have twisted everything, manipulated her into doing her bidding."

"She's not a child, Gray," Haley said. "She's a grown woman."

"That doesn't mean she couldn't be misled or manipulated or threatened," I said. "All we know is that she's working with Trinity. We have no idea what her situation is, but at the end of the day—"

"God, I hate that phrase," Haley said. "At the end of the day? We're talking about right *now*, Gray. Our sister is in trouble, and you want to sentence her before we've even—"

"I think what Gray is trying to say," Addie said gently, reaching out to touch Haley's hand, "is that even if Georgie *isn't* evil, she's still fighting on the wrong side, whether she realizes it or not."

"Thank you," I said, blowing out a breath. "That's all I—"

"And," she went on, cutting me off with a kind smile, "I think Haley is trying to remind us that no matter whose team Georgie is on, she's still our sister, and we owe it to her to give her the benefit of the doubt. To try to help her, just like you guys helped me. Just like you're helping each other."

I looked into Addie's eyes, my momentary annoyance at Haley floating away.

Haley sighed. "Addie's right. Look, Gray, the last thing I want to do is fight with you."

"Same," I admitted. "I get what you're saying about Georgie."

"And I get what *you're* saying," Haley said. "I think we

just... We can't make assumptions either way. But we also can't abandon her without trying to figure it out.

"Agreed," I said, and Addie smiled.

"Guys," she said, "I think I just broke up my first sister fight."

I nudged her in the ribs. "Don't let it go to your head just yet."

Magical or not, I was starting to think that her gifts went well beyond foresight. Addie was a natural peacemaker.

"So where do we go from here?" I asked.

Both of my sisters opened their mouths to respond, but the voice that reached my ears wasn't from either of them.

It was the dark, deadly, deep-fried twang of the only man I hated worse than the hunters.

"I'll tell you where you're *not* going, Miss Desario," Sebastian drawled. "How about we start there?"

With fire in his eyes, he snapped his fingers, and every witch in the kitchen disappeared.

TWELVE

GRAY

Instinct took over.

In a blur of movement, I grabbed my knife and leaped over the counter, lunging for him, fangs and blade bared.

But even with my vamp speed, I was no match for the prince of hell. A single raised hand, and I slammed into an invisible wall, my knife clattering to the floor.

I scrambled to my feet. "What have you done with them?"

"Relax," he said. "I've safely relocated them to another part of the lodge, where they will remain, none the wiser, so long as you give me the right answers."

"I'm not answering anything until I know for sure they're safe."

His eyes turned completely red, the vein at his temple throbbing with barely-contained rage. "I'm sorry, blood-sucker. Have I given you the impression that you're in any position to negotiate?"

I backed off, but I didn't back down. I had no idea how he'd found out about my vampire transition, but now that he had, I had to play this very carefully.

"What can I do for you, prince?" I asked, folding my arms across my chest.

"See? Civility. That's much better." Patting his stomach, he glanced around the kitchen, his eyes returning to normal. "I suppose I can't expect hospitality, though. What have you got to drink in this dreadful establishment?"

I didn't respond.

"Never mind. I'll help myself." He rummaged through the cupboards, locating the liquor stash and pouring himself a generous glass of bourbon. Gesturing to the table at the other side of the kitchen, he said, "Sit."

It wasn't a request.

I did as he asked, and he took the chair across from me, eyeing me up as he sipped the bourbon. I couldn't read his thoughts, and didn't dare try to influence them, lest he sense my interference. But one thing was clear—Sebastian had a lot on his mind.

"Let's get one thing clear before we proceed." He set the glass on the table, locking me in his frightening glare. "The fact that you are at present a soulless monster does not negate our deal. Soul or not, you *will* find a way to do as I demand, per the rules of your contract."

I waited a beat. Two. Three. Then, "The contract is for my soul, Sebastian. Which, as you can see, is long gone. I'm not sure we have anything left to—"

He snapped his fingers again, and my throat constricted.

It was as if I were being choked by an invisible hand. No, I didn't need oxygen, but I needed my windpipe intact.

"I think we're well past semantics, Miss Desario." He lifted the glass to his lips, watching with pure amusement as I clawed at my own throat, my eyes bulging. Saliva pooled in the corners of my mouth, my neck about five seconds from snapping in two, and still he drawled on. "I *own* you, just as I own Ronan. Body, mind, soul, blood, bones. I own those sharp and shiny new fangs of yours. I own those curls that probably drive the boys wild. I own your heart, your smile, your eyeballs. I own the soles of your feet. I own your fingerprints. I even own your thoughts."

He took another long sip, then set the glass down, finally releasing his choke-hold.

I coughed, rubbing my throat, glaring daggers at him.

He was full of shit. Sebastian was nothing if not a stickler for details—his entire organization was predicated on it. My contract was specific—my soul was promised to him. Nothing else.

"So you can see why attempting to avoid your fate is not only futile," he said, full of the kind of confidence that could only be achieved by the truly mediocre, "but extremely dangerous."

I nodded, deciding to play along for now.

"At any rate," he blathered on, "the task I've set for you doesn't require the presence of your soul, per se. Only your magic."

The lodge had fallen silent, save for the wheezing of his

breath. I couldn't even hear the ocean outside. He'd truly sealed us in a bubble.

And he still hadn't told me what he wanted, or why he'd shown up at all. He liked keeping me off balance, that was for sure.

Maybe it was time to throw him off balance instead.

"I know it's not my ancestors you're really after," I said.

"You know nothing."

"You sure about that?"

He waved away my words with a swat of his fat hand, but I saw the flicker of surprise in his eyes. He was playing games, as usual.

"Tell me what you want with Trinity O'Leary," I said, point blank.

The name itself was like a spell, unleashing all his pent-up rage. He slammed his glass onto the table, shattering it and slicing his hand open in the process. My eyes widened at the sight of his crimson blood, but the scent that followed was rotten, a stench so foul it made my stomach turn.

"I've told you once before, and this is the *last* time I'll say it," he warned. "Ronan and the other strays you've picked up along the way may be lining up to lick your boots, but you do *not* dictate orders to me. I'll reveal information to you if and when it's pertinent. Is that clear, witch?"

I glared at him, saying nothing.

"Is that *clear*?" he shouted, this time flipping the table between us. His eyes had gone back to red, his voice shaking.

Whatever my birthmother had done, her betrayal had cut deep. That much was clear.

But Sebastian's outbursts wouldn't scare me off—not this time. Despite his show of force and the choke-hold he'd sprung on me earlier, Sebastian's power over me wasn't physical. Deep down I knew he wouldn't break me. Scare me, yes. Hurt me, sure. But break me? Not a chance.

He needed me in one piece. He needed me willing. My magic wouldn't work without my intent, and my intent could not be faked.

I'd gotten him riled up, off-kilter, and unfocused. I had to press my advantage with him, however small it might be.

I decided to call his bluff.

"I know she bailed on her deal," I said, "but so do lots of people. You can't honestly tell me you'd invest all this energy into tracking down one nearly-powerless witch, especially when you've got the Silversbane heir on the payroll now."

Sebastian closed his eyes and bowed his head, folding his hands in his lap as though he were the picture of self-control. But without the table between us, I could see his legs now, the anxious bounce of his knee.

Again, I wished I could read his thoughts.

"Who made the deal for my soul?" I asked, certain it was all connected. My mother, my legacy, Sebastian's obsession with me. How could it not be?

"How could someone make a deal for a soul that wasn't theirs?" I pressed. "And why were you so willing to accept it?" Then, in a voice that came out much softer than I'd planned, "Why am I so important to you?"

Sebastian sighed. After what felt like an hour, he finally met my eyes again. He seemed to be taking a measure of me, and I forced myself not to fidget.

For the first time in our strange, antagonistic relationship, I swore I saw a flicker of sympathy in his eyes.

"The answer to each of those questions," he finally said, all his earlier rage gone, "is a long, complicated story."

"You've got a captive audience and all the time in the world," I said.

Ignoring this, Sebastian rose from the chair and righted the table he'd knocked over, then headed back to the liquor stash to fix a new drink.

This time, he returned with two.

Handing one to me, he said plainly, "Be careful what you drag out into the light, Silversbane. Some things can't be shoved back into the darkness, no matter how hard you push."

Surprising myself, I took the offered drink, clinking my glass against his before taking a sip. The bourbon stung, but after a moment, my tongue seemed to remember that it'd once liked the taste, and I tossed back a bit more.

Sebastian sat down across from me again, eyeing me with the same assessing gaze. We seemed to be on another level with each other, both of us dropping some of the bluster and mind games, though I couldn't figure out how we'd gotten there.

After another impossibly long stretch of silence, I said,

"I've agreed to your terms, Sebastian. I've made a vow to carry out your bidding. I think I have a right to know who sentenced me."

"If circumstances were different, I might agree with you." He tossed back the rest of the drink, but it wasn't enough to erase the humanity from his eyes. "I'm sorry, Gray. The story of your binding is not mine to tell."

The sincerity in his voice was utterly shocking. Now *I* was the one off-kilter and unbalanced, knowing I could never trust him, but seeing something else beneath the surface nevertheless.

In that moment, the Prince of Hell seemed ancient, as though he were carrying the secrets and regrets of every lost soul he'd ever enslaved.

"Then whose story is it?" I asked, clinging to a last desperate hope he might share some clue, some insight, as if knowing one more thing about my past could untangle every last mystery in my present.

"It's mine," came the sharp, clear reply, and I turned to see Deirdre storming into the kitchen, her eyes blazing. "This has gone on long enough, Sebastian."

Sebastian slammed his fist on the table, but the moment he met my grandmother's fiery eyes, his own softened considerably. In a voice entirely too tender for the moment, he said, "This doesn't concern you, Deirdre."

"You're damn straight it concerns me. You promised me you'd leave my granddaughter alone until it was time for her to fulfill her vow."

"That was before I knew she'd become a bloodsucker,"

he said. "I can only imagine why you didn't feel this change in circumstance warranted a discussion."

"I've only just learned about it myself," Deirdre said. She flashed her eyes at me, and I heard her warning in my mind.

Don't say another word, Gray. We will discuss this later.

I downed the rest of my drink and pressed my lips together, but that was more out of frustration than following her orders. Since I'd met my grandmother, she'd left me with more questions than answers, popping in and out my life as it suited her. At this point, I felt very little allegiance to her.

I just didn't know what the hell else to say.

"Be that as it may, Deirdre," Sebastian drawled, "my patience on this matter is just about gone. I think it's time the witch returns with me to Inferno."

All the sympathy, the humanity, the gentleness I'd seen in him evaporated, replaced once again by the oily, under-handed wheeler-dealer I'd always known.

"We've got a penthouse suite all set up for you," he told me with a smug smile, as if this was a selling point.

At this, I let out a hollow laugh. "Is that a euphemism for dungeon?"

"Hardly," he said. "As long as you do as I ask, you'll want for nothing, I assure you."

"Sorry if I don't take you at your word."

"I've given you no reason not to trust me," he said. "In fact, I've given you more leeway than any other in my possession."

In my possession...

The words crept uneasily down my spine. Technically, he *had* given me leeway. From the moment Liam had burned my life scroll, Sebastian could've called in my contract with a snap of his greasy fingers.

But I needed more than leeway now. I needed time.

Steeling myself, I said, "You and I have a deal. You agreed to grant me my freedom until I've figured out the situation here. As you can see, we're still dealing with that situation, and it's only gotten more complicated."

"I don't see you dealing with anything," he said, glancing around the kitchen. "I see a bunch of witches playing at spellcraft while the world outside falls apart."

"Sebastian," Deirdre said. "A word, please?"

"The world outside is exactly what we're trying to save," I reminded him, ignoring my grandmother's pleas. "And if we fail, your operation fails, too. No more human vessels, no one making deals... It's all just... Poof." I made a starburst with my fingers. "So I'm *real* sorry the apocalypse isn't sticking to your ideal timeline, but unless you're willing to let it all burn down—including hell and your place in it—you should probably back off and let me do what I need to do here."

"So let me get this straight," he said, rubbing his fingers over that ridiculous goatee. "You refuse to trust me, yet at every turn, you're expecting *my* trust. Demanding more and more of it. Attempting to break your contract."

Deirdre's voice echoed through my skull again. *Gray,*

that's enough. Tell him what he wants to hear and get him the hell out.

But telling Sebastian what he wanted to hear was the fastest way into another devil's bargain you couldn't talk your way out of, and I was *not* signing up for that.

"I made a vow to you that night at Inferno, Sebastian," I said. "If that vow is broken, it will be because I've made you a better offer, not because I've reneged."

After a beat, he rose from the table and came to stand beside my chair, towering over me.

Screw that. I stood up, meeting him at eye level, refusing to submit.

"Two weeks, Miss Desario," he said, his breath sharp and boozy. "That is all the time I'm willing to grant, and that is more than generous. See to it that you handle your affairs before then, as there *won't* be another extension. And should you even attempt to negotiate for more time, I won't hesitate to smoke your beloved demons out of existence."

His eyes glittered as he watched that threat hit the mark, worming its way into my mind. No matter how tall and tough I stood, I knew I couldn't hide the fear in my eyes.

I was a fool to think for even a second there was anything humane about Sebastian.

"Show yourself out, prince," I said, keeping my voice solid. "I'm sure you know the way back to hell."

I turned my back on him, feeling both terrified and more powerful than I'd ever felt in my life.

I sensed his instant departure. Just like that, the air in the room cleared.

"Gray," Deirdre said. "You must find your sisters."

I turned to look at her, shocked by the sight. She was slumped in one of the kitchen chairs, her eyes watery, her whole body radiating exhaustion.

"What's wrong?" I asked. "Are you okay?"

Deirdre held my gaze a long moment, then shook her head, a tear sliding down her cheek. "I need to speak with the three of you. It's urgent."

THIRTEEN

GRAY

I found Addie and Haley with Verona and the other witches in the common room, all of them sitting around the fireplace, chatting and laughing over tea and cookies as if the last twenty minutes hadn't even happened.

"Deirdre's here," I said to my sisters, deciding to leave the Sebastian stuff for later. "She needs to talk to us. Says it's urgent."

Haley and Addie headed back to the kitchen with me, Addie smoothing her hair on the way. She'd yet to meet our grandmother, and I had no idea how she'd feel when she finally did, but I was pretty sure this wouldn't be a happy reunion. Not for any of us.

We found Deirdre sitting alone at the table, exactly where I'd left her. She spared a brief glance for Addie as we approached, her eyes misting at the sight, but then it was like a wall slammed down over her emotions, locking the rest of us out.

Immediately, she warded the kitchen, making sure no one would disturb us.

"There is no easy way to say this, girls, so I'm just going to come out with it," Deirdre said. "I'll fill in the details after. Okay?"

She didn't give any of us a chance to disagree, or even wait until my sisters and I had gotten settled in our chairs. She just plowed on with the words that seemed to be tearing her up from the inside.

The ones I'd been afraid to hear since she'd first appeared in the kitchen, announcing that the story of my contract was hers to tell.

"Gray." She took a steadying breath, then met my gaze, her face a mask of control.

It was inevitable, what she said next, and I couldn't say it came as a surprise. All the clues had been there, and now that I looked backward, I could see them all line up neatly, waiting for me to solve the mystery on my own.

But I hadn't, and hearing it said aloud rattled me to the core.

"I'm the one who sold your soul to Sebastian," she said.

Ignoring my sisters' gasps, I closed my eyes and let the confession wash over me. Word by word, it sank into my skin, winding its way around my heart and squeezing tight.

It was one more betrayal in a long line of broken promises and shattered trusts. So why the hell did it hurt so bad?

The table cracked before me.

I hadn't even realized I'd been gripping it.

"Gray?" Haley touched my arm, gentle and kind, and I focused my energy on it, coming back into myself. Slowly, the anger receded, settling into a cold stone at the pit of my gut.

I released my death grip on the table and rose to put on the kettle, grabbing a bag of blood and some crushed hawthorn for myself. Something told me this fucked-up fairy tale was just beginning, and I was going to need a lot more than Haley's touch on my arm to keep from tearing Deirdre's head clear from her body.

FOURTEEN

GRAY

When the tea was ready and I felt like I could rejoin everyone at the table without destroying anything, I wrapped my hands around the mug and settled back into my chair, barely meeting my grandmother's eyes.

"Talk," I said, staring at a point just above her left shoulder.

"Sebastian and I go back a long time," Deirdre began. "Before any of you were even born, when I was still young and beautiful."

Is that a twinkle *in her voice?*

"Save us the trip down memory lane," I snapped. "Get to the point."

"Oh, but this is the point, Gray. Every step, every decision led to the ultimate one. I could no more unravel this thread from the story than I could undo the outcome."

I brought the mug to my mouth, biting back another nasty retort. For so long, all I'd wanted to know was who signed my contract—who sold my soul into demonic slavery, condemning me before I was even old enough to know what hell even was. But now that I had my answer, I wasn't even sure I wanted to understand the hows and whys of it.

But Deirdre didn't give me a choice then, and she sure as hell wasn't giving me one now.

"I was fairly powerful in my own right," she continued, "but hungry. Hungry to prove myself to my parents, who were well-regarded in our community but cruel and cold to their children. Hungry for bigger, more expansive magic, which always seemed to elude me. And most of all, hungry to make a name for myself. One night, after a particularly brutal fight with my parents, I was just angry and volatile enough to do the one thing I'd always known was absolutely forbidden—call upon the demon at the crossroads."

A chill went through the room, and both my sisters shivered. I wrapped my hands around my mug, willing myself to sit still. To not leap across the table and throttle her.

"At the next full moon," she continued, "I gathered up my supplies and headed out into the woods just before midnight, looking for the fabled place where two paths crossed—a dark, ominous part of the forest where most witches in my circle had never dared to venture. Once I knew I was in the right spot, I performed the ritual, spilling blood to call forth the demon servant who'd carry my plea to his master.

"Imagine my surprise when the master himself showed up. Oh, he was quite charming back then—in a different vessel entirely, mind you—and he knew exactly what to say to wrap me around his finger. I made my first deal that very night."

"You sold your soul?" I asked.

"Not then, no. Sebastian doesn't always trade in souls. There are other favors, other promises, other bits of knowledge and sacred information a witch might offer, and there were many things Sebastian wanted to know about my family. As I said, they were influential in the community, and my mother was a prominent witch from an even more prominent family. So Sebastian and I continued on in this way for years, meeting at the cross-roads in the woods, making deals. We used to joke that I'd signed my name in blood so many times I could've fed an entire vampire coven for a year." At this, she glanced at me briefly, but didn't have the courage to hold my gaze.

"Why are you telling us all of this?" I asked.

"I want you all to understand that Sebastian and I knew each other very well by the time you girls came into my life. Call me a fool for trusting the Prince of Hell, but he'd never betrayed me, which was more than I could say for my own family."

She paused to sip her tea, and I took a moment to process all of this. I didn't want to feel sorry for her—not at all. But I also knew what it was like to finally find the one person you could trust after all the people in your life—the people you were *supposed* to be able to trust—had shit on you.

But my empathy could only go so far. I knew the ending

of this story, and the person who'd gotten shit on this time wasn't Deirdre. It was me.

"Fast forward to the night your mother tried to kill you," Deirdre said. "By then I had a solid coven, backed by the power of Sebastian, who we'd been working with as a group for some time. After we succeeded in removing you four from your mother's home, we did a binding ritual on you."

"Why the hell would you do that?" Addie blurted out. It was the first she'd spoken since Deirdre had begun this story, and though she was initially eager to meet our grandmother, her demeanor toward her had flipped like a switch, as had Haley's. The three of us now sat close together on one side of the table, shoulders practically touching, staring down our grandmother on the other side, like some kind of tribunal. We were in this together now—three out of the four witches of prophecy, united after more than two decades, never to be torn apart again.

"We thought binding your powers would allow you to blend into human society more seamlessly," Deirdre explained. "But it didn't work. Already you were all too strong—even Georgie, who was only a baby then. I knew it was only a matter of time before you were truly discovered —before people in the larger magical and supernatural communities learned the truth about your legacy. We knew the witches chosen to adopt you into their care would do their best to shield you, but it wasn't enough. It would never be enough. I didn't... I didn't know what else to do."

"Sounds exactly like the kind of desperation Sebastian

thrives on," I said, draining the last of my tea. I'd added a little too much hawthorn, and now I felt it working its way into my bloodstream, quickly mellowing me out.

It was probably for the best. All that anger, all that bitterness was making it hard to think, and now that Deirdre had started weaving the full tapestry of this story, I realized I *did* want to know.

Every last detail.

"In exchange for your eternal protection, I offered him my own soul, my own blood. I'm no Silversbane, but as I said, my line is powerful in its own right, highly coveted by demon lords."

"What demon lords?" Haley asked. "I thought Sebastian was the boss."

"He has been in power a long time, Serena—"

"It's Haley now."

"Of course. Haley. But like all men in positions of power, he knows his is not guaranteed. There will always be challengers—someone hungrier, dirtier, more desperate, more willing to do whatever it takes to secure that ultimate power."

"So you thought having access to your magic and your blood could somehow help keep him in power?" I asked.

"That was part of it, yes. But more than my powerful blood, I knew I had another advantage: In all those deals, over all those clandestine meetings at the crossroads, Sebastian had fallen in love with me."

"Holy shit," Addie said. "Are you saying Sebastian is our—"

"No. Your grandfather was human, I assure you. With all the same weaknesses and frailties as the rest." Deirdre shook her head, the muscle in her jaw ticking. "He was long gone by the time your four came into the picture. In any case, I knew as well as Sebastian that my offer meant I'd become his—body, magic, and soul. There was no way he'd turn it down."

"Well, apparently prostituting yourself to the Prince of Hell wasn't enough after all, was it?" I asked. Under the table, I felt the touch of Addie's hand on my thigh, offering a gentle squeeze.

Deirdre shook her head, her eyes glistening with fresh tears. "Nothing is simple when it comes to Sebastian, and this deal was no different. He had conditions, the first being that I allow him to make me immortal."

Haley gasped. "You're immortal?"

Nodding, she said, "My soul would always be his regardless, but he wanted my body, too—and not just for however many years or even decades I had left. He wanted to be sure that I was well and truly his possession—for eternity. So yes, I'm immortal, but it's not the gift you might think. I was sixty-three when he turned me, so sixty-three I am cursed to remain."

"You agreed to this?" I asked, a flicker of warmth suddenly worming its way back into my heart for her. An immortal existence as Sebastian's lover sounded like a special kind of hell. "You traded your eternal freedom just so he'd protect us?"

She looked up at me again, a faint smile crossing her

lips. In a soft voice full of pain and regret, she said, "Understand, child. There's nothing I wouldn't do, even today, if I thought it would help keep you four girls safe. I truly believed that by sacrificing my eternity to Sebastian, you and your sisters might have a chance at living your *own* lives, far away from the legacy and all who'd seek to use it against you."

"How exactly was he supposed to protect us?" Addie asked.

"Sebastian promised to assign each of you a demon protector, charged with guarding you against hunters and —should she discover my trickery and come searching for you again—your mother. For many years, your guardians did just that, and though I quickly grew to despise Sebastian, I took comfort and joy in knowing that you were all safe. For the first time since you were born, I was beginning to feel like I could breathe again. Your mother believed you were dead. And the guardians were keeping you from danger. To me, every moment spent with Sebastian felt like an investment in your future, and it was a small price to pay.

"Sadly and regrettably, like most desperate people standing at the crossroads, I failed to read the fine print." At this, she looked up to meet my gaze again, her own burning with shame. "What I didn't realize, Gray, was that in addition to protecting you for the rest of your life, Sebastian would lay claim to your soul upon your natural death."

"All of us?" I asked, alarmed.

Deirdre shook her head. "All of you are spoken of in the

prophecy—the witches who would ultimately unite our kind. But Gray, only you are the third daughter of a third daughter. The powerful Shadowborn witch foretold to lead the covens. That was the power Sebastian most craved."

"I still don't understand how you could make a crossroads deal with someone else's soul," I said. "*My* soul. It wasn't yours to bargain with."

Inside, I felt my dark magic swirl, pulsing into my blood, looking for an outlet. My mind was screaming at me to put that woman through the wall, but apparently the hawthorn was keeping me in check.

At least, that's what I was telling myself. If not, I'd have to admit that my heart was breaking for her. That if this were merely a story about someone else's life, I'd already be cheering for the old woman to come out on top, despite all her missteps.

That she'd wanted to protect us was clear. That she'd truly believed she was doing the right thing was clear.

But none of that changed the outcome, and that's the part I just couldn't get past.

"You were a baby, Gray," she said. "A minor child."

"This isn't family court," I snapped. "Why would my minor status make a difference?"

"No. I fear you would've had a better chance in family court." Deirdre offered a quick smile, but it didn't touch her eyes. "In the court of hell, only Sebastian's rules matter. As your sole guardian at the time, I was able to assume temporary power and dominion over your soul, which allowed me to make the deal for your protection and sign it with my own blood on your behalf."

"But it's not your blood he's after now," Haley said.

"No. That honor goes to the Silversbane witches. You four, and your mother, of course, though she's managed to evade him thus far—a fact that torments him endlessly."

"What is it that makes Silversbane blood so special?" Haley asked. "There has to be more to it than magic words in an ancient prophecy."

Deirdre sighed. Under the guise of making more tea, she got up from her chair and headed to the stove, but it was obvious she was merely steeling herself for the rest of the story.

The tension in the room felt thick and sticky, and my sisters and I exchanged dark glances, just as rattled as Deirdre seemed to be. Even without speaking the words, I knew we shared the same understanding: things were about to get even more complicated—for all of us.

"There *is* more to it than the prophecy," Deirdre confirmed, her back to us as she watched the flames flicker to life beneath the tea kettle. "A *lot* more."

FIFTEEN

GRAY

Time slowed to an impossible crawl as we waited for Deirdre to prepare her tea, my sisters and I perched on the edges of our chairs, desperate to hear the rest of the story.

My mind was swirling with possibilities, none of them good.

By the time Deirdre rejoined us at the table, the only thing I knew for certain was that nothing she revealed, nothing she said, nothing she did would ever come between me and my sisters again.

"Your matrilineal ancestors lived in what we now know as Ireland," Deirdre began, and my sisters drew closer to me. I reached for each of their hands beneath the table, clasping them tightly, making physical the connection I'd already been feeling. Magic hummed in their veins, calling out to mine as we touched, wrapping us all in a blanket of support and rightness.

It felt like coming home after a day spent trekking

through the snow, that first wave of welcoming warmth as you opened the door, the rich scent of hot chocolate beckoning you to step inside and take off your boots, slide into your slippers, and come sit by the fireplace.

"They were among the first witches chosen by the elemental source as guardians of the earth's magic," she continued, and I nodded—she'd told me that part of the story the day we'd met in Las Vegas, when I'd first learned about the Silversbane prophecy. "At that time," she said, "the fae, who were among earth's first inhabitants, had already been living here for eons. They'd had their own magic, and had successfully connected with earth's innate magic to become quite powerful beings—perhaps even more so here than they'd been even in their home realms. So you can understand why they'd be reluctant to share. They were not pleased to learn that the source had gifted humans access to that magic, as well as naming them its sole guardians."

"They've always believed magic was their domain," I said. "They've never fully trusted us—that hasn't changed."

"No, it hasn't," Deirdre agreed, blowing across the top of her tea, making the steam swirl before her. "This is all legend, of course, but there is always some kernel of truth to be found there. As the tale was told to me, the fae decided that the best way to keep the magic within their sphere of influence was to mate with the first witches and mages, creating a new, even more powerful fae bloodline, melding the best of both magics."

"But witches can't become pregnant by supernaturals," I said.

"Not naturally, no," Deirdre said. "But with a bit of fae magic, all things were thought possible."

An image flitted through my mind—Sophie and Jael. I wondered if they would've had children together. Beautiful, magical babies with her gorgeous red hair and Jael's penetrating yellow eyes...

"Humans had always been enamored of the fae," Deirdre said, pulling me back to the present. "And a bit intimidated by these beautiful, otherworldly beings who'd kept themselves largely apart for so many years. When the fae rulers brought the proposal to the covens, the witches, who were quite open-minded and keen to further the protection and stewardship of all forms of magic, saw it as a great honor. And so the mating rituals began, but no children were born. Years passed, and still, not a single heir, though not for lack of trying."

At this, Deirdre smiled, lost in the story. I felt my own lips twitching into a smile; fae were rumored to be extremely passionate lovers.

"According to the old tales," Deirdre said, "a young fae prince had a prophetic dream about a witch who was recently born in the mortal realm to one of the first witches, with violet eyes and silver-white hair. In the dream, her mother allowed him to hold the child, and the moment he gazed upon her face, he fell in love with her. When he woke up that morning, he told his court of the dream and declared his intent to marry her, sending his emissaries to scour the mortal realm for the child who matched the description. She was found in Ireland, and her family was presented with the prince's proposal, along with the promise of more wealth than they could ever imagine.

"The family saw this as a high honor, and accepted the proposal, on the condition that they be allowed to raise their daughter Finnabair and keep her at home until she reached the age of twenty. The prince agreed, and the wedding date was set.

"But the prince, who dreamed of her nightly, grew impatient. When the child was only four years old, he sent his emissaries to her home to request that she be released into his care immediately, vowing to raise her himself until she came of age, at which time they would marry as planned. Horrified at the thought of losing their precious daughter sixteen years sooner than they'd agreed, her parents outright refused." Deirdre's eyes misted. "The emissaries slaughtered her parents and siblings, kidnapping the girl to the fae realm and presenting her to the prince anyway."

Deirdre paused to sip her tea. Next to me, I felt Addie curling inward, her shoulders hunching. After everything she'd just been through, I wasn't surprised the story was upsetting her.

"Addie, do you want to get some air?" I asked softly, squeezing her hand. "We could take a walk."

My sister shook her head. "I want to hear how this ends."

"I'm sorry to upset you," Deirdre said kindly, "but

know that this particular story has a happy ending—at least for Finnabair. You see, she was a clever child, and though the prince had treated her kindly, and sworn his love and loyalty until the end of time, she still remembered her homeland, and what had been done to her family on his orders. Biding her time, she waited until midnight the night before her twentieth birthday—what was to be her wedding day—and made her escape, knowing it would cause the prince the most pain to lose her so close to the moment she was set to become his for eternity."

"Fucking badass," Addie said, and we all laughed, breaking up the tension a bit.

"Oh, but the story doesn't end there," Deirdre said. "The prince did not take her departure lightly. The moment news reached his ear that his bride-to-be had run away, he called in a favor to an allied court in the north, rumored to have the most powerful and destructive army in the realms. The ally sent him four elite fae warriors, and the prince sent them to hunt Finnabair down. He wanted her executed on site, and as proof that they'd completed their duty, they were to return with her long silver braids as both a trophy and a lesson to anyone who might think to betray the prince in the future."

"So much for his so-called love and loyalty," I said. "Asshole."

"Though the prince claimed issuing such an order broke his heart," Deirdre said, "he could no longer trust her, and could not allow such a betrayal to go unpunished, for to do so would be a sign of weakness, and his rule would most certainly be challenged."

I rolled my eyes. It always came down to the same thing with these guys—power. They spent their whole lives coveting it, and once they got a taste of it, they spent the rest of their lives trying to hold on to it before the next upstart got his claws in. It was a vicious cycle with no end and no winners.

Beyond that, something else about the story was making me uneasy, though I couldn't quite put my finger on it. A question struggled to form from the mist of my mind, but no matter how hard I tried to focus, it wouldn't coalesce.

"The soldiers tracked her down in a matter of days," Deirdre went on, "for though she was clever, and very much at home in the forests of fae she'd essentially grown up in, she did not know how to get back to the mortal realm. But despite their training and the prince's orders, none of them could bring himself to execute her. They continued to send dispatches back to the prince that they'd yet to locate her, hoping they could buy themselves enough time to figure out what to do, but they were running out of options. Eventually, Finnabair cut off her own hair, soaked it in animal blood, and had the men send it to the prince, declaring they'd done their duty—that she was well and truly dead and buried. But the prince knew this was another trick, and demanded the soldiers return to him immediately. If they refused, he would consider it an act of war from the allied court—the soldiers' homeland—which would leave him no choice but to retaliate."

"Please tell me they told him to fuck off," Addie said.

"Essentially, that's exactly what they did. The soldiers had fallen in love with Finnabair. They refused to turn her over to such a cruel fate."

"So wait—all four of them fell for her?" Haley asked.

"Yes."

"Hmm." Haley nudged me in the ribs, laughing. "Where have we heard this story before?"

"What happened next?" I asked, ignoring Haley's teasing.

"The prince followed through on his threats, and a long, bloody war ensued. There are differing accounts as to how it turned out, but one outcome was certain: the allied court was completely ostracized. They were branded as traitors, their reputation destroyed along with most of their lands and a good deal of their people. Despite the skill of their armies, they could not defend against the prince and the other allies he'd rallied against them."

"I thought you said this story had a happy ending?" Addie said.

"For Finnabair, yes." At this, Deirdre smiled. "Ironically, the union of the warrior fae and the silver-haired witch was the first of its kind to create a child. From their love, a new bloodline was born."

"Silversbane," Haley whispered, and a shiver rolled through my body. Silence floated between us, and I closed my eyes, walking backward through Deirdre's story, back to the start. I'd been so caught up in Finnabair's tale, I'd forgotten why we'd started talking about it in the first place.

And now that I was thinking about it more clearly, the nagging question I'd been chasing finally reared it's big, ugly head.

I opened my eyes, meeting Deirdre's across the table.

"Which court?" I asked, my voice low, my jaw tight. Deep inside, where magic and intuition lived, I feared I already knew the answer, but I had to ask anyway.

Deirdre nodded slowly, her smile fading. She'd known this question was coming. "You're asking about the northern allies. The warriors."

"Our ancestors, Deirdre," I clarified. "Aside from Finnabair, whose blood runs through our veins?"

"Your lineage can be traced back to Darkwinter," she confessed. "That is why you're so powerful. You—all of you —are descendent from the powerful union of a daughter of a first witch and the warriors who sacrificed everything they'd ever known and cared for to keep her safe."

Addie was out of her chair, pacing the kitchen before her. Haley got up to get her some water, but I was pretty sure nothing would ever wash away the memories of what she'd suffered. The memories of the torture and torment Orendiel and his knights had doled out.

"Understand, girls," Deirdre said, "Darkwinter were not always as they are today. Their hallmark hatred and violence —that was made, not born. Your line was not created from such darkness, but its opposite. The Knights of Darkwinter called upon by the prince were brave and true. That they loved Finnabair, that they protected her, that they sacrificed so much to keep her safe—*that* is where the true source of the magic of Silversbane lies. The friendship, love, and union of the fierce witch and her brave, honorable fae… All of it came together to create the most powerful bloodline in history."

"That may be so," I said, "yet somehow along the way, that line became corrupted."

"I will not excuse Darkwinter's actions now, but as I said, that hatred was born of war, evolving over centuries of being ostracized and attacked on the orders of a cruel, vicious prince bent on power."

"Do they know who we are?" I asked, my head spinning from the direction this crazy story had spun. "Orendiel and his army of glitter-dicks? Do they know they're hunting their own…" I trailed off, unsure what to call it. Blood? What the hell did that even mean anymore?

The word itself felt strange to me now, its meaning so diluted it may as well have been a foreign language. Did it mean family? A bond? A promise? Or was it no more than the red stuff oozing through us all—the stuff that made my heart beat? The stuff Darius and I and others of our kind needed to swallow in order to survive?

"They know of the stories, I'm sure," she said. "It's part of their ancestral lore as much as it's a part of yours. But you have to remember, Gray. It's not as if you're *fae*. We're talking about thousands of years, hundreds of generations of blending bloodlines. They don't necessarily know that you girls are the four Silversbane descendants—the witches of prophecy."

My sisters joined me back at the table. Seeing Addie's red, puffy eyes made me want to stab something.

"I think it's time for you to go," I said to Deirdre. I'd been caught up in the story about Finnabair, but that didn't change the fact that my grandmother was the one who'd sold my soul to Sebastian. I understood her reasoning— why she thought she had no other options—but no matter how hard I searched my heart, I just couldn't find forgiveness there. Not for her. Not yet.

"Gray, I understand you're upset with me," she said, "and you have every right to—"

"I'm not upset," I snapped, but that was just a reaction. The moment the words were out, I knew they were true. All the anger I'd felt when Deirdre had first begun this confession had somehow evaporated.

I wasn't upset. Wasn't mad. Wasn't even marginally annoyed.

The only emotion swirling in my gut now was disappointment.

Again, I thought of Finnabair. Not the woman who'd fallen in love with the fae warriors sent to execute her, but the violet-eyed, silver-haired newborn the prince had first dreamed of.

Deirdre had glossed over that part of the story, but in my mind, it was the most important part. The origin, without which the tale could not have unfolded as it did.

Emissaries of the fae prince had arrived with promises

of prestige and money, and without a second thought, Finnabair's parents made a deal. She was days old, and they'd agreed to trade her away, completely trampling her sovereignty, cashing in her future for their own personal gain.

And right here in America, thousands of miles and thousands of years away from Finnabair's Ireland, the same cycle played out again when a sixty-three-year-old witch made a bet on the devil and lost.

I looked at my sisters, wondered again at the abuses they'd suffered, both at the hands of the same men. Hunters who'd been trying to kill us for millennia. Fae who had no idea they'd been chasing down their own descendants.

I thought of Norah, a witch so many others had trusted and venerated. A witch who later turned over her own kind to the enemy, trading their lives, their blood, their souls for a shot at saving her own ass.

I thought of my rebels. I thought of all the battles we'd faced so far, all the power games we'd been forced to play and play again, all the fights still banging on our door, looking for a way in.

We had so many enemies, yet in the end, the people with the greatest power to destroy us weren't our enemies at all.

They were our own flesh-and-blood families. The ones we hadn't chosen ourselves. The ones who hid under the twin banners of blood and loyalty while they sharpened their swords, waiting for the day when they'd shove them straight through your heart.

"Girls, what can I do to make this right?" Deirdre asked. "What do you need from me? Please tell me."

In her eyes, I saw the same desperation she must've felt when she'd realized her granddaughters would never be safe—the same desperation that had driven her to Sebastian —and I knew she'd meant what she said earlier. That she would do absolutely anything, even now, to help keep us safe.

All I had to do was ask.

I reached for my sisters' hands, holding them tight, the three of us a unified front. The tight, unbreakable bond of our magic flowed between us, connecting us, strengthening us.

I had a single thought, and in that moment, I knew my sisters shared it.

"We need you to leave, Deirdre," I said. "Permanently."

SIXTEEN

ASHER

"Ace of Cups. Drink."

Tossing the Tarot card on the discard pile, I pushed a glass of whiskey toward Gray, amber liquid sloshing up over the sides.

Clear-eyed and resolute, she held my gaze and downed it, never blinking.

"That's not how Tarot works." Haley rolled her eyes. "You can't just say *drink* every time you draw one of the cups cards, Ash."

"And *you* can't ask me to give you guys a reading and then tell me how to interpret the cards." I picked up another one from the pile on the table between us. "The Fool. Oh, this one's got your name all over it, Barnes. Drink up."

"No way," Haley said. "I'm tapping out. Two is my max, and I've already had three."

"I'll take one for the team," Gray said, downing the glass I'd set up for her sister.

I shook my head, flashing her a grin. "You're a lot harder to drink under the table as a bloodsucker."

"Bloodsucker *fae*," she corrected.

"That too." I'd been sticking to beer, but now I poured a round of whiskey for myself and picked up the glass, lifting it in salute before downing it. When I finished, I caught her gaze again, seeing right through the jokes to the soft parts inside her—the parts that still felt like the lost, confused kid who'd first washed up in Blackmoon Bay all those years ago. Couldn't blame her, though. Seemed like every time she finally solved another piece of her mysterious origins, she uncovered another betrayal. Another painful tale she wished she could close the book on for good.

But shit didn't work that way. We didn't get to flip through the fairytales of our lives, picking out only the best ones, the happy ones to keep. They were all part of us, the good as well as the terrible.

I just wished she'd gotten a few more good ones lately.

"Pick another card," Addie said. "It's my turn."

"You got it." I did as she asked, revealing the next card in the deck—Three of Cups. This one had three women sitting side-by-side on the rocks before a lotus pond, the full moon shining down upon them. They each held a chalice, and their eyes were closed, heads bent as if they were casting a spell.

"It's you three for sure," I said.

"Does this mean we all have to drink? I think it does."

Without waiting for an answer, Addie reached for the bottle and poured three shots, then downed hers like a champ. "Cheers, fae bitches."

"I should've quit while I was ahead," I said. "I'm no match for three drunk-ass sister-witches, especially if you keep ganging up on me."

"The big bad incubus is afraid of three little girls?" Haley teased. "That's rich."

"We should totally start a band," Addie said randomly. "Drunk-Ass Sister Witches. It has a nice ring to it, don't you think?"

"I'd definitely pay to see that show," I said.

"Your turn, Ash," Gray said, flashing a smile I know she didn't totally feel, despite my best efforts to cheer her up. To cheer them all up. "Pick a card for yourself."

I picked up the deck, giving it a good shuffle before turning over my card.

"Seven of Swords?" I picked up the card for a closer look. There was a dude on the front, with black angel wings, kneeling in the snow to pick up two swords, one of which he'd grabbed by the blade—total fucking amateur. Five ravens circled him, each one holding its own sword. The storm clouds behind him felt pretty damn ominous to me. "This guy looks shady as hell. What's his deal?"

"Oh, you know," Gray said. "Deception, trickery, the usual." She folded her arms across her chest, eyeing me up and down as a sexy-ass grin stretched across her mouth. "Maybe the cards are warning me to watch my step around you, incubus."

I reached for my beer again, tipping it back to take a swig. "You needed the cards to tell you that?"

Still grinning, she slid out of her chair and joined me on the other side of the table, straddling me, seemingly oblivious to the fact that we weren't alone. "I'm not so great with learning lessons. Maybe you should teach me the hard way."

I wrapped an arm around her back, ensuring she wouldn't wriggle away. "Why the fuck are you so sexy?"

"And on that note... *Barf.*" Haley stood up, making a show of yawning and looking at her phone. "Wow, would you look at the time?"

Addie laughed. "Subtle, girl. Real subtle."

"Stay for the show if you want," Haley said, "but the two of them have enough chemistry to set the whole lodge on fire, and trust me, you don't want to be at ground zero when it happens."

"Alright, alright." Addie stood up and grabbed her glass, along with the unfinished bottle of whiskey. "You two kids have fun. Try not to incinerate anything."

"No promises," Gray said.

And then two of the three drunk-ass sister witches were gone, leaving me alone with a woman insisting on being taught the hard way.

Emphasis on hard.

Gray leaned forward, licking a path across my lips.

Three, two, one, and... yep. Hard as fuck.

"You taste like beer," she said, her voice low and sultry.

I kissed her again. "You taste like trouble."

"Mmm. We make a good combo, don't we?" She looped her arms around my neck and sighed, her breath warm on my lips. "A vampire-fae-witch with the worst gene pool in history, and an incubus with... well, let's just call it your garden variety mysterious origins."

I laughed. "My origins aren't all that mysterious, Cupcake. You take one incubus, find him a succubus mate, throw 'em together, shake well, and garnish with a cherry."

"That's it?" she asked.

I shrugged and ran my hand up her spine, cupping the back of her neck and pulling her mouth to mine. Kissing was better than talking. Always had been.

But eventually she broke our kiss, pulling back and staring into my eyes in a way that completely undid me. She wanted to know more. She wanted to know *me*—all the things I'd never told her, the things I'd been trying not to tell myself.

"Last I heard they were somewhere in Italy," I said. "I haven't had any contact with them for at least a hundred years, give or take."

Her mouth fell open, and she stared at me for a good full minute before finally finding her voice. "Ash, your parents are still *alive*?"

"No idea, but I haven't heard otherwise, so that's my assumption."

"You don't talk to them at all?"

I reached for my beer again, tossed back another slug. Normally the booze kept the memories at bay, but every once in a while they snuck back in.

Like whenever I had to watch Gray live through some fucking trauma her own family had caused. That shit always stirred up old ghosts.

Hundreds of years wandering this forsaken rock, and I'd never understand why so many of the world's worst people in existence insisted on procreating. Most of the population—human and supernatural alike—had no business bringing kids into this world.

"Alright, Cupcake," I finally said. "You want the whole sob story? You got it."

I sighed and closed my eyes, breaking off her intense gaze. Saying the words was one thing. Seeing her eyes change from sexy and flirty and curious to sad and pitying was another—one I wanted no part of.

"My parents never bothered to tell me what I was. I grew up thinking I was a regular kid with serious fucking problems."

"How did you finally figure it—oh. Oh, fuck, Asher." She leaned forward, resting her forehead on my shoulder, and in that moment I knew she'd answered her own question. "The girl," she said softly. "The one from your drawings."

"The one and only." The same girl I'd drawn night after night for decades, though the drawings had stopped not too long after things heated up between me and Gray. Somehow, whenever I tried to draw her after that, I'd end up drawing Gray instead, which was just fine by me.

"I saw her," she said. Confessed. "The night I… When I had your soul. I saw the whole thing."

"I figured as much." The night she'd taken my soul to save me from the devil's trap in Norah's attic, our souls connected. She relived my worst memory as though it were her own, and I was pretty sure it'd haunted her ever since. "If I could erase that from your memory, I would."

"I'd erase it from yours, too."

"My parents thought they'd have more time, but they waited too damn long. If they'd just been honest with me from the start, I could've learned to control it. And I *damn* sure wouldn't have gotten involved with a human girl. Fuck, Gray. Carina was innocent, and I just…"

I held Gray close and clenched my jaw, willing the wave of memories to recede, but of course they wouldn't. *Carina…* It was the first time in centuries I'd said her name out loud, and in doing so, I'd called forth her ghost.

Every single memory I'd ever shared with her came crashing back, from the first day we met at her father's farm stand, to the last in that wheat field.

"You loved her," Gray said softly.

At this, I pulled back and opened my eyes to meet her gaze. There was no jealousy there. Only empathy.

There was a time when that look in her eyes would've sent me into a rage. When *no one* got behind my walls without a fight.

But who the fuck was I kidding? This woman had crashed through those barriers the very first night she sat across from me at her own kitchen table, slinging the cards that revealed my nature to her.

I looked into her eyes, losing myself in their twilight

blue depths. "Yeah. I loved her, Gray. I loved her, and then I killed her."

My throat tightened, barely keeping the tears at bay. The guilt.

"I never even got the chance to tell her I was sorry. To go to her funeral. To tell her father what had happened, man to man. My parents whisked me away in the middle of the night, forbidding me to talk about her. To this day, I'm sure her father thought she'd run away." The tears gathered, then spilled. Hastily, I scrubbed a hand across my eyes. "That was the worst of it. The man hadn't even known his daughter had died."

Gray took my face in her hands. "It's not your fault, Asher. You didn't even know what you were."

"Neither did she. So why am I the one still walking around? Still breathing and eating and drinking and fighting and fucking... Falling in love. I just..." I closed my eyes, reining it in. "She doesn't get a do-over, Gray."

"No, and that's not fair. Really. But Ash, even if she'd never met you, right now? Tonight? She would've already been dead for centuries."

"If you've got a point, Cupcake, I'd appreciate you getting to it."

In a voice so soft it nearly broke me, she said, "Why are you still carrying her on your shoulders?"

I felt another tear slide down my cheek, hot and bitter, and willed myself to end this. To change conversations, get us back onto neutral territory. Back to fake Tarot readings and teasing and kissing.

But Gray wouldn't let me. And in so many ways, I didn't want her to.

I loved her. With my whole fucking heart. With my soul, however tarnished and tattered it was.

So this part of me, this deep dark well of regret and pain... I had to let her see it. The worst of me. The best of me. All of it.

"I can't put her down," I whispered. "Carrying her, remembering that moment, watching the life leave her eyes... That's my punishment. My penance."

"That's just torture. You're torturing yourself."

"What else can I do?"

"Forgive yourself, for starters."

I grabbed her hands, pulled them against my chest, pleading with my eyes for her to understand. Why was this so fucking hard?

"Ash, you have to—"

"I can't, Gray. I just can't."

Gray shook her head, her own eyes reflecting my pain. My anguish. "I love you. That means you don't get to carry this burden by yourself anymore. You say Carina doesn't get a do-over, and you're right. But you *do*. Every day you wake up alive, it's a do-over. You decide every minute, every second. *You* choose. So if you can tell me that you're honestly not ready to put her down, or that you're not quite sure how to forgive yourself, I will accept that, and I'll do my best to help you through it any way I can." She reached for my face again, her eyes blazing with new fire. "But you don't get to say 'can't.' Not anymore. Not about this."

"Good advice, Doc. So how's that grandma of yours? You ready to forgive her yet?"

It was a low blow, a desperate move to get off the topic of Carina, and I regretted it the instant the words fell out of my big, dumb mouth.

Gray didn't take the bait, though. Instead, she just shrugged. "A traitor, a dark witch, and goddamn liar. The devil's playmate. I'm still on the fence about whether she's evil incarnate or not, but I'll keep you posted."

"Gray, you can't—"

"What did I just say about that word?" She leaned forward, stealing a kiss I was all too eager to give her anyway. Beneath the heat of her thighs, my cock stiffened again, ready to pick up right where we'd left off.

When she pulled back again, she said, "You know what? Let's not talk about our fucked-up families for the rest of the night. Deal?"

Gray and I had both cut a little too damn deep—I knew she sensed it, too—and it seemed we'd both had enough soul-baring for one night. It would've been so easy to give in to her touch, to laugh at her joke, to let her soothe the ache that tore through my heart, just as I would do for her.

But I was done taking the easy way out. There was something I needed her to know, and it went beyond the love I felt for her, beyond the guilt and shame I'd felt about Carina, beyond the rage I still felt toward my parents.

One thing all of that had taught me was that standing around with your dick in your hand when you should've been telling someone how you truly felt was a one-way ticket to endless regret.

Immortal or not, none of us ever knew how long we truly had.

"Gray, listen to me." I slid my hands into her hair, fisting it, holding her steady. I'd never seen anyone so beautiful, so fucking incredible, and the fact that she loved me—that she'd continued to stand by me night after night—that blew my fucking mind. "The people who gave birth to me? They aren't my family. Darius, Ronan, Emilio, Spooky? *They're* my family." I pressed a kiss to the corner of her mouth, whispering close. "*You* are my family, Gray. The one I choose, every day I wake up alive."

The admission felt big, important, more vulnerable than anything I'd ever admitted to another being. Family—the kind I was talking about? It was so much more than being in love. Yeah, that was part of it for me and Gray. But it was friendship. It was respect. It was calling each other out on our bullshit, and holding each other close when everything got to be too much. It was being vulnerable and scared because you knew and trusted your heart was in good hands.

It was everything I never had growing up, and never dared to dream I'd have now. Not until the first time she'd told me she loved me.

A tear rolled down her cheek, and she smiled, her eyes twinkling. "You're my family, too, Asher. Always."

She kissed me then, deep and passionate and wild, and I wrapped her legs around my hips and rose from the kitchen chair, carrying her into the common room. The few witches who'd been hanging out in there vacated the moment they saw us coming, closing the French doors behind them, and now we had it to ourselves. I laid her on one of the couches and kissed my way down her throat, loosening the buttons on her shirt as I went, the fire roaring beside us.

I'd just unveiled her sexy-as-sin black lace bra when I sensed an unwelcome intruder standing over us.

"I thought I smelled fire," Darius said. "Apparently I was correct."

I tore my mouth away from Gray's silky-smooth skin and glared up at him. "So you're, what? Swooping in to dump some cold water on my nuts?"

Gray laughed. "You and your visuals."

"You've got two options here, bloodsucker," I said, repositioning myself between Gray's thighs. "One—turn around, go back to your coffin, and we'll all pretend this never happened."

He folded his arms across his chest, gracing us with his smug grin. "What's choice two?"

I cut my glance back to Gray, her eyes glittering like twin sapphires. The smile on her lips felt like a dare.

"Yeah, incubus," she teased, arching up against me until I was about ready to come right there. "What's option two?"

"Ladies choice," I said, giving it right back to her. I rolled my hips, grinding my thoroughly-hardened cock against her clit, wishing I'd thought to take her jeans off before the shirt. "You wanna play with fire, Cupcake? Be my guest."

"Oh, I do, and I will. Darius?" she called out, never taking her eyes off mine, her smile never slipping. "Get naked. *Now*."

The command in her voice made me weak in the best fucking way.

The vampire was naked in a heartbeat. By the time I flicked my gaze up to meet his, he was already hard as fuck, a slow grin sliding across his face.

"Alright, little vampire," he said, kneeling down beside us. "I'm here and at your service. Does this mean I'm well and truly forgiven for last night's oversight in the woods?"

"Hmm." She looked at him with a wicked gleam in her eye that told me we were both about to be in some serious trouble. "I'll let you know later. Now shut up and kiss me before I change my mind."

SEVENTEEN

GRAY

The fire crackled before us, bathing my incubus and vampire in a flickering orange glow. They were naked, stretched out on their backs on the bearskin rug before the hearth, the French doors shut tight against intruders—including poor Sunshine and Sparkle, who'd been taking turns pressing their muzzles up against the glass as if they'd been utterly abandoned.

Ignoring the pang in my chest at locking my loyal beasts out, I knelt between Ash and Darius, one hand on each of their muscled chests. Outside, the icy wind was doing its damnedest to shatter the bay windows along the front wall, but nothing could break this moment between us.

"You're so beautiful," Asher said, his eyes glazed with emotion that belied the ever-present bad-boy smirk on his face.

Darius nodded his agreement, reaching up to stroke my

171

thigh. "I'm not sure what we've done to deserve you in our lives, Gray Desario, but not a moment goes by that I don't thank the universe for you."

"I love you both," I said, emotion tightening my throat. We'd started this thing teasing each other, but now, seeing them together, both of them looking up at me like I'd painted every last star in the sky, I was overcome with gratitude. Asher was right—we were family in the true sense of the word. In the only sense that mattered. "More than you could possibly realize."

Before they could respond, I pressed my fingers against their lips. I didn't need to hear the words returned; I knew how they both felt. It was written in their eyes, glittering with the reflection of the firelight. It was laced through every touch, every kiss, every soft sigh I felt against my skin.

I'd once heard that the human body completely regenerates itself every seven to ten years. It sounded like myth to me, but in the last week alone, I'd already felt like I'd been through several iterations. I was a witch. I was a vampire. My blood contained that of the very fae we were hunting. Each revelation had unveiled countless others, until I no longer knew which way was up and which way was down.

Now here I was, a composite whole of all the various parts, sometimes breathing, sometimes not. Sometimes hungry, sometimes not. My heart never beat the same pattern for more than a few moments anymore. And each time I looked in the mirror, I found new facets, new scars, new shadows.

The only constant in my life now was this—my rebels. No matter how much I'd changed—physically, magically, emotionally—they'd stood by me through it all. Darius had asked what they'd done to deserve me in their lives, but I was the who'd been truly blessed.

Without their kindness, their loyalty, their bravery, their sacrifice, I'd still be a little lost girl shivering in a boat, floating in the harbor of a strange city she'd never even known was her home.

With tears in my eyes, I climbed on top of Asher, straddling him as Darius knelt behind me, kissing a slow, teasing path up my spine. My incubus was hard as steel, and I was wet and ready for him, lowering myself onto his length, taking him all the way in. Behind me, I felt the press of Darius's erection against my backside, just as eager, just as ready, but his turn would come later.

Unlike me, Darius had infinite patience.

Wrapping his hands around my hips, he guided me into a slow roll that had Asher fisting the rug at his sides, his breath catching in his throat.

"Fucking hell, woman," Asher groaned. "That's…"

"Bloody brilliant," Darius whispered, nipping my shoulder, his fangs teasing my hyper-sensitive skin. I leaned my head to the side, exposing the tender flesh of my neck, inviting the bite I knew he was dying to give me.

"Are you certain?" he whispered, nipping my earlobe.

Bearing one of my most vulnerable spots to him was the ultimate sign of trust, and therefore, forgiveness. He knew what I was saying with that gesture, and it wasn't just about the exquisite pleasure I knew would follow.

"Yes," I breathed. "Absolutely certain."

As Asher's hands slid up to palm my breasts, Darius sunk his fangs into my flesh, and I let out a cry of pure ecstasy. Warmth pooled on my skin, and he licked it seductively, taking his time as he swirled his tongue over my super-sensitive flesh, every delicious stroke making my blood simmer.

Asher sat up, capturing my nipple between his lips, sucking me hard as his hand slid down between us, fingers brushing my aching clit.

The two of them played my body like an instrument they'd mastered together long ago, touching and teasing and caressing until my nerves were humming, my thighs aching, my core throbbing, and still, they gave me more.

I didn't want it to end, but I was quickly losing the capacity to hold back. I pushed Asher back down, hands on his shoulders, our eyes locked in a fiery gaze as I slowed my movements, rolling my hips, taking him in deeper and deeper until I brought him to the brink.

Clenching his teeth, he arched upward, driving in deeper, his hands gripping my thighs, fingers digging hard into my flesh.

"No," I commanded. "Not yet."

Asher blew out a breath, but I was in charge tonight, and I knew he wouldn't come. Not until I was ready to make him.

I leaned forward and captured his mouth in a deep kiss,

slowly sliding off his cock. Inch by inch, I kissed my way down his body—his chin, his jaw, his collarbone, the impressive ridges of his abs, my tongue tracing lines along his tattoos as I went. When I finally reached my destination, I fisted the base of his cock and took him into my mouth, slowly teasing the tip with my tongue before taking him deeper.

I arched my backside, brushing against Darius's cock, an invitation as much as a demand. Without hesitation, Darius slid into me from behind, filling me as I took Asher deeper into my throat. Our connection was unbreakable; the pure pleasure of taking both of them inside me at the same time made me dizzy. It was all heat and fire and love and a perfect rhythm that drew me closer and closer to that pure, white-hot bliss.

I'd intended to tease Ash a little longer, but now I was the one who couldn't hold out. I sucked him harder, bobbing my head, bringing him right back to that razor-thin ledge I'd left him on as Darius brought me to the same place.

"Fuck, Gray. You're killing me." Asher slid his hand into my hair, fisting it, guiding me to take him in deeper, slower, then fast, then slow again. I loved the way he tried to grasp the very last vestige of control, even as he was absolutely losing it.

I couldn't hold out another second. Raking my nails down his thighs, I sucked him in deep once again, and he finally lost the battle, shuddering against my mouth, his moans of pleasure setting off my own orgasm. I arched back against Darius, who grabbed my hips and slammed into me harder, faster, chasing his own release and turning mine into an explosion of stars and fireworks that couldn't be contained.

The sounds that came out of my mouth… I was pretty sure I'd never heard anything quite like that before.

Finally, I crawled back up to rest my head on Asher's chest, collapsing in his arms as Darius collapsed on top of me, the three of us making the perfect sandwich, the echo of their heartbeats a beautiful song that I would carry with me for eternity.

"Are you cold?" Asher asked a little while later, rubbing my bare arm. The fire had faded to a soft glow, and a slight but icy draft snuck in around the windows.

"Not possible." I laughed. Curled up against his chest, with Darius spooning me from behind, I was thoroughly cocooned, my body as hot as if we'd been lying out in the summer sun.

We'd gotten up to grab a quick shower and let the poor hounds in to sit by the fire, but other than that, we'd been tangled together on the bearskin rug for the last couple of hours.

I didn't want the sun to rise.

"You're shivering," Ash said.

"Your fault," I teased, tracing a circle around his nipple.

His skin erupted in goosebumps. "Both of you make me lose control."

"It's a gift," Asher said.

"One that keeps on giving," Darius said, pressing a kiss to my bare shoulder.

"I'm just glad you finally gave in at all," I teased. Looking up at Asher, I told him about Darius's ridiculous demands about how our first time would be. "You should've heard him, Ash. 'It will be in *my* bed, blah blah blah.'"

Asher laughed. "I take it your first time didn't go as planned?"

"No. We were in the Shadowrealm, of all places. And I *still* haven't seen his actual bed."

"To be fair," Darius said, "we're dealing with extenuating circumstances. That aside, I assure you, I *would've* taken you in my bed. In fact, I still might."

"Whatever you need to tell yourself to get through the night," I said, earning myself a playful slap on the ass and a nip on the shoulder.

"So you really remember everything from before?" Asher asked Darius. A note of wonder echoed in his voice. "All of it?"

Sometimes, I still couldn't believe it myself. I'd tried to have faith, but for so long, I truly believed the old Darius was gone. That we'd have to rebuild everything we'd had from scratch, with no guarantee that it would turn out the same. I loved him; I was willing to try anything, even if it meant falling in love with him all over again, but I couldn't say I didn't miss the man I'd fallen for in the first place.

In the end, we didn't have to go down that road. Somehow, he'd come back to us.

I turned over onto my back and reached for his hand, lacing our fingers together.

"I do remember." Darius nuzzled the crook of my neck, his hand sliding across my belly. "Thanks to the tenaciousness of this crazy witch and her many blood spells."

"It wasn't just the blood spells," I corrected. "They definitely got the ball rolling, but the real magic was in the bite at the cemetery. I had no idea it would work like that."

"It was our blood bond," Darius said. "And you were the one who figured out blood was the key to—"

"Everything," I said suddenly, then I gasped, struck by a new realization. "Blood spells! Oh my God, that's it!" I turned on my hip to face my vampire, a smile stretching across my face. "Darius Beaumont, you're so brilliant I could kiss you."

"Allow me to save you the trouble, love." He claimed my mouth in a possessive kiss, and for a minute I almost lost myself again, a soft moan escaping my lips as heat rekindled in my core. Asher slid his palm over my hip, his fingers brushing across my belly, then down between my thighs. He was hard again, his cock thickening against my backside in a way that had me dreaming of all new ways for them to share me...

No. That particular pleasure would have to wait. I had work to do.

Disentangling from their embrace, I hopped up from the floor and hunted around the room in search of my clothes.

"Wait, what?" Ash laughed. "Why the fuck are you getting dressed? I was just getting warmed up again."

"Raincheck," I said. "I've got an idea, and it can't wait."

"Yeah," Ash said. "Obviously the worst one ever."

"Blame Darius," I said.

He turned to glare at the vampire, who held up his hands in mock innocence.

"Don't blame me, Asher. You heard the woman. She said I'm so brilliant she could kiss me."

"Maybe *she* could kiss you, bloodsucker," Ash sneered. "But *I* could kill you."

"You could try."

"Time and place, brother. Time and place."

"Simmer down, boys." I glanced around the room, exasperated. "Where the hell did my underwear end up?"

"Pretty sure the bloodsucker stashed them in his pants pocket," Ash said.

"What?" Darius blustered. "I did no such... Well, this is just preposterous. I demand a trial of my peers."

Glaring at Darius, I picked up his jeans from the couch, fishing my underwear from the back pocket. "You're incorrigible."

"Where are you going, Gray?" Ash stood up and grabbed my elbow, steadying me as I stepped into my underwear. "Seriously."

"First? The kitchen. I need supplies."

"Supplies?" he asked.

"Water, candles, crystals, salt, a glass bowl, and some herbs." Picking up my T-shirt, I answered his question, but I was mostly talking to myself, figuring it out as I went. "I'm thinking mugwort—it's good for clairvoyance and ancestor work. Maybe some wormwood as well. Oh, and something sharp and pointy."

"Mmm." Asher tugged the T-shirt out of my hands and dragged me back into his embrace, kissing his way up my neck, damn near convincing me to stay. "Kinky little witch, aren't you?"

"You don't... know the... half of it." I closed my eyes, temporarily sinking into the pleasure of his mouth on my flesh. Each kiss unlocked another image of the two of them inside me, a fantasy, maybe taking both of them in the same place at the same time...

Oh, God...

No. No, no, *no*. I *had* to concentrate.

"Pause button," I breathed. "I... I mean it. I need to find my... Oh, fuck. What was I even talking about?"

"No idea," Ash replied. "Do you remember, bloodsucker?"

"Funny, incubus. I seem to remember everything *but* that."

"Sisters!" I shouted, forcing myself to stay focused—a task that was growing more impossible by the second. Damn, Asher's mouth was something to behold. "You guys need to wake up my sisters and tell them to meet me in the kitchen."

"Why?" he asked. "I think we're doing just fine on our own."

I finally wriggled out of his embrace, yanked my shirt from his hands, and pulled it on over my head.

"Because as skilled as you guys are in the carnal arts," I said, grinning, "blood magic is not in your wheelhouse." I kissed each of them in turn, short and sweet, then called Sparkle and Sunshine and headed to the kitchen. "Don't wait up, boys. This might take a while."

EIGHTEEN

GRAY

The flames of a dozen candles flickered around us, throwing eerie shadows on the walls and illuminating my sisters' faces in the darkness. The three of us sat together inside the salt circle we'd drawn on the kitchen floor, grounding ourselves, tapping into the magic of the earth and air, fire and water, silently calling forth the elements to help us on our quest for answers.

Behind us, Darius, McKenna, and Verona stood guard, ensuring no one disturbed us—from within the lodge or from wherever our visions took us tonight. Verona had been especially concerned about outside interference, and had insisted we place black tourmaline, labradorite, and black obsidian in every corner to help shield us from psychic attacks, just like we'd done during the blood spell we'd performed on Darius.

That night, Haley and I had inadvertently tapped into a vision with Trinity and Georgie. It was short-lived, no more than a side effect of the blood magic intended to restore Darius's memories, and we hadn't even recognized what it was at the time. But my hope was that by doing the spell together, with the full intention of connecting with our mother and sister—our blood relatives—we could hold the vision long enough to get some solid information.

"And so we begin," Haley said, calling us back to the moment. Verona had prepared an incense of wormwood and mugwort, and Haley lit it now, fanning the smoke with a raven's feather before setting the bowl to her left.

Unsheathing her athame, she glanced up at me. "Are you sure you're okay with this?"

"You're totally safe," I assured her. At Darius's insistence, I'd fed before we began the ritual. Neither of us believed I'd attack my sisters, but if I felt even a pang of thirst, there was a good chance I'd get distracted by freshly spilled blood and ruin the ritual.

Addie and I unsheathed our athames, following Haley's lead. At her direction, we all sliced our palms, then squeezed our blood into the glass bowl at the center of the circle, three crimson streams merging into one.

The tang of their blood filled my senses, making my mouth water. But I stayed focused, magic tingling inside, warming me.

Addie placed a piece of bloodstone inside the bowl, and I sprinkled African dream root powder on top.

Haley instructed us to touch our fingers to the rim, and then we recited the spell she'd crafted.

"Blood of Silversbane, blood of fae
On ancestors past we call today
Seeking your guidance, your wisdom, your love
Without and within, below and above
Bestow upon us the vision we seek
That we may hear the words they speak."

After our seventh incantation, we released the bowl and clasped hands, my skin tingling as our blood and magic connected and bound us. A sense of belonging washed over me, and though I was still getting to know Haley and had just met Addie, I felt the years of our separation melt away, leaving only the unbreakable bond of our sisterhood.

Blinking away tears, I glanced down at the bowl, the blood inside rapidly changing before my eyes.

Glowing brightly at first, it darkened to near-black, then, ever so slightly, began to swirl around the bloodstone. Entranced, I let my eyelids flutter closed, then followed the tug on my consciousness.

The sensation was similar to swimming in a calm, warm ocean—drifting along on gentle waves, weightless. But then the tide turned, an undertow sucking me further from the shore, pulling me down, down, down…

When I opened my eyes, I found myself standing in the center of a familiar home. I knew I'd been there before—recently, too—but I couldn't place it. There was no furniture, and though the room was freshly cleaned, it was also damaged. Floorboards were missing, walls bashed in, windows taped up.

"Norah's house," Haley said suddenly, and I turned to find her standing at my right side. Addie was on her other side, the three of us still holding hands.

It took me a beat to realize she was right. The last time I'd been here, the guys had basically destroyed the place fighting off a pack of rogue vampires while I saved Asher from a devil's trap in the attic.

"How did we get here?" I asked.

"It's just the vision," Haley said. "There must be something we need to see here."

"Is there anything that can see *us*?" Addie asked.

Haley shook her head. "We're basically in the astral realm. Come on."

We followed her into the dining room, where a lone woman sat at a large dining table with her back to us. Dark blue fingernails, manicured into sharp points, tapped impatiently against the table. Every few seconds, she glanced at her cell and sighed.

Creeping around to the side of the table, I turned to look at her from the front, gasping at the sight.

Too much eye-makeup. Dark hair pulled into a severe French twist. Lips pressed together in perpetual annoyance.

"It's you," I blurted out.

"She can't hear you," Haley said.

I turned toward my sisters. "It's her. Trinity."

Haley nodded. She'd seen her before, too—the night we'd done the blood spell for Darius. But Addie seemed shocked into silence, her mouth hanging open, her fingers wrapped so tightly around the back of one of the dining chairs, her knuckles had turned white.

I put a gentle hand on her forearm. "Addie?"

"That's our... She threw me into the creek." A tear slid down her cheek.

"You remember?" Haley asked.

Addie rubbed her forehead, her face pained. "Just flashes. Gray was begging her not to throw me in. Delly, you guys called me. 'Delly can't swim,' Gray kept saying. Over and over and over, and that woman just... She didn't even care. She wanted us gone."

Addie was shaking now, staring at Trinity with a mixture of fear and hatred.

"But you *did* swim, Addie," I said, rubbing her back. "You pulled yourself out of there, and you screamed your head off until a neighbor finally heard. You're the reason she didn't succeed."

"I can't believe it's her," she said absently.

I turned to stare at the woman who'd given birth to us. She was almost beautiful, and maybe had been at one time, but there was something off about her features. She reminded me of someone who'd had too much plastic surgery, and now tried to mask it with too much makeup. Parts of her skin drooped and sagged unnaturally, her brows and forehead unmoving. Her collarbone jutted out at an odd angle, as if it'd been broken and set improperly.

She reminded me of Jonathan, of the side effects of all the experiments he'd done on himself, constantly chasing the perfect hybrid combination that would make him strong and immortal. Trinity may have been immortal—she was a vampire now, after all—but something told me strength had eluded her. Her hands trembled, and her back hunched over as if it wasn't strong enough to hold her up.

It was hard to believe this woman had almost killed us.

It was even harder to believe she was our mother.

"She can't hurt us here," I said, turning back to Addie, offering what I hoped was a comforting smile.

"No, she can't." A calm steel edged into her voice, and now Addie moved to stand behind Trinity, attempting to wrap her hands around the woman's neck. They passed right through her, as if Addie were no more substantial than mist. "And we can't hurt her, either, which is a shame."

"Guys, someone's coming." Haley gestured for us to join her on the other side of the room, giving us a full view of the table and the entrance from the kitchen, through which four more figures emerged—three fae and one human male.

"That's gotta be Talia," I said, nodding toward the fae woman as she took the chair to Trinity's left. I recognized her wine-colored hair from Emilio's description. "She's on the Council. The fae dude with the scar on his cheek looks like a Darkwinter Knight." He was dressed in a black uniform, with a black-and-gold insignia on the armband. He took the chair on the other side of Trinity, spreading out a bunch of maps on the table before him.

I wondered if he was the soldier Jael's sister Kallayna had pretended to fall in love with.

I wondered if she was even still alive.

"Who do you suppose the other fae is?" Addie asked, nodding at the male settling in on Talia's other side. He was dressed in dark gray robes, with long, stark-white hair woven into several intricate braids. Whomever he was, he had an air of importance about him.

"If that's Talia," Haley said, "a hundred bucks says Mr. Self-Importance is Fenlos."

"Who the fuck is that?" Addie asked.

"He and Talia were higher-ups on the Council," she said. "Jael sensed their magic that night we got into that crash on the highway. They killed some poor truck driver."

I glared at the pair of them, wondering what it was going to take to kill them.

"And the human?" Addie asked, and I glanced to the opposite end of the table, where the human male was settling in and booting up a laptop. He was short and broad-shouldered, with a weathered face and a scraggly whitish beard.

Everything in me turned to stone, except for my heart, which pounded so hard it made my chest ache.

You and your kind will burn, witch…

The last time I'd seen him, that beard had been blond.

The last time I'd seen him, he'd slit Calla's throat before my eyes and ordered his son to kill me.

"Phillip Reese," I managed to choke out. "Jonathan's father. The hunter who murdered my mother. My *true* mother."

I felt my sisters seething beside me, our pain and anger shared. Each of us had been wronged by the people in that room. Each of us had scores to settle. If we could've lit that room on fire and butchered everyone in it, I'm certain we would have.

But we weren't really standing there in Norah's dining room. We weren't really standing *anywhere.* And so my sisters and I clasped hands, infusing each other with love and support, and allowed the meeting of our enemies to unfold before our eyes.

NINETEEN

GRAY

"You're late. Again." Trinity glared at the doorway as the final attendee scampered in—another fae, dressed the same as the first guy, but with a lot more bling pinned to his shirt. Medals, no doubt, for all the witches he'd killed.

"Orendiel," Haley said. "The fae fucker in charge here. He and Phillip took over in the cave prisons when Jonathan went AWOL."

"The same fae fucker who killed Emilio at the warehouse raid." My fangs protruded, the magic inside me stirring. It was only the warmth of my sisters' hands that kept me still.

"Apologies, mistress." Orendiel offered a small bow before taking the chair to Phillip's left. "I was detained in the warehouse district. There was a small—"

Trinity cut him off with a single raised eyebrow. "Perhaps, Orendiel, you are under the false notion that my time is less valuable than yours."

"Quite the contrary, mistress." Orendiel lowered his eyes. "It won't happen again."

"See that it doesn't." Trinity finally tore her glacial gaze away from the fae and looked at Phillip, not thawing a bit. "The report, if you please, Phillip. Despite what you all seem to think, I'm not here this evening for my entertainment."

Phillip pulled up a file on his laptop, then began. "I've received confirmation from our generals in each of our west coast targets that the teams are in position and awaiting the final order."

"Which cities, specifically?" Trinity asked.

"Seattle, Los Angeles, Portland, San Francisco, and San Diego, to start. We're expecting confirmation from Denver and Santa Fe by the week's end."

"Excellent," Trinity said. "And the east coast?"

"Our teams in Boston, New York, and Miami will begin roll-out as part of phase three," he continued. "We'll have more information in the coming weeks, along with reports on cities where we're still trying to establish a foothold."

"Do keep me informed," she said.

"Of course, mistress."

A chill ran down my spine. So many cities, with many more to come. So many people dead smack in the path of destruction. We'd already known that the shitstorm in Blackmoon Bay was merely a testing ground—that they'd planned to branch out, spreading their poison from sea to shining sea—but we had no idea that they were so organized, or that things had already progressed so far.

"They've been working on this a lot longer than we thought," I said. "Seems like Trinity's been running the show the whole time, too."

It jived with the info Asher and Ronan had uncovered in Trinity's office in the crypt. Trinity—our birthmother—truly was the mastermind behind all of this.

My stomach turned over, and I swallowed bile.

"And what's with the mistress shit?" Haley asked. "Why would they just allow her to take over the Council like that? This whole thing is giving me the creeps."

Addie opened her mouth to say something, but the other Darkwinter Knight was pointing something out on his map. From my vantage point, it looked like the area around Luna's Café.

"Blackmoon Bay is nearly ready to fall," he said, tapping the map. "Everything will branch out from this point here —ground zero. Once we've received confirmation that the operation was successful, we'll put the external teams on standby for imminent orders in each city."

"And local law enforcement?" Trinity asked

"We don't anticipate any issues," Phillip said. "Most of the local units have been fully infiltrated and replaced. The holdouts will be taken care of soon enough."

I glanced at my sisters. Holdouts? Was he talking about human cops? Shifters like Emilio's team, who'd remained loyal despite the Darkwinter invasion?

"How soon do you anticipate beginning operations on the east coast?" Trinity asked.

"After the successful completion of our objectives on the

west coast, everything will begin to move at a much faster clip," Phillip said.

"Picture the whole country lined with dominoes, coast to coast," the other fae said. "Most of the work will take care of itself. It's merely a matter of knocking down the first one."

"Blackmoon Bay." Trinity smiled, her teeth gleaming, the heavy makeup cracking around her eyes. "What have we left to do here, then? As you can imagine, I'm anxious to remove myself from this festering city as soon as possible."

"The warehouse district is finally secured," Orendiel said, "Along with most of the residential neighborhoods. There are a few remaining strongholds in the Rockport area, but it won't be long before they surrender.

"Witches, I presume?" Trinity asked, her lip curling in disgust. "What, precisely, is the issue?"

At this, Fenlos gave a slight bow of his head. "They've been strangely resistant to the glamours, mistress. Furthermore, it seems the remaining witches in the area have banded together, making it nearly impossible for us to have any effect whatsoever."

I squeezed my sisters' hands, the first hopeful thing we'd heard yet. If witches remained in the Bay, and had gathered together to resist the invasion, they might be able to help us get inside.

I looked at Trinity, waiting for her to unleash her ire on Fenlos, but it never happened. She simply shook her head, clucking her tongue as though she could barely stand the weight of such disappointing news.

"Georgina really needs to work on gaining their trust," she said. "Where *is* that stupid girl?" She rolled her eyes, then shouted at the ceiling, "Georgina!"

My heart leaped. *Georgina*. She was here. Our sister was here, right upstairs.

That was two pieces of good news in the last minute alone.

At least, I hoped it would be good news. We still didn't know whose side Georgie was really on.

"Setting aside Georgina's oversights for the moment," Talia said, her tone even icier than Trinity's, "have you made any progress with her sisters?"

The three of us immediately tensed.

"I don't mean to question your authority, mistress," she continued, her tone suggesting that she'd meant to do *exactly* that. Unlike the men in the room, she did not appear to be the *least* bit enthralled with Trinity. "But you assured us the full cooperation of all four Silversbane witches. That was a condition of your appointment. This plan will not work without them—not in the long term."

"There's no cause for agitation, Talia." Trinity lowered her eyes, her fingernails running along a crack in the table.

Was she actually nervous?

"I'm getting closer to them each day," she said.

Like hell you are.

"So you've said," Talia replied, glancing at Fenlos as if to say, *see what I mean?* "At every meeting this month, you've made your empty promises. Yet we've seen no evidence that you've even *attempted* to reach the others, let alone gotten closer."

"Georgina knows. Ask her." Trinity glanced at the ceiling, as if my sister would apparate from thin air. "Georgina! Get down here! Now! You're—"

"Trinity," Fenlos said, calm and steely, "How can you be so certain they'll follow you?"

Trinity looked at the man as if that were the dumbest question ever uttered. "I'm their *mother*, Fenlos. Of course they'll follow me."

At this, Orendiel finally spoke up. "Forgive me, mistress, but I'm not so certain we should presume their loyalty just yet."

Yeah? Good call there, glitter dick.

Trinity folded her hands on the table in front of her, her eyelid twitching. She looked about three minutes away from core meltdown.

"What was that, Orendiel?" she asked, her lips stretching into a menacing smile.

Orendiel shifted uncomfortably in his chair and lowered his eyes, but he didn't back down. He simply cleared his throat and began again. "From my limited observation, Morgan and Serena are *extremely* loyal—not just to each other, but to the demons, the vampire, and the wolf. Somehow this motley assortment has convinced a great many others to join their cause—primarily witches—and after the losses we suffered at the cemetery, it's my opinion that we are underestimating their strengths, their numbers, and their ability to pose a serious challenge to our plans."

Morgan and Serena. Me and Haley. How the hell did everyone at this table seem to know so much about us?

How long had they been watching? How long had they been planning, plotting, killing?

"My understanding," Orendiel went on, "was that your daughters were removed from your care at a young age, raised in separate homes with no knowledge of you or each other. There's no guarantee they will even *remember* you, let alone agree to follow you into a cause that flies directly in the face of everything they now stand for."

"Agreed," Fenlos said, and Talia smiled at Trinity, vicious and vindictive.

"A mother's love for her children is a bond that cannot be broken," Trinity snapped, and again I tried not to puke, but she was just getting warmed up. "Not by time or by distance," she ranted on, "not by magic or rumors or lies, and most *certainly* not by creatures so vile as demons, vampires, and shifters. Yes, my daughters and I have some things to work through, as any family would after a prolonged estrangement. But as I've said countless times before, I'm confident that once we clear up those misunderstandings, we will be united again as a family."

"Tell me they're not buying this crap," Addie said, but for now, it seemed they were doing just that. Talia and Fenlos had settled back in their chairs, and if any of the others thought to challenge Trinity, none of them said it out loud.

I could barely believe my eyes and ears. Could our

birthmother really be that delusional? Clearly, she'd been drinking her own Kool-Aid for far too long.

The question was... How the fuck had she convinced the others sitting around this table to drink from the same damn jug?

Commotion at the front door snagged my attention, and all three of us turned to see someone enter the house in a frenzied rush, her dark brown hair windblown across pink cheeks, glasses askew on her face.

Georgie.

My eyes misted. In that moment, I didn't care whose side she was on. I loved her instantly, and I suspected Haley and Addie felt the exact same way.

"We have to help her," I said.

"There's nothing we can do here," Haley said. "Let's just see what we can find out, then we'll go back home and make a plan."

"But she's—"

"Gray." Haley nodded at the table. "Shh. Just listen."

"Sorry," Georgie panted, rushing into the dining room, tracking snow through the house. "I was in Rockport trying to figure things out with the witches. I tried to get home faster, but this weather is insane."

Trinity arched an eyebrow, spearing our sister with her patented frosty glare. "Tell me you've made progress on that front, or you may turn around, march right back out the way you came, and try again."

Georgie removed her snow-crusted winter coat and draped it over one of the empty chairs, then flopped into the seat, her shoulders slumping. In a small, watery voice, she said, "It's not that easy, Mom. They don't trust me."

"And who's fault is that, Georgina?" Trinity asked.

Desperation crept into Georgie's eyes. "I tried to tell you before, but—"

"Enough!" Trinity silenced her with a raised hand, making her flinch.

The unknown fae started rambling on about maps and coordinates and supplies, but I barely heard him. I was so focused on Georgie, so shocked that she was here, right in front of us, alive and whole and beautiful and just... real.

And now, I knew without a doubt she was *not* here by choice. I could sense it in her reactions, in her movements around Trinity. And there, beneath the fear and desperation, a flicker of the fighting spirit I sensed in all of my sisters. In myself.

However Trinity had found her, whatever she had done or said to convince her to follow her, Georgie was a prisoner now. Again, I felt the anger rise inside me, the rage so close to the edge I could taste it.

Rage at my mother, who'd tried to murder us. Rage at Deirdre, who'd signed away my soul and separated me from my sisters. Somehow, she'd believed that if we were never reunited, the prophecy could never come to fruition. That the four of swords could never rise and fulfill our true destiny. That breaking up our family—our sisterhood—would somehow keep us safe.

I thought of all the witches back at the lodge, and all the witches here in Blackmoon Bay, and all the witches across the entire world who'd been forced to endure the same tortures, and I knew that we would *never* be safe. Not until every witch was free to live the life she chose, without the constant threat of hunters, dark fae, and power-hungry monsters like the woman sitting at the head of this table, desperate to claim what was never hers.

"Gray," Haley whispered, her hand on my lower back. "You need to calm down and pay attention. We need this intel."

I nodded, shaking out of the funk and re-focusing on the conversation. Haley was right. Already we'd learned more in fifteen minutes of spying than we'd managed to piece together over the last few weeks with the guys.

"What of the Grinaldi vampire?" The Darkwinter Knight asked.

"He's talking about Fiona," I said to Haley and Addie. She turned out to be a surprising ally, and was presently recovering back at the lodge with the others we'd rescued from the crypt.

Phillip waved away the question. "Useless to us now. As I suspected, her loyalty to Jonathan was thin at best. Sources tell us she's now firmly entrenched with the enemy."

"We can't just forget about her," Orendiel said. "She knows too much about Jonathan's plans—*our* plans."

"I will personally deal with her if and when it becomes necessary," Phillip said. "Our immediate concern is launching the operation here in the Bay, then relocating our core team to the permanent base in Seattle."

"And what of the units in Europe and Asia?" Trinity asked.

"Once the United States is converted and fully within our control," Phillip said, "it will only be a matter of time before the other countries fall."

Fear and frustration simmered in my gut.

"When?" I shouted, slamming my hand into the back of one of the chairs, but of course my touch passed right through. I could no more cause a physical action here than I could make the monsters sitting around the table answer me.

Still, I didn't know what else to do. If we had any hope of preventing whatever horrors they'd planned to unleash upon the world, we needed a damn timeframe

"When?" I shouted again. "When the fuck is—"

"When?" Georgie asked suddenly, and I gasped, my eyes darting back to her.

She was looking straight at me

"Georgie?" I asked.

"She can't see or hear us," Haley said.

I waved my hands. Georgie didn't blink.

But she didn't look away either.

"She heard me," I said. "I know she did. Guys, she knows we're here."

"What did you say, Georgina?" Trinity asked, her voice barely audible, yet shaking with rage.

Georgie's face was ashen.

She broke our gaze and looked back at Trinity, then lowered her eyes. "I just... I was just wondering when we... When you thought we would be leaving Blackman Bay?"

Good girl, Georgie. That's what we need to know.

"Do you have urgent business elsewhere?" Trinity asked.

"No, mother."

The fake smile came back out. A shark's smile. "A date, perhaps? With a boy?"

"Of course not," Georgie said, her cheeks darkening. But despite her obvious fear, she persisted. "I just wanted to know when we'd be heading up to Seattle."

"Our target date is in three weeks," Phillip replied. "But that's assuming—"

"That's enough, Philip." Trinity turned those dagger eyes back on my little sister. I wondered if she was using her vampire influence, but Georgie didn't flinch. Didn't blink. I sensed the tremble in her body, but she held her chin high, her shoulders squared.

Fucking fight her, little sister. You're a Silversbane witch. You've got this, and we've got you.

"It's a simple question, mother," Georgie said.

It happened so fast, none of us even realized it until my sister was already bleeding.

Georgie gasped, tears springing to her eyes. She pressed her fingers to the fresh gash on her cheek, wet with blood.

The same blood dripping from Trinity's dark blue fingernails.

Georgie met my eyes again.

"I'm sorry," she said, and I knew in my gut her apology was meant for us.

I no longer had control over my body—I no longer cared. All I saw was Georgie's blood dripping from Trinity's nails, and I was in motion, launching myself across the table, gunning for the bitch who called herself our mother.

"Gray, stop!" Addie shouted, and then it was like someone had hit us with a sonic wave. I was falling, spinning, sucked through time and space, everything around me disintegrating…

When I opened my eyes, I was pinned to the kitchen floor back at the lodge, Darius and Emilio trying to steady my thrashing limbs.

"She's awake," Emilio said. "She's okay. Gray? Gray, can you hear me?"

I nodded, blinking away my confusion and trying to sit up.

"That's it, love," Darius said, helping me up. "Nice and easy."

My sisters were standing in front of us, still inside the salt circle that I'd managed to break through, taking several candles down with me.

"What happened?" I asked. "How did we get out?"

"We didn't *get* out," Haley said. "Someone pushed us."

"Georgie," I said, adamant. "She knew we were there. I'm telling you, she could hear me. She knew we needed a timeline. That's why she asked. She pushed us out to protect us."

"Let's hope it was her. Because if Trinity or any of the

others knew we were in there, then everything we've just seen is useless, and they're going to double their efforts to shield themselves now."

"I'm sorry," I said. "I know I shouldn't have blown up like that. I just... I saw Georgie bleeding, and then *all* I saw was red. I wanted to claw that bitch's eyes out."

"Your protective instincts are strong, Gray," Darius said. "That's not something to apologize for."

"No, it isn't." Haley offered a smile, but it quickly melted, and she knelt down to blow out the remaining candles. "It wouldn't have done any good, though. We were there on the astral. Georgie might've sensed us—I'll give you that. But that's about it."

"Only it *isn't* it. Not by a long shot." I held out my hand, unfurling my fist to reveal a chunk of Trinity's dark hair.

TWENTY

GRAY

In so many ways, it felt as if an entire year had passed since I last stood in the common room to rally the witches for a battle they never should've had to fight.

An entire year since I'd asked them for their support against an enemy bent on our complete annihilation.

An entire year since they'd given it freely.

In truth, it had been less than two weeks.

And now, the night after Haley's blood spell had given us a glimpse into the darkest corners of our enemies' minds, I found myself standing in the same spot at the front of the same room, looking out at a familiar sight.

The crowd was larger now—including the new friends and allies we'd rescued from the crypt and several more Raven's Cape area witches Verona and her people had rallied to the cause—but everything else about this moment felt exactly the same.

A room full of friends and allies gathered before the fireplace, some huddled on the couches, others standing near the fire, all of us trying to find a moment's warmth in an otherwise inescapable winter.

The men I loved, wordlessly sending me their unwavering support. My sisters standing by my side.

And in my shirt pocket, close to my heart, the objects I'd taken to carrying as gentle reminders of those who'd gone before me—those who were with me still: the Page of Cups card for Sophie, the High Priestess for Calla, and the granite heart Liam had given me, carved with the raven's feather that would always remind me of Death, my teacher, my guide.

Borrowing their strength, I steadied myself for the task ahead.

The fire popped, and a heavy silence descended on the room.

It was time.

"We have some news about our enemies in the Bay," I began. "Before we get into specifics, let's just rip off the Band-Aid." I paced in front of them, trying to meet each and every person eye-to-eye. I wanted them to know we were in this together, no matter what. "Ten nights from tonight, whether we're ready or not, we are going to war."

A murmur rippled through the group, the tension in the room rising. I could feel the spike of their heart rates, smell the hit of adrenaline that flooded their bloodstreams as soon as I'd said the words.

But the sharp, pungent scent of fear? Completely absent. Two weeks ago, a month ago, three months ago, we had no idea what was coming for us, and that fear of the unknown was enough to drive a person mad.

Knowledge was ammunition, and now, we had a stockpile.

"You guys followed me into hell once before," I said. "Some of you are still recovering from that night at the crypt—and others never will. You put everything on the line that night, and now, I'm going to ask you to do it all over again."

"You don't have to ask us *shit*," McKenna said from the back of the room. "We've got your back, girl. No question."

The others quickly voiced their agreement, and I smiled, grateful for the boost.

"The same caveat we established before still applies," I said anyway, just in case. "And this goes for new friends, too. Anyone who wants to tap out can do so, no questions asked. You will always have a home here, so long as the rest of us are able to provide and protect it. But I have to be honest with you, guys. This is a balls-to-the-wall, all-hands-on-deck kind of situation. If ever we needed the numbers, it's now."

"We're here for you, Gray." This from the yellow-eyed witch who'd been imprisoned in the caves with Haley and McKenna. "We're here for each other. I know I speak for everyone in this room when I say that. This is family now. *You're* family."

"Here, here," came another call, and a few witches let out a whistle, showing their support.

"I... I feel the same," I said, emotion threatening to cut

off my words. I swallowed past the tightness in my throat, then continued. "The fight at the cemetery was hard-won—for those on the front lines as well as for the brave souls who'd been imprisoned there. But from the enemy's perspective, the cemetery was just a minor outpost. Blackmoon Bay is ground zero for their entire operation, and it's no longer simply the home we're trying to take back. It's the spark that will eventually set the whole world on fire.

"I know we talked about this last time, but it bears repeating: this is not just about our own lives, but the lives of everyone we've ever loved. If we fail, we will *all* die. Witches, shifters, vampires, demons, fae, *and* humankind. None will be left standing. Not one soul but the few who've masterminded the entire collapse."

Haley and Addie joined me at the front of the room, and together we passed along all of the pertinent intelligence we'd gathered from the blood spell vision. Emilio, Elena, and detectives Lansky and Hobb shared their thoughts on the likely scenarios we'd face once we got past the fae's magical borders and into the city proper, assuming we could get in at all. And those who'd been imprisoned shed more light on the types of hybrids they'd encountered inside, along with details about the fucked-up weaponry both Jonathan and his father had been working on.

"Well," I finally said, certain the picture we'd painted couldn't get any bleaker, "I'm afraid that's all the good news we've got for you tonight."

Everyone laughed, breaking the tension just a fraction.

"If that's the good news, what's the bad?" Detective Hobb asked.

"We're outta booze and the roads are fucked," Asher said, inspiring a chorus of groans and more laughter from the crowd. "That's about as bad as it gets in my book."

Taking advantage of the levity, I closed my eyes and took a moment to reset. Again, I thought about all of the people gathered here before me, all the people counting on me. I thought of my two sisters standing beside me, strong and beautiful women who I'd only just found again after two decades of separation. I thought of Georgie, trapped by a delusional, dangerous psychopath. I thought of the men that I loved, the men that I wanted to build a life with.

My heart expanded in my chest.

When the noise died down again, I opened my eyes to find the entire room looking at me, their smiles encouraging, their gazes serious but hopeful. No doubt they were thinking about their own loved ones, their own dreams of the future, their own reasons for fighting against these nearly impossible odds.

They were counting on me—each and every one of them. In that moment, amidst the laughter and the tears, the darkness and the light, I felt the weight of their collective hope settle firmly on my shoulders. It was, I realized now, mine to carry.

But it wasn't a burden.

It was an honor. I would die for them. Not just the men I loved, not just my sisters. But every one of the witches and allies gathered in this room.

And I suspected they felt the same way. Darkness had brought us together, but through that togetherness, we would fight our way back to the light.

I blinked away tears before anyone saw them fall. When it came to translating messages from the heart, words were a limited medium.

But I had to try.

"Despite what the Silversbane prophecy says about leadership and uniting covens and all that stuff…" I shook my head, those limited words crashing into each other and getting stuck on the way out. "Guys, I'm not really one for big speeches. I just want you to know that I appreciate each and everyone of you so much. I know what we're facing, and I know it won't be easy. I don't really have any big inspirational words or battle cries, but I can tell you what always helps me keep the monsters at bay. It's pretty simple, really." I looked at each of my men in turn and smiled. "You just remember the ones you love, and know that everything you're doing is for them. And if you're on your own right now, then I want you to look in the mirror tonight before you go to bed. Take a good look. Truly *see* that woman looking back at you. Memorize the color of her eyes, the shape of her face, the sound of her laughter. When things get dark out there, when things are at their most hopeless and bleak, know that whatever demons we face, whatever bombs are dropped at our feet, whatever evil befalls us tonight or tomorrow or ten years from now, that woman is *always* worth fighting for."

TWENTY-ONE

GRAY

From that moment forward, we went hard and fast on all fronts, pushing each other and ourselves to our absolute limits.

Potions and poisons. Protective amulets and charms. Darkwinter lore. Combat training. Mental acuity and shielding. Cardio. Strength-training. Weapons—God, so many weapons—all of them lethal, and not just to our enemies. Asher's fae swords would do a lot of damage against the Darkwinter Knights—the right hit would kill them on contact. But they would also decimate the shifters, as Emilio could attest to first hand. I'd grown particularly fond of a fae staff Ronan had taken from the crypts, but using the staff meant giving up the sword. Ash was immune to devil's traps, but Ronan could easily fall prey; we had no idea whether Jon's original devil's trap nanotech was just a prototype or if it'd been replicated on a larger scale. Darius and I, along with the other vampires we'd liberated from the crypts, could only fight at night, and we had to be particularly careful around fire and sharp swords. On the most basic physical level, the witches and Liam—the humans among us—were at the greatest risk, but all of us had weak points.

It was a lot to account for, and we had very little time to plan. If the intel we'd gathered was accurate, and the enemy's plans were still on track, we had about two weeks before all hell broke loose. The only way we were going to survive this, reclaim our home, and save the rest of—well, existence—was by working together, sticking together through the shit of it, and seeing it through to the very end.

Despite the risks, there was excitement in the air, a crackling charge I could feel everywhere I went. Though we'd only just learned about Trinity's plans, this battle has been a long time coming, and there was something to be said for knowing the end was on the horizon.

No matter what that end would bring.

We might very well be slaughtered in Blackmoon Bay, but after being forced into hiding for thousands of years, we were damn well ready to fight—and fight hard.

Fuck *anyone* who thought we'd go out quietly.

A few nights after our training had begun in earnest, Ronan and I took a break from sparring with Elena and Emilio to take the hounds for a walk along the shoreline, sneaking in some long overdue alone time.

We walked in silence for a while, keeping as close together as our curse would allow. It was our new normal—the "almost" we'd adapted to, almost without realizing it.

He could *almost* brush a lock of hair behind my hear. I could *almost* lean up on my toes and kiss a path along his beard. He could *almost* wrap me in his arms, push me against the wall, and…

"Ronan, we can't wait any longer."

He nodded without meeting my eyes, knowing exactly where my mind had gone. Where it *had* been, ever since the blood spell.

The moment I realized I'd yanked Trinity's hair out of the astral plane and into our reality—that I'd captured physical proof that we knew of her whereabouts—the wheels began to turn.

We had leverage now. A new bargaining chip to offer Sebastian.

"We're heading into the Bay in six days," I said. "This needs to be settled up before then."

Ronan nodded, but didn't respond.

I stopped, turning to meet his eyes. "I need to see him. It's our best shot."

Ronan held my gaze for only a moment before cutting away, his eyes roaming the dark, choppy sea, a stiff wind blowing the hair in front of his eyes. When he finally turned to look at me again, he said simply, "We."

"We what?"

"*We* need to see him. We're doing it together, Gray, or not at all."

I bit back a smile, toeing the ice with my boot. "So that's how it's gonna be, huh Vacarro?"

"That's how it *is*, Desario." He shot me another quick

glance, catching my smile, his own crooked grin making me dizzy. A hundred, a thousand, a million years from now, I had no doubt he'd still have the same effect on me.

"So tell me something," he said, continuing our walk. "Once the Prince of Hell lets you out of your deal, what's your endgame?"

"Ronan, he's not going to let me out of the deal. Not even for Trinity." I swallowed my disappointment, stopping our forward motion and meeting his eyes once again. "Do you... Do you really think that's what this is about?"

Ronan sighed, raking a hand through his hair. "No. Just had to be sure. It's a big risk, Gray."

I looked deep into his eyes, so familiar, yet still so mysterious. There was so much more I wanted to know about Ronan—about his past, his human life, all the times and places our lives had intersected.

Before all of this started, some part of me assumed that no matter what had happened between us, we would always be friends. That we'd grow old together in Blackmoon Bay, even though Ronan wouldn't age. It was a nice fairytale picture, one that used to get me through the dark days.

But that felt like a million years ago. Now, I was immortal, too.

Now, I knew what dark days really were.

"You were born for this, Gray," Ronan said, once again sensing the direction of my thoughts. "I've always known it."

But I didn't want to talk about the war we'd yet to face,

about the witches back at the lodge, about all the crazy shit still brewing on the horizon.

"I was born for *you*," I said. "Born to fall in love with you. Born to build a life with you. Born to... to *touch* you." I reached for his face, the wind blowing the tips of his hair against my fingers—an all-to-brief tease that made my heart ache even as it strengthened my resolve.

If Sebastian accepted my counter-offer, I would never take Ronan's touch for granted again. Never push him away. Never shut him out.

It didn't matter whether we had days, weeks, or a thousand years together. I would never let him go.

I closed my eyes, the frozen sea mist coating my lashes, the truth settling deep in my heart. Even if Sebastian refused, and our curse remained for the rest of our immortal days, that wouldn't change the way I felt. Ronan was mine, and I was his.

"What are you thinking?" he asked softly, and I opened my eyes to look at him again.

The moonlight glittered in his eyes, a sad smile pulling at the corners of his mouth. I could taste the depth of his ache, the loss we both shared each time we looked at each other.

"I want to spend the rest of my life with you," I said.

He reached for my face, but stopped short, just as I had, tracing the shape of my jaw a hair's breadth from my skin. "And you will."

"Let's just hope the rest of our lives last more than—"

"Hey." He touched a finger to my lips, ever so briefly.

Heat sparked, but didn't ignite. "Shhh. Right now, in this moment, we have an eternity."

His hazel eyes blazed bright, calling to my heart, to that place deep inside where my love for him burned.

There were no words for it. All I knew was that I'd never wanted his kiss as badly as I had in that moment, and I wanted him to know it. Closing my eyes, I let my influence gently touch his mind. He dropped his guard immediately, and I sent him an image of my desire, real and passionate and all-consuming. Enough to melt all the ice from the shoreline and chase away this eternal winter for good.

Ronan leaned in close and whispered against the shell of my ear. "Me too, Gray. Always."

I nodded, offering him another smile. "I'll spare you the rest of that vision tonight. But as soon as we get back, you're getting the director's cut."

"I'd better." Ronan laughed, but eventually, his smile faded, and he turned away to watch Sparkle and Sunshine, who were trying to outrun the frigid waves about a quarter-mile down the shore. When he turned back and caught my eye again, he said simply, "I've already summoned Sebastian. He'll be here tomorrow night."

I nodded once, grateful. I should've known Ronan was already on it.

"We'll have five minutes to convince him," he said, "so let's make it count."

"I always do, Vacarro." I sent him a quick flash—a sneak peek of just what I had in store for him if we could entice

Sebastian to take the deal. "Just in case you needed evidence of my commitment to breaking this damn deal."

Ronan groaned, then glanced down at his jeans, now bulging. "And now you've got evidence of mine, too."

I cracked up, wishing we could play this game all night, because I definitely would've won. But back in the direction of the lodge, a figure had emerged from the mist, running toward us. The breeze carried the sound of my name.

"Who is that?" Ronan asked.

"I think it's McKenna." I called the hounds back from their chase, and the four of us made our way back toward home.

"Gray," McKenna said when we'd caught up, her cheeks red from the cold, her eyes bright. "Okay, don't freak out, but we've got a *slight* problem."

"Define slight and define problem," I said.

"It's… It's probably best if you come see for yourself."

TWENTY-TWO

LIAM

Gray stood at my bedside, her face inscrutable, though her anger was quite palpable. Even my comparatively dull human senses could discern as much; her energy was so fierce, I feared my bed would ignite, with me in it.

"A concussion?" she demanded. "You got a *head injury*?"

"The pain is not unbearable," I said, which was only partially untrue. "To be fair, McKenna doesn't believe it's a concussion. We just have to ensure I don't fall asleep for a prolonged period tonight, but that is merely a precaution. In most of these cases, I'm told the patient—"

Gray held up her hand, silencing me. "What happened? The short version, if you don't mind."

"Your sisters were sparring with the detectives, trying to learn the best techniques for defending against shifter attacks. Were you aware that most shifter communities follow complex hierarchical structures that dictate—"

"Liam. What is it about the phrase 'short version' that's so unclear?"

"Right. Of course." My cheeks warmed under her scrutiny, but I pressed on. "Detective Hobb, in his wolf form, had set up on one side of the beach, with Haley and Bex on the other. He'd been alternating between them, charging straight for them while Detective Lansky instructed the women on defensive maneuvers. On this particular turn, Lansky wanted Haley to run straight at the wolf instead of waiting for him, but as she did so, she twisted her ankle. Down she went."

"Oh, shit," Gray said. "Is she okay?"

"Your sister is completely fine," I assured her. "As for me, well... I'd been timing them on the sidelines, taking notes and making observations, as I do. But the moment I saw her go down, instinct took over. I leaped in front of Hobb to prevent the inevitable collision, and..." I shrugged, knocking lightly on my head.

"You jumped in front of a charging wolf?" Gray nearly exploded. I'd never seen her so upset, so worried. "You're lucky you're still alive! You can't do things like that anymore, Liam. You're human. Understand? Not Death. Not the Great Transformation. Not a bird or a bat or a wisp of cloud on the breeze. You are a *man*, with breakable bones and spillable blood and a head that could crack open like a melon if you hit it too hard."

Shame burned a hot path up my spine and I turned my head, unable to hold her gaze. "As much as I appreciate the detailed enumeration of my many weaknesses, I assure you, I'm fine. So if that's all, I'd like to be alone now if you don't mind."

Undeterred, Gray waltzed over to the other side of the bed, once again capturing me in her gaze. From those twilight eyes, I could no more look away than I could've defended myself against the inertia of the rapidly charging wolf.

But now, her eyes were soft. Wounded. Gentle. "That's... that's what you think this is about?"

"It matters not what I think. These are merely facts, Gray. I can no longer protect you or any of the people I've come to care about. Not the way the others can. I am a liability in the truest sense of the word." I gestured toward the window, against which the wind sang winter's incessant song. "Despite the fact that I've brought much of this chaos to your doorstep, I am no longer in a position to help you defend against it. Despite the shame in my heart, I've lost the ability to right those wrongs or any of the—"

"Stop. Just... stop." She took my face between her hands, her thumbs sweeping over my cheeks. Tears shone in her eyes, and when she finally spoke again, her voice had lost all of its anger, though none of its ferocity. "It's about losing you, Liam. I can't... I told you that night at the cemetery—you're family. Losing you is not an option."

Family. The word echoed in my mind, suddenly bigger, grander, greater than it'd ever been. In truth, I'd wanted nothing more than what she was offering, but now, I felt as if I were the runt of the litter, the one who'd constantly need looking after while the others risked their lives to keep me safe.

But Gray was having none of my self-pity. She stripped down to nothing but her T-shirt and undergarments, then gestured for me to move over.

"What is this?" I asked. "Not that I'm complaining, mind you. It's just… a bit unexpected."

"As it should be." She flashed me a quick wink, then climbed into the bed beside me, sliding beneath the blankets, her bare legs tangling with mine.

The brush of her soft skin against mine was a balm for all that pained me, physically as well as emotionally.

We lay on our sides, face-to-face, and there we remained for many long moments. There was a time, however briefly it'd lasted, when it felt as though I could read the thoughts swimming in the depths of her eyes. But tonight, whether it was the loss of my greater powers or merely the shifter-induced scrambling of my soft human brain, I could no longer anticipate the direction of her mind's many wanderings.

"Please tell me what you're thinking," I finally said, my voice breaking, though I couldn't have said why. Some strange, uncomfortable emotion had climbed into my chest and taken hold of my heart, making it skitter and stall.

I hated that I'd disappointed her.

Gray ran her fingers through my hair, and I closed my eyes, settling into the comfort of her gentle caress.

"You're not weak, Liam," she said softly. "You are brave and strong and wise beyond measure. But you are accustomed to immortality. *Eternal* immortality. You don't have that self-protective instinct that humans develop. Your instinct is always to protect those you care about, and I appreciate that more than I can even express. But you have to balance that with common sense. What happened today with Detective Hobb... What if something like that happens in the Bay? What if it's not friendly shifters next time? What if you're not surrounded by witches with healing magic?"

I opened my eyes to meet hers once again. "Then I shall do my best to outwit them."

"That's not good enough."

"I will not allow you to fight these battles while I cower in the shadows. That is not up for debate, little witch."

"I'm not asking you to sit this one out, Liam. I'm just asking you to know yourself. Not as Death, but as a mortal man."

She was right, of course, and I promised her I would do as she asked. This seemed to appease her, and she drew closer to me, the crease between her eyes smoothing once again.

I traced an infinity symbol on her forehead, and she sighed, her eyelids fluttering closed.

"Tell me what you're thinking *now*," I said.

"Just that I miss our philosophical talks." Then, opening her eyes again and turning a bright smile my way, "But that just means we'll have lots more to talk about when all of this is over, and we can finally breathe again."

"I am looking forward to that day more than you

know." I traced my thumb around the curves of her mouth. "I love you, Gray Desario."

She parted her lips to reply, but I cut her off with a kiss, drawing her closer, hoping she could feel just how much I'd meant those words. I would've been quite content to kiss her for the rest of the evening, but Gray pulled back.

"That day on the beach," she said, "when we first kissed? Do you remember?"

"I remember everything about that day. About you."

"You told me you'd never done anything like this before. Does that mean you haven't..." Her words trailed off, but her intense gaze didn't waver, and I knew exactly what she was asking about.

Again, heat flooded my cheeks, and I found myself babbling in the wake of her question.

"I... I have studied human anatomy as well as that of the animal kingdoms of several realms, and I'm quite knowledgeable about the physical mechanics of—"

"Liam. That's not what I meant, and you know it. But if you'd rather not talk about—"

"No, it's okay. It's just... I'm not exactly sure how to answer your question. Presumably, you're wondering as to whether I have ever engaged in sexual intercourse."

Gray's tender smile made my heart flutter. "I probably would have chosen to word the question differently," she said, "but yes, that is what I'm asking."

I considered her question, uncertainty creeping into my chest. But with Gray, there was no need for shame or nervousness. I'd betrayed her, and somehow she'd seen fit to forgive me. To welcome me back into her life, into her arms. From now on, I would only be open with her. Honest, no matter the topic.

"Perhaps my vessel has," I said. "And perhaps I, as a human all those eons ago, engaged in such pleasures. The truth is, Gray, I cannot recall much of that time. For all intents and purposes, I suppose I'm what you might consider... inexperienced."

She trailed her fingers down my arm, her touch sending electric tingles throughout my entire body. In a gentle voice, she asked, "Is that an experience you might like to have? With me, I mean?"

I swallowed hard, my heart trying its best to climb into my throat. "Is that something *you* might like? With me, I mean?"

Gray bit her bottom lip and nodded, her cheeks darkening.

I cleared my throat. "How would we... I mean, do we just... I'm sorry. This is... I suppose I am a bit out of my element." I offered her what I suspected was a rather awkward smile. For all I knew about human anatomy, for all I knew about a great many subjects both large and small, nothing had prepared me for this moment.

"Let's just figure it out as we go," she said, wriggling beside me as she stripped away her remaining clothing, and I did the same.

She shifted closer, our bodies touching. A brilliant warmth radiated from deep inside her, the complex magic pulsing like a second heartbeat, calling to me as it always had.

I was instantly erect.

I touched her face, capturing her mouth in another kiss as I shifted to lie on top of her. Gray parted her thighs and arched her hips, reaching for me, guiding me, and suddenly I was inside her, sliding into her wet heat, the feel of it unlocking ripples of pure, exquisite pleasure.

I gasped, unable to hold back, and instinctually, my body moved, faster, deeper, desperate for more of her. For all of her.

"Slow," she whispered, smiling up at me. "Let's go slow."

I did as she suggested and forced myself to slow my movements, though everything inside me was screaming to push harder, faster, to chase this feeling of pure bliss until it exploded inside me like a newborn galaxy.

"Breathe, Liam," she whispered, the touch of her palm against my cheek bringing my attention back to the moment. Back to my breath, which I now realized I'd been holding for far too long. I exhaled slowly, and I looked into her eyes, letting my gaze wander down the slope of her nose, across the planes of her cheeks, down to her dark pink lips.

I'd seen the sun rise and set upon every country in this realm. I'd seen the very bottom of the deepest part of the sea, and followed the winds across the highest mountain peaks. I'd watched the stars die and be reborn.

Yet I'd ever seen anything so beautiful as the look upon her face as I made love to her.

It was almost too much to bear—the warm silk of her skin, the sweet taste of her kiss, the soft moans escaping her lips, all of it creating a symphony of sensations that conspired to stop my heart. No matter; if this was to be my final hour in this mortal vessel, I could think of no better way to depart from this realm.

Eventually, I relaxed into the rhythm of this divine act, and just as Gray had suggested, we figured it out. Soon I sensed a shift in her demeanor, her hips arching, her own movements quickening.

"We can go fast now?" I asked, hope rising inside.

Gray laughed, soft and sweet, her cheeks flush, her eyes sparkling. "Yes, Liam. We can go fast."

At her words, I quickened my movements, my body taking over, bringing us closer and closer to the final act in this seductive dance. In so many ways I wanted to prolong that inevitable ending, but the mere idea of it felt like standing in the ocean and trying to hold back the waves with your bare hands.

"Liam," Gray breathed, her eyelids fluttering closed. I sensed she wanted to be touched, and I slid my hand between us, fingers seeking her most sensitive flesh, knowing we were both mere moments away from letting go.

She moaned softly at my touch, then gasped, her body clenching me in a grip so tight, so perfect, it made the stars dance before my eyes.

No, not the stars, I realized then, but Gray's eyes, open once again, locking fiercely with mine, her gaze full of love and passion that mirrored my own.

And then, as she shuddered beneath me, my name no more than a sigh on her breath, I finally lost the tenuous hold on my own control.

I kissed her, everything inside me exploding in pure, white-hot pleasure as the world crashed out of orbit, sending me spiraling into another galaxy, another time, another universe.

And through it all, we looked deeply into each other's eyes, a connection so deep and intimate it stole my breath.

There were tears in her eyes, and when she looked up at me and smiled, my heart was utterly full.

* * *

"How do you feel?" she asked later. Minutes, hours, I could not have said. In those precious moments in her arms, time had lost all meaning for me.

"It's not an exaggeration to say that I now understand why humans have gone to war for such a thing."

Gray laughed softly, a sound that made my heart sing. "Hmm. And this was just our first time."

"You mean... We get to do that again?"

Now, her laugh turned hearty, so full it made our bed tremble. "I love you, Liam Colebrook. You know that, right?"

"You've left no doubts, little witch." I cupped her breast,

stroking her nipple with my thumb. In the span of a single heartbeat, I was hard for her again.

"About that whole 'doing it again' bit," I said, pulling her on top of me, "do you think we might…"

"Yes, Liam." She lowered her head, her lips alighting on mine as the dragonfly alights upon the lotus. Then, with a wicked gleam in her eye, she smiled and said, "I think we might."

TWENTY-THREE

RONAN

In all the time I've been with Gray, from the moment I was assigned as her guardian to this moment right now, I'd been dreaming of the day when I'd have leverage over Sebastian —just enough to break his hold on Gray. Just enough to loosen the binds of her contract. Just enough to let us find that final, indisputable loophole.

All the fucking wishes and dreams in the world, yet in my mind, they'd always ended the same way.

Sebastian, laughing me out of his office, reminding me to remember my place.

Sebastian, threatening me with eternal banishment, with harming Gray, with assigning her a new guardian, with finding crueler and more heartbreaking ways to keep us apart.

He was a monster, and we were his prey.

Until tonight.

"What is so urgent," Sebastian demanded, "that I had to

take time away from running my operations to come see you in person?"

It was the night after our walk on the beach, and one hour after our agreed-upon meeting time, he'd simply appeared at the kitchen table, where he now sat with his arms folded across his chest, his face pinched in annoyance.

I glanced at Gray, who was standing next to me, and she nodded once.

I tossed a paper bag onto the table in front of him.

"What's this?" he asked, barely glancing at it.

"A new deal," Gray said.

The D-word piqued his interest, as it always had. Keeping his eyes locked on Gray, he opened up the bag, fishing out the chunk of hair she'd yanked from Trinity's head, along with the passports we'd discovered in her crypt office.

Sebastian's eyes glowed red with rage.

I took a step closer to Gray.

"How did you come by this?" he demanded, pressing the hair to his nose and taking a deep whiff. "Answer me!"

As it had so many times before, Sebastian's total lack of emotional restraint gave him away, and for the first time since I'd traded away the ability to touch the woman I loved for a chance at keeping her safe, a spark of hope flickered to life inside my gut.

Hope that the Prince of Hell might actually agree to this.

Hope that tonight, rather than sleeping next to Ash as he touched her, rather than listening to her soft moans and Darius and Emilio brought her to the edge, rather than seeing her shy smile and swollen lips as she crept out of Liam's bedroom just before sunrise, rather than dousing myself with icy showers as I replayed the images she'd implanted in my mind, I might be able to share her bed again without burning her alive.

"How we came by it is irrelevant," Gray said. "What's important is what we're offering—*if* you're willing to negotiate."

Sebastian placed the items back inside the bag and set it on the table, feigning indifference, but it was too late for that. He couldn't hide the desperate desire smoldering in his eyes.

"You're bargaining with me, Silversbane?" he asked.

"There's nothing in my contract that prevents it," she said. "Besides, aren't you the king of the deal?"

"Get to the point."

"Ronan and I share a deep love you couldn't even *begin* to understand," she said, surprising me. I hadn't expected her to get so personal there, but Gray was on a mission, and wherever the hell she was going with this, I trusted her. "You had no right to take that from us."

"Oh, but I did," Sebastian said, condescension dripping from his voice. "It's all there in black and white. Ronan agreed to my terms, no tricks, no take-backs."

"You left him no other options, and you did it all for sport," she said. "You gain absolutely nothing by keeping us apart—nothing but your own sick amusement."

"What you call 'sick amusement,' Silversbane, I call managing my assets, which I'm free to do as I see fit."

Sebastian folded his hands over his belly, offering a smug grin, assuming he'd gotten the upper hand.

But Gray wasn't done yet. Not even close.

"When I first met you," she continued, "I thought you'd never loved anyone in your life. How else could you be so cruel? So casual about destroying *our* love?"

Sebastian rolled his eyes. "In case you haven't noticed, girl, I'm the Prince of Hell. Love is not my primary motivator."

"It was once though, wasn't it?" she asked, her tone softening. "A young witch at the crossroads, a favor here, a favor there, and before you realized it, you'd given away your heart."

Bullseye.

I'd never seen the Prince of Hell turn so white. Gray had hit him right where it hurt.

Sebastian exploded, jumping to his feet in a rage. "I didn't come here to be manipulated and cajoled by—"

"Ronan and I know of Trinity's whereabouts," Gray deadpanned, once again hitting her target.

Sebastian's mouth dropped open. He tried to recover, reclaiming his seat and smoothing his hands over his pants, but once again, she'd tricked him into showing his hand.

"We know where she's been hiding," Gray continued. "We know who's been protecting her, we know who's given her an army, and we know about her plans for a major power grab that—if successful—will leave you unemployed and homeless."

"Are you suggesting she has the power to claim hell?" he asked, incredulous.

"Oh, I'm not suggesting it, Sebastian. I'm straight-up *telling* you. But if you'd rather bury your head in the sand and pretend your power and position come with an immortal guarantee, be my guest."

I coughed into my hand to hide my damn smile.

Fucking Desario. She had him by the balls, and all three of us knew it. I'd never been so proud of her.

When he didn't respond, she pressed on.

"My team and I intend to capture Trinity, decimate her army, and return her to your care, at which time you may deal with her as you wish."

He narrowed his eyes, but it was clear Gray wasn't bluffing, and he damn well knew it.

"And in exchange?" he asked.

"It's simple," Gray said. "I want to be able to touch the man I love. To take him in my arms—in my bed—whenever I damn well please. I want you to break that wretched curse, and I want you to do it right now."

"Now? But how do I know you'll uphold your end of the bargain? How do I know you'll succeed?"

"You don't, but those are my terms." Gray leaned across the table until her face was just inches from Sebastian's, her blue eyes blazing like midnight fire. "Stop interfering in our relationship, demon. We both know you have bigger things to focus on, as do we."

He glared right back at her, but just when I thought he'd explode in another fit, his gaze softened. It was only for a split second, but I saw it—a brief flicker of humanity in his otherwise cunning, cutting eyes.

"You remind me of her," he said to Gray, his voice so soft and tender I actually thought his vessel had been possessed by some other demon.

For her part, Gray looked absolutely stricken. "Trinity? I'm nothing like—"

"No—your grandmother," Sebastian corrected. "Deirdre."

If Gray felt one way or another about the comparison, she didn't show it. "And?"

"*And*," he said, "I haven't yet decided if that's endearing... or a liability."

"Maybe a little of both," she said.

"Maybe." A crooked smile touched the bastard's greasy lips. "Don't disappoint me, Silversbane."

And then he was gone.

TWENTY-FOUR

GRAY

I dropped into a kitchen chair and blew out a breath, the relief instant. Sebastian's presence had sucked up all the air in the room.

"Gray." Ronan knelt before me, his eyes glazed with emotion. "Did he…?"

"I don't know," I whispered. My heart hammered in my chest, my magic tingling inside.

Tentatively, Ronan reached for my face, stopping just short of touching me.

"Well, there's only one way to find out." He sighed, but didn't move any closer. "I don't want it to hurt."

"It's not too bad if it's just a quick burn," I said.

Ronan closed his eyes. "It's not the burn I'm worried about."

He was right. A burn would be nothing compared to the agony we'd feel if Sebastian had walked without granting my request. And so we hesitated, floating together inside this fragile, bubble-thin moment where hope still existed, where there was still a chance.

"You have to touch me," I finally whispered, the words aching in my throat. "We have to know."

Opening his eyes, Ronan sighed again, his warm breath teasing my skin. Slowly, he brought his fingers close to my lips.

"I love you," he whispered. "No matter what."

And then, swallowing hard, he touched me.

Quickly at first, then again, and then once more to be certain. This last touch lingered, and he held his breath as we both waited for the sizzle that never came.

Beneath his fingers, my lips stretched into a grin, tears spilling down my cheeks.

Ronan pulled back and glanced at his fingers, a gasp escaping his throat. He looked back at me for half-a-second, his beautiful leaves-in-autumn eyes the last thing I saw clearly before he crashed against my mouth.

Our kiss was endless, all-consuming, a vortex of relief and laughter and passion and love into which I gladly fell. Ronan could barely breathe, so intent was he on keeping his mouth on me at all times.

"Just so you know," I finally managed, panting between his increasingly demanding kisses, "if you ever... make another deal with him... like that again... I'll..."

"I know."

"We have to find other ways... to protect... each other. Ways that don't involve..."

"I know."

He scooped me into his arms and got to his feet, lifting me with him, still devouring me with kisses.

"And Ronan, you can't—"

"I *know*, Gray. I know." He shut me up for good with a searing kiss that I felt all the way in my toes, igniting a fire inside me that—for the first time in far too long—had nothing to do with hell's curses.

Ignoring the glances of everyone in the common room as Ronan carried me past, we headed upstairs and locked ourselves away in my bedroom, giving ourselves permission to forget the rest of the world for just a little while.

Still kissing, we stripped out of our clothes and tumbled onto the bed, touching each other everywhere at once, skin on skin, lips on lips, our breath mingling as we entwined beneath the sheets.

Ronan pushed the hair from my face and kissed my forehead, my eyelids, my cheeks, the tip of my nose. His eager mouth finally found its way back to mine, and there he lingered, his tongue exploring every soft curve of my mouth as if he were experiencing it all for the first time.

In so many ways, he was.

"I missed the taste of you," he finally breathed.

A tear slid down my cheek, and I pulled back, taking his face between my hands. The touch of his beard tickled my palms, and I closed my eyes and memorized the feeling, the shape, the texture. "I missed the *everything* of you."

"Nothing will ever come between us again," he said. A proclamation. A promise. "I mean it, Desario. The whole fucking world can burn for all I care, as long as you're still with me—you and the guys. That's who matters now. Call me selfish, but there it is."

I wouldn't—*couldn't*—call him selfish, because I felt the exact same way. My rebels and I were soul mates in the truest sense of the word, a single bright soul divided into six beings, always meant to find our way to one another, always meant to be together, in this realm and the next.

With no more promises to be made, I parted my thighs and pulled him on top of me, arching my hips up to meet him as he sank blissfully inside me.

Beneath my touch, the muscles in his shoulders and back rippled, and Ronan shivered, rolling his hips and sliding in deeper, filling me completely.

My body took over, and I matched his stride, eager for more. Harder. Faster.

"No," he said, stilling inside me, rubbing his thumb across my lower lip. "We've got all night, Gray, and I intend to take advantage of every last minute of it."

"But the training, and the others—"

"Can wait." He flashed the crooked grin I'd fallen in love with. "World burning, selfish demon, misses his woman—remember?"

Laughing, I gave in to his demands, relaxing my muscles, both of us easing our way back in.

Ronan kissed my shoulder, my collarbone, slowly making his way to my breasts. Each brush of his lips set my skin ablaze, and though we'd both agreed to take things slow, the physical sensations proved too much, too intense, too perfect.

I felt him trying his best to hold back, to make this reunion last, but it was a losing battle for us both.

"Ronan," I breathed, sliding my hands into his silky hair, "we don't need all night. We've got the rest of eternity now."

He nodded, running his nose down along my neck, tracing a new path with his tongue as his hips rocked forward, his body brushing my clit. He pulled out slowly, then slid back inside, and that was all it took to unravel the very last of my control. I dug my nails into his shoulders and arched my back to meet his final thrust, taking him in fully, sending him over the edge. He came in a white-hot rush as my own orgasm exploded inside me, and I cried out in pleasure, in relief, in bliss.

In that moment, the world very well could have burned, and neither of us would've known about it until we walked outside later and saw the ashes.

Ronan rolled onto his back, pulling me on top of him, my head nestling against his chest. I found the familiar, steady beat of his heart and followed it home, back to where he and I had begun, and a sense of rightness wrapped around us like a warm blanket,

We were meant for this love, this passion, this friendship. We were meant for this moment, and everything that had come before, and everything that would come after.

"Welcome back, Ronan Vacarro," I whispered, and he ran his hand down my bare back and sighed, content and happy.

I wanted nothing more than to spend the rest of the

night in his arms, but the truth was, the world really *was* in danger of burning down, and we really *did* have a responsibility to try to prevent it. So, after another slow, lingering session, we reluctantly showered and headed back downstairs to see what else needed to be done, who else needed help, what other potions could be mixed, which weapons could be sharpened, what intel could be pieced together.

But as we descended the stairs, our fingers interlaced, our smiles still firmly in place, the sight in the common room stopped me dead in my tracks.

"Jael!" I bolted down the remaining stairs and basically launched myself at him, yanking him into an impossibly tight hug. I hadn't seen him since the night I'd been turned, and seeing him here tonight, safe, knowing he'd risked so much to protect my soul... I didn't have the words for the emotion suddenly swirling inside.

"It's so good to see you," I said, pulling back to meet his cat-like yellow eyes.

Jael offered a thin but genuine smile, the skin around his eyes crinkling, those fine lines a bit deeper than I'd remembered. "You as well, Gray." Then, glancing at Ronan, he gave a brief nod. "Both of you."

"Thank you for... With the moonglass," I said, not sure what exactly to say. He'd saved my soul, risking his own life in the process.

"Seeing you healthy and well is all the thanks I need," he said. "Vampire looks good on you."

"Thanks. I'm still getting used to it." I watched him a moment longer before I finally realized Ronan and I had interrupted a meeting already in progress. Verona, McKenna, and several of the other witches had gathered around the couches, with Elena and Emilio standing beside the fire.

No one was smiling.

"What's going on?" I asked. "What did we miss?"

Jael clasped his hands in front of his body, the last vestiges of his smile finally fading. "My sister was able to get a message to me last night," he said. "I'm here with news from home."

"Good news?" I asked, but deep down, I already knew the answer. I could see it in the way the witches sat hunched, knees drawn to chests. I could read it in the bend of Emilio's shoulders, in the heavy sadness on Elena's sigh.

Jael shook his head, looking at me with the pale, haunted eyes of a man who'd seen the future and witnessed the very end of our days. "Blackmoon Bay is burning, Gray."

TWENTY-FIVE

EMILIO

Blackmoon Bay had been many things to me. An escape when I had nowhere else to go. A refuge and a haven. The home I'd made, the community I'd served and protected.

Then, later, it became the place where I'd connected with the guys. Through Ronan, I'd met Asher and Darius, and finally, Gray. Years later, I'd come back into her life there following the murder of her best friend.

Blackmoon Bay was the place where I'd fallen in love. Where I'd begun my family.

And now, our home was nearly in ruins.

Luna's Café. Illuminae. The historic buildings that housed the police precinct and other government offices. The harbor. Johnny's Seaside Pizza. Bloodstone Park. Every neighborhood and every location, every home, every street corner bore the mark of Orendiel's dark army.

According to Kallayna, it wasn't the result of the coordinated, full-scale attack we'd been expecting—the one Gray and her sisters had learned about during their blood spell.

No, this destruction was born of the resistance.

Somehow, the witches remaining in the Bay had hooked up with the few remaining supernaturals who hadn't fallen prey to Darkwinter's mind games, and together they'd executed one hell of a sneak attack, stealthily killing several hunters and a handful of fae knights, saving a few additional witches who'd been captured and imprisoned by Phillip Reese.

But Phillip did not take the attack lightly. He retaliated immediately, sending in his armies, decimating anyone who even *looked* like he or she may be sympathetic to the witches' cause.

Jael told us that the hunters and fae had swept through the city like wildfire, slashing and burning, putting down the resistance with a show of force like nothing we'd seen before. Like nothing we'd predicted.

Jael had no idea how many survivors were left in the city overall, and whose side those survivors might be fighting on now—his sister's message was cut short before any additional details could be shared. At this point, he wasn't even sure Kallayna had survived the night.

But as far as I was concerned, even if there was just one soul, one heartbeat, one being still clinging to life and hope in our city, we would find them. We would protect them. We would help them rebuild.

Gray wouldn't have it any other way. None of us would.

Not long after Jael's visit, I found her on the upper

balcony of the lodge, looking out across the winter-ravaged sea. The twisted fae magic had altered the climate conditions again, and waves of solid ice rose high above the shore, only to shatter and crash back down in a rain of glass.

Again.

Again.

Again.

By sight and by sound, it was as terrifying as it was beautiful.

I approached her slowly, not wanting to disturb her from whatever thoughts had taken up residence in her mind. Her face was turned down, her eyes focused on a Tarot card in her hand. After a beat, I cleared my throat to let her know I was near, but she didn't move at first.

Then, with a deep sigh, she finally tucked the card into her back pocket and turned to me, offering a sad smile.

"Can't sleep?" I asked, then shook my head, realizing my mistake. Gray slept during the daylight hours now, if she slept at all. "Sorry. Still getting used to your new routines."

"Me too." She leaned into my embrace, tilting her face up to meet my eyes. "I still climb into bed at the same time every night, only to remember I'm supposed to sleep during the day now."

"You always were a night owl, though," I said, brushing my lips across her forehead. "So it shouldn't be too much of a hardship."

She smiled again, but it didn't quite reach her eyes. "No brownies tonight, huh?"

I raised my hands in surrender. "It's not my fault—I swear. We're out of chocolate, if you can believe that."

"House full of witches? Yeah, I believe it."

"I brought you something else, though."

A gust of icy wind lashed us both, blowing her hair into her face. She swept her loose curls back, gathering them together at the base of her neck.

Steadying myself for any number of possible reactions, I retrieved the envelope from my shirt pocket, opening it up and tipping the contents into my hand. "This belongs to you, *mi querida*."

Gray gasped at the sight of it, her eyes glistening with tears.

"Elena was able to retrieve it from the station," I explained. "They've closed the case on the Landes murder, naming Jonathan as the primary suspect, officially believed deceased."

She reached for my hand, slowly closing her fingers around the crescent-moon amulet.

"Thank you," she whispered, pressing her hand to her chest.

"Would you like me to put it on you?"

She nodded, handing it back so I could fasten the delicate chain around her neck. The crescent moon came to rest just beneath her collarbone, glowing faintly against her skin.

I smiled. "It seems Calla is still with you."

"Always," she whispered, fishing the Tarot card from her back pocket. "I asked for a message just before I came out here. Some sign that we'd be okay, that we were on the right path."

She turned the card so I could see it. It was the High Priestess, a woman dressed in blue robes, surrounded by tiny butterflies.

"This card always shows up when I'm thinking of my mother. My *real* mother," she amended. "Calla."

"I remember it from the night we dug up your book of shadows," I said. "It slipped out when you opened it for the first time."

Gray nodded, her smile softening. "I don't see or hear her like I do with Sophie sometimes, but I sense her in other ways. Namely through the card. Sometimes I'll dream of her, though, and then I wake up and smell her perfume."

"I sense my parents, too. More lately, since Elena and I have started to reconnect." I tucked her hair behind her ear, my hand lingering on her cheek. I had Gray to thank for bringing my sister back into my life. It was just one more thing I loved about her, one more thing that made my heart feel full every time I looked into her eyes.

"I love your sister," she said. "She doesn't take any shit from you."

"She loves you, too." I pulled her close again, inhaling her scent, her familiar sweetness mixed with the salty tang of the crisp ocean air. In my mind, an image danced through unbidden—my sister, crying tears of joy, helping Gray make adjustments to her wedding dress.

The image was so startling I nearly gasped, but it felt comfortable, too. Inevitable. The thought warmed me.

"Do you think they're really with us?" she asked. "Watching over us or something like that? Or is it just wishful thinking?"

"I don't know, Gray." I sighed, pressing my lips to the top of her head. "That sounds like a question for Spooky."

Gray laughed, but it trailed off quickly, and she pulled out of my embrace to look into my eyes once more. The amulet around her neck still gave off a subtle white light.

"We have to send Reva in tomorrow night to see if there are survivors," she said. "For all we know, Trinity is still planning the full-on attack. I don't want to wait another day."

I nodded, totally in agreement. "She's ready for it, Gray. Liam's been working hard with her."

"Oh, she's totally ready. I just..." She sighed, looking out again over the white sea. "I guess I just wanted her to have a shot at normal. The shot the rest of us never got."

"She will, Gray. You've given her that."

"Letting her be our eyes and ears on this... We have no idea what she'll see once she gets in. But I do know that whatever it is, Emilio, she'll never be able to un-see."

Gray was right, and there was nothing I could say to ease her mind.

"When this is over," she continued, "I was hoping she might want to live with us. I mean, if you're all cool with that. I just thought..." She trailed off, finally turning to meet my gaze again. Her eyes were full of love. Hope, however fragile in this moment, the relative calm before the storm.

"Gray, there's no question, *querida*. Reva is family. *Everyone* here is family, and we take care of each other."

This got a smile—a real one—and she drew me close again. "Yeah, but just so we're clear? *Not* everyone here gets an open invitation to our house."

"Our house," I echoed. "I like the sound of that."

"Do you think it will happen?"

The wind kicked up again, bringing with it a wet, icy blast of slush, coating us both. But neither of us flinched, and I held her gaze, my heart pounding fiercely, the words fighting their way out against the onslaught of weather.

"I love you so much it scares me," I said.

"I'd tell you not to be afraid, but I feel the same way." She shivered in my arms, then laughed. "In a good way."

"In the *best* way." I dipped my head to kiss her, sighing against her lips. "I know you usually sleep during the daylight hours, but I was wondering if you might do your favorite wolf shifter a favor tonight?"

"What are you asking me, wolf?"

"Come to bed with me. Just the two of us tonight."

Wearing matching conspiratorial smiles, we snuck back into the lodge and found a small, windowless bedroom currently being used to store dried herbs and a few other bulk supplies. It wasn't pretty, but it was warm and quiet, tucked away from the main bedrooms, unlikely to be disturbed or even noticed.

As surreptitiously as I could, I retrieved a couple of

extra blankets from the other bedroom closets, then returned to roll out a makeshift mattress for us.

We stripped out of our wet clothes, and there in the quiet darkness of our secret room, I made love to her, soft and slow, savoring each tender touch and kiss, each smile and sigh.

We spent the next few hours talking about our dreams, about the future, about what our someday house would look like. She told me about the herb garden she wanted to plant, and I told her about all the different recipes I wanted to try, and on and on we chatted, until one by one, the others found their way into our little hovel.

Asher first, who could always sense whenever someone in the vicinity was getting intimate. He curled up on the other side of Gray, nuzzling the back of her neck.

The three of us had just gotten comfortable when Darius appeared, staking out a patch of blanket behind me.

Liam and Ronan came in last, neither saying a word. Like the others, they simply found their place among us. Their place in our family.

There, in that tiny windowless room on our last night before our military operation began in earnest.

It felt right. It felt familiar. It felt real. And I allowed myself to hope, for the briefest moment, that it would be. That when all of this was done, we'd find that house Gray and I had painted in our minds, and the six of us—seven, if Reva accepted Gray's invitation—would make it our own.

As the others slowly dropped off to sleep, I forced

myself to stay awake, wanting to watch over them, especially Gray.

She may have been a powerful vampire, a prophesied witch, heir to an ancient fae legacy that she and her sisters were still struggling to accept. But there in my arms, her eyes closed, her lips red and puffy from my kisses, she was just a woman. The woman I'd fallen madly in love with. The one who'd made me believe—no, who'd made me *know*—that as long as we all held on to one another, as long as our family stuck together, we'd find a way through this darkness.

"We will survive this," I whispered into her hair, a promise for us all as I finally drifted off to sleep.

TWENTY-SIX

LIAM

More than anything, I wished I could take Reva's place. Or Gray's, or Haley's, or any one of the witches gearing up to invade Blackmoon Bay in the coming hours.

But I was human now. My strengths, my magics came in other forms. An encouraging smile, a hug, a touch. Information passed on from one generation to the next. A whispered promise against the bare flesh of the woman who'd made me remember what it meant to be human. To love, completely and with abandon.

To believe in something greater than one's own ends.

"I'm worried about her," Gray said now, doing a final check of the potions Verona had issued her. It was the night after the six of us had fallen asleep together, and now she and I were alone in the kitchen, the others doing final weapons checks and strategic planning and many other things that had to be fast-tracked as a result of the riots in the Bay and our now-shortened attack timeline.

Though none of us had dared to move from the peaceful serenity of that room until well after sunset this evening, we all knew ours had been a momentary peace. A bubble made of moonglass, destined to shatter at the first onset of our reality.

That reality was now upon us. In thirty minutes, Reva would be traveling amongst the shadows of Blackmoon Bay, searching for survivors. Searching for a way in. After that, the rest of us would make our move together, hoping that by sheer number and combined magics, we might overpower their fae cloaking spells—as well as the armies themselves.

Many of us would not survive to see the sunrise of another day.

"I know she's powerful," Gray continued, "and determined, and probably braver than any of us." Her smile softened. "But she's still just a kid. A witch who would do anything to protect us, not even realizing she was putting her own life at risk."

I couldn't help but laugh at that. "I think it's fair to say we've all done just that, and we'll all *continue* to do just that, as often and for as long as any of our loved ones are in danger. To expect anything less from Reva is frankly a bit naive."

Gray smiled softly. "Touché, Liam."

"And there's something else you need to know about Reva," I said. For the past few days, I'd grappled with the best way to reveal this information, but now seemed as good a time as any other. "Reva is not just a kid, as you say. She is a Shadowborn, Gray. Like you."

I watched her eyes, certain that through them I could read the thoughts dancing in her mind, all the little moments replaying, all the puzzle pieces about Reva that were now adding up to the complete whole.

"She will likely come into her full powers in the next year or so," I explained, "simply because she's been nurturing her connection with magic for years."

"Reva," she whispered, then nodded, the final pieces clicking into place. Her eyes twinkled with something that looked an awful lot like pride.

"So what does this mean for her?" she asked. "Who will train her now that you're no longer Death?"

"I must train her still," I said. "To the extent that my human limitations allow, anyway. I may not be able to travel with her to the Shadowrealm or interact with the remaining soul ferriers, but there is a great deal of knowledge I shall endeavor to impart upon her. And none of us truly knows what her unique powers will be, nor what her role will be in the absence of Death, where souls cannot readily pass on through the realm as they once might have."

"Does she know?" Gray asked.

"I haven't discussed it with her yet, no. I've yet to find an appropriate time, and I don't want her to be overly concerned about her future, particularly now, when she needs to focus on getting into and out of Blackmoon Bay undetected. As you might recall, learning that you have the power to influence death and manipulate soul energy is not always an easy thing to process and accept."

A smile curved her lips. "You mean, I wasn't all in with your whacky theories from the start?"

"If by 'all in' you mean refusing my many invitations at every turn, causing trouble wherever you went, and generally upheaving the universal order, then yes. Of course you were all in, Gray."

Gray laughed in earnest, but before she could ask any more questions, Reva entered the kitchen, her mouth set in a grim line, her shoulders squared.

"When am I going in?" she asked.

Gray closed her eyes, cursing under her breath. But then she, too, squared her shoulders, and by the time she turned to face Reva, her eyes were once again shining with pride.

"You ready?" she asked.

Reva gave her a thumbs-up.

"Come here," Gray said. "There's something I need to give you first."

Reva did as she asked, and Gray unclasped the amulet from around her neck, fastening it around Reva's instead. She pressed her fingers against the crescent moon and whispered a protective spell that made the charm glow brightly.

"Reva, I know you can do this," Gray said, once the amulet had dimmed again. "I wouldn't send you in there otherwise. But there's no shame in retreating. The goal of connecting with any remaining Bay witches and sussing out the situation? That's our second priority tonight. *You* are our first. The minute you feel scared or uncomfortable, the minute you get even the *slightest* vibe that something isn't right, you pull back. Got it?"

"I will. I promise."

Reva turned her bright eyes my way, and I put my hands on her shoulders, kneeling down before her, again wishing I could protect her with magic or sheer force of will.

But all I had now were words, and I offered them freely.

"Remember everything we talked about," I told her. "The shadows are your domain. You are not bound by physical constraints, by the natural laws of the universe. But while your astral body cannot be harmed in the way that your physical body can, fae magic is treacherous, and could very easily sever the cord that connects the two. You must avoid Darkwinter at all costs—their traps, their servants, their spies. You must keep to the shadows and avoid being seen by anyone but the witches and known allies."

"I remember," she said. "I won't let you down. Either of you."

At this, Gray pulled the girl to her chest, capturing her in a fierce hug. "You could never let us down, Reva. No matter what. Just come back to us."

We brought Reva into the common room, where Verona had blessed the space and set up protective charms and crystals throughout the room. Reva took a position before the fireplace, and all around her, the witches formed a half-circle, joining hands, whispering more protective chants and Reva stared into the fire.

All of us watched as she slipped into a trance-like state, her eyelids fluttering closed, her shoulders drooping as her consciousness departed her physical body.

As the witches continued their protective whispering, I stood to the side with Asher, Darius, Emilio, Ronan, Jael, Emilio, and Elena, all of us exchanging glances, no one daring to speak.

Other than the witches, none of us made a sound, though I was certain the vampires in the room could hear the frantic thumping of my heart, the fraying of my nerves. I felt as if I'd stopped breathing, and wouldn't dare to start again until Reva was wholly returned, her astral and physical selves united and safe.

An hour passed. Two. And then, just before the passing of the third, when I was certain one more minute would have us all charging blindly into the Bay to right whatever wrongs had most certainly been committed against her, Reva emerged.

Her face was as blue-white as the full moon shining on the snow.

"Reva," Gray said gently, kneeling beside her in front of the flames. "Are you okay?"

Reva blinked rapidly, then turned to look at Gray, her eyes going wide with shock. "I... I couldn't stay," she said. "Not more than a day."

Gray nodded, deciding not to tell the child that she hadn't even been gone three hours by our reckoning. Another trick of the fae magic.

"Why couldn't you stay?" Gray asked.

"There weren't enough shadows."

"What do you mean?"

At this, Reva looked up and met my eyes, her own clearing a bit as the shock receded. "It's morning there. All the time now. There's no snow, no fires, no armies, no darkness. There are flowers blooming on every street, and birds singing, and warm breezes coming in off the Bay… It's like… It's like this weird, twisted paradise."

"What of the people?" I asked. "Did you see anyone?"

"I saw everyone," she whispered. "Witches, vampires, humans. Everyone was smiling. Happy. Chatting with their neighbors, riding bikes through the park. But the thing is, something felt off about their smiles. They seem kind of like zombies. Well, not the kind that eat people. Just the spaced-out kind. I tried to talk to one of the witches and tell her we were coming, but the woman just kept asking me if I was lost, over and over again, even when I told her I lived in the neighborhood."

"Are you sure you traveled to Blackmoon Bay and not to another location by mistake?" I asked her.

"Yes. I saw Norah's old house, and the café where she used to take me for peppermint mochas sometimes. Not Luna's—the other place."

"Covington's Cup," Haley said. "It's around the corner from Norah's."

Reva nodded. "It was definitely home. Just… super messed up. And not in the way Jael said. I swear, you'd take one look at it and think that nothing bad had *ever* happened there."

"It must be glamoured," Jael said, "and heavily at that. Kallayna didn't mention it during our last conversation, so I presume it's a relatively new situation—one that makes our endeavors that much more challenging."

"Can you undo it?" Gray asked. "We really need an accurate picture if we've got any hope at sorting out friend from foe."

"I won't know until we're in there and I get a sense for the complexity of the spell weave," he said.

Gray got to her feet, turning to face the crowd. The collective energy in the room rose considerably, the air suddenly electrified.

We all knew what was coming next.

"Alright, guys," she said, meeting each of our gazes in turn. Then, with a resolute nod of her head, "Let's move out."

TWENTY-SEVEN

ASHER

Gray wasn't out for power. Hell, she'd had a hard time accepting her own magic, let alone trying to control anyone else's. World domination? It just wasn't her style.

But seeing her take charge of the troops, unflinchingly directing us into the Bay where we'd face our ultimate enemies... She had truly come into her own. She was, as Ronan had always believed, born for this.

Our girl was a total badass, and truth be told, I was kind of fucking turned on.

Unfortunately, I'd have to stash that thought for later.

On this night, there would be no sneak attack. No standing around in the snow with our thumbs up our asses, waiting for the signal. No more planning, no more plotting, and no more talking.

There would only be doing.

All of us were out for blood.

From the moment Gray ordered us to move out, we

were in motion, loading into the emergency vehicles Elena had commandeered from the RCPD, caravanning east to Blackmoon Bay.

Gray had been confident that with so many witches concentrating their power and intention to a single outcome, we'd be able to override the fae cloaking spells that would otherwise send us in circles.

Her theory proved correct. After a tense drive, we found ourselves driving across a bridge that led straight into the center of the warehouse district.

Ground zero.

We met no resistance. Not on the drive over, and not as we pulled in behind an abandoned warehouse, stashing the vans down a narrow alleyway.

The vampires had ridden in a van with tinted windows, uncertain as to how the Bay's perpetual sunlight would affect them. Now, I watched as Gray and Darius stepped out first, gingerly stretching their hands into a patch of sunlight.

Nothing happened.

"Remember, it's glamoured," Jael said. "None of this is real. Not even the sun. But that also means that when the real sun rises, we won't necessarily know it until it's too late. You all need to keep a very close eye on the time."

Gray glanced at her phone. "It's nine p.m. now. That means we've got a good ten hours until sunrise, but I don't want to take any chances. Vampires, we all need to be back here or seek other appropriate shelter by six a.m."

"Clear," Darius said, and Fiona nodded.

Gray and I checked all the vans, making sure everyone had their weapons and whatever magical items the witches needed. We made a formidable force—witches, vampires, shifters, demons, and our resident human, Spooky. Even Reva was in line, carrying a short blade, her blue eyes wild.

No one had stayed behind, and no one was unprepared.

"That's everyone," I said, giving Reva a fist-bump.

We moved quickly after that, the whole crew slipping inside the warehouse for cover. This part of the district had always been a ghost town, and so far, we hadn't spotted any people—human or super—but we weren't taking any chances.

Certain we were all secure inside, Gray turned back to Jael. "So, can you undo the glamour?"

"I need an hour, but yes, I can do it. Just remember, Gray —the moment I break the spell weave, they'll know we're here. Not necessarily where we are, but they will eventually find us."

"Or," she said, flashing a sly, ready-for-anything grin, "we'll make it easy on them."

"How do you mean?" he asked.

There was a fae sword strapped to her back, but in her hand, she gripped the staff she'd been favoring during the training. Raising it before us, she looked us over, taking our measure—her dark rebels, her fighters, her friends, her lovers, her hellhounds—and her magic crackled to life, arcing along the wood.

"Let's show these motherfuckers who's coming home tonight."

TWENTY-EIGHT

GRAY

Blackmoon Bay is burning…

Jael's earlier warnings echoed, but they had not done the situation justice.

As the fae glamour fell away, taking with it the sunshine and the birds and the bright, cloudless sky, my whole body froze in sheer horror as I took in the scene.

The *real* scene.

Our home, as we'd known it, was well and truly gone.

Luna's café had been leveled, leaving no more than a smoking husk in its place. The magical boundary that had protected it had clearly evaporated. I thought of Ella, the cute fox shifter I'd last seen behind the counter, how she'd always saved the last chocolate macadamia cookies for me. I hoped she'd gotten out alive.

The boats that hadn't been blasted ashore were frozen in the icy bay, smashed and sticking up at odd angles, unmoving. They were so still, it looked like a photograph.

The warehouse around the corner that had served as the base of operations for Waldrich's Imports, the black-market employer Ronan and I had shared, was little more than a steel frame now. The Waldrich's van I used to drive—the same one the guys and I had driven to Norah's house to rescue Asher—was tipped on its side in the middle of the street, all of the windows smashed.

Everywhere we turned, destruction and chaos reigned supreme. Fires were still smoldering. Buildings we'd visited and passed by thousands of times had been reduced to rubble and ash. Stores and homes and restaurants, parks and plazas, trees, all of the places that had made Blackmoon Bay something more than a name on a map...

I swallowed the tightness in my throat. Those places no longer existed.

But the most frightening sight of all wasn't the burned-out husks of buildings or the rows of decimated houses.

It was the people.

Human and supernatural alike, they walked the streets in the same glassy-eyed daze as Reva had described. The same as when everything had still looked shiny and new, as though the glamour had so thoroughly transfixed them, they'd never again be able to see things as they truly were.

One of them passed by me now, brushing against my arm as if she hadn't even noticed me—a woman in a bright green sundress, her arms loaded up with flyers, the bare skin of her legs black with frostbite she didn't seem to feel. I reached out and took her hand, stopping her forward momentum.

At this, she finally turned around, her glassy eyes fixating on me as if she were waiting for me to cue up her lines.

"Are you okay?" I asked. Stupid question with an obvious answer, but in that moment, I couldn't form a logical thought.

She cocked her head, her smile unbroken. "Would you like to come to our meeting? Please bring a dish to pass." She handed me a flyer from the stack in her arms, then moseyed along, disappearing around the corner.

I glanced down at the paper, my heart twisting.

> Unhappy with your lot in life?
> Wishing things could be better?
> WITCHES ARE THE PROBLEM.
> The good news? Problems can be solved.
> But only by taking ACTION.
> A better, happier, richer life can be yours.
> Find out how!

There was an address and phone number, followed by a lengthy, small-print essay delineating all of the awful, terrible, very bad things witches had allegedly caused—everything from unemployment and economic crashes to STDs and the brainwashing of our nation's youth.

I didn't have the heart to tell the woman she, too, was a witch, just like me.

She, too, was part of the alleged "problem."

I crumpled the paper and tossed it onto a burning pile of trash, resolute.

No, this crazy disaster area wasn't the Blackmoon Bay of memory. But it was still home. *Our* home. These aimlessly wandering people, however bespelled in the moment, were our neighbors.

And when I turned and looked back at the guys, at the witches, at all the living, breathing, passionate, loving souls who'd followed me into this hell, I knew we were all thinking the exact same thing.

We're not giving up on our home.

I met Darius's eyes, and he nodded once. It was time.

I brought my hands up and closed my eyes, calling up the magic of home, the magic of my birthplace, the magic of the city we loved. It was still there, pulsing beneath the burning streets with a fire all its own, ready to be channeled, ready to consume anything in its path.

I drew it up into myself, then pushed it out into my staff, where it connected instantly with the weapon's fae magic, twining into a bright blue arc twice as powerful as anything I'd ever called upon, anything I'd ever wielded.

I pointed it at the warehouse on the corner across from us, a storage facility owned by the marina operators that was typically stocked with marine fuel and all kinds of other flammable shit.

And then I let loose my magic.

The warehouse exploded on contact, lighting up the docks and sending out a beacon bright enough to be seen from space.

The message was clear.

The Silversbane witch was here—right fucking *here*—and she'd brought an army of witches and rebels who weren't going down without a fight.

Scratch that. We weren't going down at all.

I tightened my grip on the staff and looked back at my guys one more time, my lips stretching into a grin as I felt the drumbeat of a hundred enemy boots hitting the docks, finally barreling toward us.

It was time to take out the trash.

TWENTY-NINE

GRAY

Hunters and dark fae, hybrid shifters, rogue vampires… Every foul beast we'd ever faced now converged before us, their teeth sharp, eyes bright with menace.

Together with my rebels, my sisters, my hounds, and all the witches and supernaturals who'd come to fight at our side, we broke upon their army like a wave crashing against the shore.

All around me, the colorful explosions of different magics lit up the snowy night, including the familiar yellow-orange signature I knew belonged to Deirdre. She hadn't traveled here with us—I hadn't even spoken with her since I'd sent her away. But she'd shown up when it counted, and for that, I was grateful.

The fae forced the hunters to lead the charge against us. Eager for the kill, Sparkle and Sunshine cleared a path right through them, mauling their prey without a second thought. Blood ran red in the gutters as I blurred into action behind them, slicing through my enemies as though my staff were a hot blade and their bodies no more substantial than butter.

Against the deadly combination of my vampire speed and the magic, the hunters and even the hybrids were no match for me.

The fae, on the other hand, posed more of a threat, as did the vampires, and after I'd taken out almost as many hunters as my hounds had, I found myself surrounded by much more formidable opponents. All around me, I saw my rebels facing their own battles, the demons teaming up on other fae, Darius leading the RCPD shifters against the hybrids, the witches grappling with the remaining hunters.

I was on my own, but I wasn't alone. I took strength from them, just as they took it from me.

Steeling myself as the enemy closed ranks around me, I raised my staff, infusing it with the magic that hummed inside me.

"You're gonna die slow," one of the vamps said, but before he could pop off another useless threat, I swung hard, sending a burst of magic into the staff just as it connected with his head.

Blue flames ignited, quickly engulfing him. It'd happened so fast he hadn't even had time to scream.

The others lunged for me all at once, but I was faster than them, faster than Darius, faster than any vamp we'd ever come upon. They were no more than smudges in my peripheral vision as I darted and danced, keeping them at bay with the threat of blue fire.

One of the fae soldiers lunged for me with his blade, but I dodged easily. As his momentum carried him past me, I spun around fast and swung for his head, connecting hard. The force of the blow reverberated into my hands, jarring me for a brief moment before he dropped to the ground, dead weight.

The other fae watched me in shock.

Fae weapons were powerful in their creators' hands, but I had fae blood running through my veins, too.

"Take her down!" one of the soldiers ordered an unseen assailant behind me, and instinctively I dropped to the ground. A sharp pain bit into the top of my shoulder, but I'd dodged a deadlier thrust, and now I used my position to my advantage, grabbing the soldier by the knees and knocking his feet out from under him.

He hit the ground with a thud, and I leaped to my feet and bashed his skull in with the tip of my staff.

The two Darkwinter Knights remaining quickly turned tail, charging into another skirmish that had broken out behind us, hoping for an easier target with the witches.

Obviously, they'd never seen witches fight.

I scanned the crowd for my sisters, catching sight of Haley just as she sliced open her hand. She was on her knees, and now she pressed her bleeding palm to the concrete, calling forth a line of yellow fire that separated the witches from the hunters and fae who'd been attacking. The enemy leaped backward to avoid the path of that blood magic, but it had distracted them just enough to give the witches another advantage. Channeling their active powers, the group fighting with Haley pummeled the soldiers with a coordinated magical attack, lighting up the darkness.

"Gray! You good?" Ronan appeared at my side, his eyes black, a gash across his forehead, but otherwise unharmed. He eyed my blood-soaked shirt, but the wound at my shoulder had already knitted back together.

"Vampire healing for the motherfucking win," I said, and he nodded once, then charged back into the fray. I was close on his heels, taking out two hybrid panthers who'd tried to double up on him from behind.

Together, Ronan and I fought our way through a tangle of hunters, easily dodging their comparatively weak human attacks. I'd just turned around to get a read on the rest of the group when I saw six vamps circling a couple of witches, herding them down an alley away from the rest of the fighting.

Away from anyone who might protect them.

"Ronan!" I shouted, but I didn't wait to see if he'd heard me. I was already racing toward the vampires, unwilling to consider any outcome but their immediate destruction.

They had Verona and my sister, Addie. There was no way they were going to survive this.

Charging in at vampire speed, I slammed into the first one from behind, bashing the front of his skull against the brick exterior. He spun around, grappling for me even as blood streamed into his eyes, but I was faster, my staff already igniting.

Without a word, I touched it to his chest, lighting him up.

Movement just behind me, and I slid the staff backward, catching another vamp hard in the groin. He dropped to his knees, and I spun around, swinging. The staff cut through his neck, melting away muscle and bone, thoroughly decapitating him.

Four left, and two of them were taunting Verona and Addie, but the witches were holding their own, defending themselves with a combination of Verona's potions and the hawthorn stakes Addie had brought. I saw her slam one into an attacker's chest just as the other two grabbed me.

My staff clattered to the ground.

I twisted out of their grasp, but these two were relentless, coming at me again and again, both of them stronger than me, nearly matched on speed. One of them finally got his hands around my upper arms, and then the other grabbed a fistful of my hair, wrenching my head backward.

Behind them, I caught a glimpse of Ronan charging down the alley, fire in his eyes, fire in his steps. But just before he reached me, he stopped and smiled, and a Darkwinter Knight stepped out of the shadows, shoving his blade right through Ronan's heart.

It was Emilio's death at the warehouse all over again, and I screamed in horror as Ronan went down. He dropped to his knees, his blood spilling on the street before him, his eyes going vacant.

He caught my gaze for the briefest moment, then fell forward.

Dead.

It had happened in an instant.

Fear and grief overwhelmed me, twin serpents that slithered around my chest and threatened to choke the life out of me.

But... *no*. It wasn't real. It *couldn't* be real. I blinked rapidly, feeling the logical part of my mind trying to claw its way through a sticky haze. Ronan wouldn't have been caught unaware like that, wouldn't have stopped to smile, leaving himself exposed. He'd fought too many battles, lived too many lifetimes to make such a rookie mistake, especially after he'd seen Orendiel take out Emilio with the same dirty trick.

My instincts kicked in fully, and every last one of Darius's lessons on shielding came flooding back.

These bloodsuckers are fucking influencing me.

I blinked away the image of Ronan lying face down in a pool of his own blood, and I ground out a string of curses, forcing the rogue vamp out of my head. I shook with the effort—he'd already embedded his poison quite deeply by the time I'd realized what was happening—but eventually, my thoughts became my own once again.

Ronan's lifeless body, no more than a figment of my vamp-infiltrated imagination, vanished.

Rage-induced magic surged into my limbs, and I wrenched myself from their vicious grip, slipping out from between them. I had just enough time to grab the fae sword I'd strapped to my back before they were coming at me again, but this time, neither would lay a hand on me.

I blurred out of their reach, then doubled back, swinging at the first one with all I had.

His head dropped to the ground with a wet thud.

I felt the invasive touch of the other vamp's influence again, and I forced my eyes to go glassy, a fake whimper escaping my lips. Standing perfectly still, I let him approach. Let him get cocky. Let him scent my fear.

And then I smiled, shoving my sword through his throat.

He choked and gasped, dropping to his knees. I yanked the sword back out and swung again, serving him the same fate as his buddy.

The other two vamps were still engaged with Verona and Addie, and now I crept behind them, taking down one in the same grizzly manner while Addie and Verona staked the other once again, then lit his bloodsucking ass on fire.

"Everyone okay?" I asked.

Verona and Addie were panting from the effort, blood and sweat and grime coating their faces, but they smiled now, nodding briefly and squeezing my hands before they took off in the direction of the main fight still unfolding in the streets.

I had just finished re-securing my blade on my back and grabbing my staff when new movement at the end of the alley caught my eye. Now, Ronan did appear there, he and Asher fighting off a pair of Darkwinter Knights. Sparkle was in the mix, too, her muzzle dripping with blood as she tore chunks of flesh from one of the fae's leg.

I tightened my grip on the staff and darted toward them, eager to help dispatch the two fae. But there was another figure behind them now, emerging from the swirling snow.

The sight of his white beard stopped me cold.

Even at a distance, I could see the eager glint in his eye. Casually, he raised his arm and took aim, and the moment played out before me like a slow-motion horror movie I was powerless to stop.

Phillip pulled the trigger.

This time, when I saw Ronan go down, I knew it *was* real.

Just as I knew Phillip's gun wasn't just a regular gun with regular bullets.

"No!" I screamed, but it was too late. Ronan was on his knees, leaving Asher to grapple with the Darkwinter Knights.

Phillip had already vanished.

I charged toward Asher, my staff raised and hungry for death. I cracked one of the soldier's skulls wide open just as Ash had gotten a hold of the other guy's head, giving it a sharp twist.

Both soldiers dropped.

Asher and I exchanged a quick horrified glance, then got to our knees, both of us reaching for Ronan.

"Devil's trap nano," he managed. "In the bullets... Smart."

The poison was already working its way through his bloodstream, sapping his strength, wringing the life from him before our eyes.

"Fucking hell!" Asher shouted.

"Listen to me," I said to Ash, shoving my fear into a tiny little box and burying it deep inside. Ronan didn't have much time; there was no room for anything but action. "Your blood... It's in your blood. You can fix this. You're immune to the devil's traps."

Asher immediately got my meaning, and without wasting another heartbeat, he scooped Ronan into his arms and got to his feet.

"Get him somewhere safe and find one of the witches with healing magic," I said. "They'll figure out a way to make an infusion from your blood."

Asher nodded, and I took Ronan's face between my hands, staring deep into his eyes. They were shifting back and forth from hazel to black, his body convulsing.

"I love you," I said. "And if you don't come back to me, I swear to Sebastian himself I'm going straight back to Hell to hunt your ass down. So don't you pull any shit, Vacarro."

Asher lowered his head, capturing my attention. I saw the promise in the depths of his ocean-blue eyes even before he said the words. "I got this, Gray. Go find that filthy hunter and fucking butcher him."

I pressed my mouth to his and stole a kiss. "You can count on it."

THIRTY

EMILIO

The dark fae were absolutely everywhere, skittering across the streets like cockroaches, clashing with our witches and shifters as we all fought to reclaim the city.

Some of Elena's men and the witches had already been injured, but Liam had set up triage in an abandoned restaurant, and he and the witches with healing magic were doing their best to keep our people safe.

Twenty minutes in, and everyone was already bloody and exhausted, but I knew no one would give up. This was too important, too real. I was certain Gray's earlier words weighed heavy on all of our hearts.

Blackmoon Bay is ground zero for their entire operation, and it's no longer simply the home we're trying to take back. It's the spark that will eventually set the whole world on fire...

This is not just about our own lives, but the lives of everyone we've ever loved. If we fail, we will all die. Witches, shifters, vampires, demons, fae, and humankind...

And so we fought, holding true to the bond that had brought us all together, fighting for our lives and the lives of anyone and anything that ever mattered. Witches lit up the streets, vampires blurring in and out of sight, shifters and hounds tearing flesh and breaking bone.

And still, more came. More fae. More hybrids. More rogues.

But then, a light in the brutal darkness, more witches arrived.

Three dozen at least, charging up the street in formation, their steps quick and determined, their magic at the ready.

They needed no introduction. These were the witches of Blackmoon Bay, and they were ready to take back their freedom.

Side-by-side, they fought with our witches, all of them united in this purpose, in this singular mission. With their help, our side quickly regained our advantage, and slowly but surely, the enemy's numbers began to thin.

In the midst of the battle, my sister and I were a team in the truest sense of the word, never leaving each other's sides as we fought our way through hunters and hybrids alike, dodging the fae and their deadly silver weapons at every turn.

But there was one Darkwinter Knight we couldn't— *wouldn't*—avoid.

Elena and I had a score to settle, and the moment we caught sight of him, we were on the move.

"There!" she said now, nodding her head toward an

alley at the end of the street. "He's down there. Three other fae are with him."

"You sure?" I asked.

Elena nodded. "I'll never forget Orendiel's face."

Checking to make sure the others were holding their own, we broke away from the main battle and headed in the direction she'd last seen the general, keeping our eyes peeled for any would-be ambushes.

By the time we reached the entrance to the alley, the sounds of clashing blades and the cries of the fallen had softened to a din behind us, and we leaned our backs against the exterior bricks, taking a quick moment to regroup. I knew this section of town; this was the First American Bank, and the alley cut through to Hodge Street on the other side.

The fae could be anywhere. Still, we had to try.

My sister had gone quiet, slipping into the darkness of her own mind. I didn't like that one bit.

"Talk to me, Lainey," I whispered, nudging her elbow. "What's on your mind?"

"Just that I'm… I'm glad it's you," she said. "If I have to die tonight, I want it to be fighting side-by-side with my brother."

"You always were a drama queen." I grinned at her and rolled my eyes, needing the levity as much as I knew she did. "*No* Alvarezes are dying tonight. Not on my watch."

"From your lips to all the saints in the sky."

"You ready?"

Elena blew out a breath, then nodded, and together we stepped into the alley, ready to end it, one way or another.

The strip was empty, but a commotion at the other end of Hodge caught our attention. More fighting, fae blades clashing, magic lighting up the wintry mist.

"It's Jael!" I said, quickening my pace. He was fighting alongside two women—one I recognized as his sister, Kallayna. The other looked just like them, but slightly older. Not so much by physical age, the way a human might, but by stature. By wisdom.

She was, I realized in an instant, their mother. Queen Sheyah.

Whether they'd asked for her help or she'd simply arrived, I didn't care. What mattered now was that she knew how to swing a sword, and she and her children made a formidable force against the tangle of fae enemies gathered before them.

Not waiting for an invite, Elena and I shifted into wolf form, leaping into the battle, taking down two Darkwinter Knights before anyone had even realized what'd happened.

The Queen swung a blade like a seasoned warrior, icing two soldiers in one shot, then pivoting to catch another in the chest. Her blade melted through their armor, eating down to the bone like acid.

I'd never seen anyone fight so ferociously. So calmly. I wondered how many battles she'd fought.

Together with the fae on our side, Elena and I continued to tear through the enemy, dodging their weapons, spilling their blood.

And then, backing away from the melee, a defector. A traitor to his own blood. A fucking coward wearing the uniform of a general, turning tail and trying to make his escape.

"Go," Sheyah ordered, taking down another soldier, and Elena and I were off at a good clip.

I reached him first, launching myself onto his back and slamming him to the concrete. He struggled to reach his weapon, and just as his fist tightened around the pommel, I sank my wolf fangs into his forearm, his scream of agony washing over me like a symphony.

Elena bit his shoulder, but despite his cowardice, Orendiel was not easy prey. He fought hard and scrappy, beating us back with his boot, with a rock he'd picked up, with anything he could.

He managed to get to his feet, once again reaching for the deadly blade at his side.

But Elena was having none of it. She shifted back into her human form, the sudden appearance of her nude, powerful body distracting Orendiel just long enough for us to get the upper hand.

Elena grinned at him. As if I could read my sister's mind, I locked my jaws around his ankle, biting until I heard the bone snap. Just before he dropped in agony, she swiped his sword.

Orendiel hit the ground, blood pouring from his wounds.

I pinned his legs with my massive form, and without hesitation, Elena shoved the fae blade into his throat.

"That's for my brother, asshole."

Certain he was no longer a threat, I shifted back into my human form, and together my sister and I loomed over the body as his skin melted away, the magic of the sword eating straight through. He writhed in agony, and I watched him burn, knowing full well the pain of that particular wound.

I couldn't say I was sorry.

After several long moments, Orendiel finally stilled, his eyes dimming, the white mist of his breath disappearing into the night.

I felt nothing but relief.

We made our way back toward Queen Sheyah, Jael, and Kallayna, who were fending off the last of the soldiers. Several lay dead at our feet, and Elena and I—still nude from the shift—stripped off some of their clothing, quickly covering ourselves.

We rejoined the fight just in time to watch Kallayna behead the last fae standing.

In the momentary calm that followed, the five of us stood silent, almost reverent, taking in the scene. Fae corpses littered Hodge Street, blood pooling and running in rivulets down the pavement.

"Thank you, your Highness," I finally managed, breaking the silence and offering a slight bow of gratitude. "I don't know how you came to join us here, but I'm beyond grateful."

"The Council has rotted from the inside," she said, her voice laced with a sorrow that surprised me. I did not take her for an emotional woman, but she sounded truly regretful. "It was not supposed to be this way. I am here to right that wrong."

I bowed again, then introduced my sister to the Queen and Kallayna.

"I'm glad to see you safe," I said to Kallayna.

"Me too," she replied, then squeezed her brother's hand. Jael's eyes were misty with unshed tears.

"This war is just beginning," Queen Sheyah said now. "Dark fae are crawling through your cities like rats."

"And we've just killed the biggest rat of them all," I said.

The Queen nodded. "Orendiel should not have risen to such heights unnoticed. Like the Council's darkness, I simply refused to see it. I assure you, that will not happen again."

I nodded, knowing she meant every word.

Gathering her children at her side, the Queen led them back toward the main battle, leaving me a moment alone with my sister.

"The fae gear looks kind of badass on you," I said.

"I know, right?" Elena started to laugh, but her smile quickly fell, her face crumpling into a look of abject horror as the events of the last few moments finally caught up with her.

She glanced down at her bloody hands and gasped, and I gathered her into my arms, rubbing her back, whispering promises into her hair like I'd done so many times before.

But this time, when I told her the worst was over, when I told her we'd survive this, when I told her I *knew* we'd be okay, I wasn't feeding her platitudes or trying to find the right words to make up for past mistakes.

I was laying the foundation for our future. For our family.

And this time, when her tears finally dried and she'd come back to herself, she looked up into my eyes and smiled, saying the words that for two decades, I hadn't even realized I'd needed to hear.

"I love you, Meelo. Just so you know."

THIRTY-ONE

GRAY

The instant I was back in the crush of the battle, I found Dirty Beard, shouting orders at his hunters to attack the triage area Liam had set up.

Grabbing Darius along the way, I sped toward the group, both of us barreling into them at top speed, knocking them down like bowling pins. I pinned one to the ground, baring my fangs and tearing out his throat.

The touch of his foul blood on my lips sparked an ancient instinct, and this time, rather than repressing it, I welcomed the bloodlust, letting it fuel me. I destroyed two more filthy hunters in the same manner, looking up just in time to see Darius tearing into another.

In minutes, we cleared through the lot of them, leaving only Phillip alive, gaping at us with wide eyes.

He turned to bolt out of there, but Phillip and I?

We were just beginning.

You no longer need your weapon, Phillip Reese. Lower your

*arm, and surrender it to the woman standing before you. She will
know what to do.*

I focused my will and intent on sending him that
message, my influence pulsing through his mind, already
making him question his own instincts.

He turned back around slowly, confused, as if he'd just
run into a room and forgotten what for.

*That's it. Nice and easy. That weapon is dangerous, Phillip.
It's best to turn it over.*

Phillip nodded, then finally handed over the weapon,
and I shoved it into the back of my waistband.

In his cloudy haze, Phillip had lost all common sense,
and now he allowed Darius to approach him, totally
unchallenged.

Without ceremony, Darius drove a fae sword into the
man's gut, bringing the bastard to his knees.

But Phillip wasn't dead yet. Just bleeding.

Darius yanked out the sword and lifted it overhead,
intending to finish the job with a clean swipe—a quick and
painless decapitation.

But *this* job was mine, and there would be nothing quick
or painless about it.

That was a promise.

I glanced up at my vampire, our gazes locked in a fierce
battle of wills. Logically, I knew it didn't matter who killed
Phillip, or any of our enemies, so long as it got done and we
stopped their ultimate plans.

But I couldn't let Darius take the man who'd murdered
my mother. Who'd set our home on fire, trying to burn me

down inside. Who'd shot the man I love with a devil's trap his own twisted son had invented.

Darius read my thoughts, finally lowering his sword. "Whatever you need to do, Gray, make it quick."

I nodded. My mouth was already full of hunter blood, but there was another whose blood I'd taste tonight. Another whose blood needed to be spilled by my hand.

I knelt down beside Phillip and sank my fangs into his neck, taking exactly what I needed—not a drop more.

Phillip choked and sputtered, his body failing.

"Are you afraid?" I asked him.

No response.

I leaned in close, whispering in his ear. "Good. You should be." Then, glancing up at Darius, "I'll be right back."

The blue runes carved into the gates of the Shadowrealm pulsed brightly, its stone archway looming overhead. Here in my realm, the night sky was cloudless, glittering with stars.

It seemed fitting that he would die here—die by my hand, by my power. Die in a place he and all hunters feared —a place of a witch's true power.

"Do it," he hissed, kneeling before the rune gate, writhing beneath my grip on his shoulder. But his efforts were weak. He'd already lost too much blood. All he had now were his nasty words, his filthy lies.

He was going to choke on them.

"Do it!" he tried again, but I shook my head, a sense of rightness and calm washing over me.

This man, if I could even bring myself to call him that, had murdered my mother. I was also holding him at least partly accountable for Sophie's death, considering that his passionate hatred of witches ultimately drove his son mad. Phillip's torments had set Jonathan on a fruitless, lifelong quest to prove himself by any means necessary.

"You cut my mother's throat," I said plainly, "and you set our home on fire."

"Your mother was the devil's whore," he spat, "just like you."

Ignoring this, I said, "I watched her blood spill. I watched her bones turn to ash. I pissed myself waiting for you to come back and light me on fire next, but you never did."

"That woman needed to burn, and *you* will, too. Maybe not tonight, but soon enough."

"For more than a decade," I continued, still calm, still serene, "I've seen that moment in my nightmares, in my waking hours, in the bitter darkness. It took me years to accept that it wasn't my fault. That there was nothing I could've done to save her, just as there's nothing I can do now to bring her back. But there *is* something I can do to get that image out of my mind—for a little while, at least."

Phillip coughed up blood, but his eyes still burned with vicious hatred. "How do you plan to do that, sorceress?"

I smiled.

Then I removed the dagger from my boot, grabbed a fistful of his hair, and cut his throat. Not too deep. More of a nick, just like Ronan had shown me how to do. It was an art, really, getting it just right. Just deep enough to watch his artery pump out his blood, slow and steady, but not so deep he bled out too quickly.

I wanted him conscious for this.

Phillip growled at the fresh pain, his taunts quickly turning into moans of agony.

I took a step back, looking down on him and meeting his gaze.

"This is for my mother, Calla, and all the other witches you've tortured and killed. This is for Sophie, my best friend and the bravest witch I know. And this is for every witch and every woman who's ever had to hide her truth, her heart, her soul from the world because of men like you."

Then I reached into my pocket, pulled out a lighter, and lit him on fire.

There were no words for the sounds that came out of his mouth then. No words to describe the smell of his burning flesh.

From the moment I'd brought him here, I thought I'd want to watch, to wait until the flames consumed his body, until the very last smoldering ember died. I thought I'd want to spit on the ashes of his bones.

But hearing his screams? That was enough.

I took one more glance at his burning body, his twitching limbs engulfed, then turned my back on him.

And there before me, gaping at the burning mass of the former king of the hunters, was his son.

Half beast, half something else entirely, the hunter formerly known as Jonathan dragged himself closer, his eyes full of inexplicable agony.

He fell to the ground before the fire, keening, the sound making the hairs on the back of my neck stand on end.

That Jonathan would grieve for the man who'd ruined him was a testament to the power of manipulation, the weaponization of love by those completely incapable of feeling it.

It was tragic. Logically, I knew that. And maybe there was a time when I would've felt bad at how things had ended for them. For Jonathan, the first boy I'd ever loved.

But I had no compassion left for the Reese family. The best I could offer Jonathan now was a quick death. And this time, I'd be sure it stuck.

"You're the last of your line, hunter," I said to his back. "And this is the end of yours."

Jonathan didn't move. I grabbed his head and twisted hard. Fast. Bone snapped, but a broken neck was only a setback for Jonathan. He was, after all, a vampire now, however mutated.

I retrieved the sword from my back. Gripping it tightly, I swung hard and true, decapitating him instantly.

As Jonathan's blood dripped from my blade, I watched just long enough for the flames to lick across the grass and catch his body, swallowing him in the inferno, the blaze burning father and son out of existence.

Feeling lighter than I had in years, I walked back along my path, taking in the whole of my realm—the black skeleton trees, silver eyes glittering from the branches. The scents of lilac and lavender. The rolling meadow, and the lake that seemed to appear and disappear at will.

I loved this place. It had brought me back to my magic when I was certain I'd never feel its warm touch again.

But now, it was time to say goodbye.

I sat down on the path, digging my fingers into the dirt, and closed my eyes, slowly releasing my hold, slowly letting it go.

When I opened my eyes, I was back on the material plane with Darius, right where I'd left him. It was clear that only moments had passed here, just as I'd intended.

He pulled me into his arms, pressing a kiss to the top of my head.

"Ronan?" I asked. "Have you seen him?"

Darius shook his head. "Let's go find him, shall we?"

We headed back to the side of the street where another skirmish had broken out, weaving through a cluster of witches and hybrids, helping them take out the last few enemy shifters.

We dispatched them quickly, and I was ready to be on my way again. But a flash of movement in the shadows in the alley beside us caught my eye, and I turned just in time to see her.

Alive. In person. Real.

The woman who'd once called herself my mother.

Her eyes locked on mine, gleaming with pure, unadulterated hatred.

"You *die*, Shadowborn filth," she announced.

But in that terrible, soul-wrenching instant, I realized it wasn't me she was after tonight. Not yet, anyway.

She charged toward us in a blur, plucking a witch from the group and sinking her fangs into her neck. It was over in an instant. She dropped the witch like a rag doll, sparing me a quick, bloodstained smile before blurring out of sight.

My heart shattered, exploding in a million tiny shards inside my chest.

I couldn't feel my legs, my lungs, my face. Nothing was working. Nothing would ever work properly again.

Because the witch lying broken on the street, blood leaking from her artery as she sputtered and gasped for her final breaths, was Reva.

THIRTY-TWO

LIAM

Darius charged after Trinity, disappearing around the corner as Gray dropped to her knees beside us.

Her heartbreak mirrored my own, and as she wept for the child that'd become like a fourth sister to her, I felt the weight of her impending loss bearing down on us both.

It stole the very breath from my lungs.

"I love you, Gray," Reva choked out. "You're... You're my sister in all the ways that... that count."

"Reva, don't talk." Gray held the girl's hands, pressing them to her heart as if she could bring Reva back from the brink with the force of her love alone. "Save your strength. We'll fix this. We have to fix this."

"It's too late," Reva said. "Don't—"

"If you say I'm your sister, then you have to listen to what I say," Gray snapped. "And right now, I say it *isn't* too late." She scanned the street in both directions, frantic.

"Damn it. Where is McKenna? We need healing, now. Liam, find—"

"Gray, I… I need to talk to Liam alone." Reva's voice was faint, but her eyes were calm and clear. Resigned.

"Shh," Gray said. "Just be still."

"You have to let me go." A tear tracked down Reva's cheek, and Gray gasped, sensing the end was near.

"It doesn't have to be this way," Gray said. "I can… I can fix this." She closed her eyes, then shook her head, as if she were talking herself out of something terrible.

Or, more likely, *into* something terrible.

Immediately I sensed the direction of her thoughts, and I placed a hand on her shoulder, bringing her back from the darkness.

"No, Gray," I said softly. Gently. "Your heart is in the right place, but you mustn't act on it."

We both knew Reva wouldn't want Gray to turn her into a vampire, or to manipulate her soul energy, even if it meant saving her life. Even as Gray's skills had improved immeasurably, there could never be a resurrection without loss.

Reva would certainly lose something—some part of herself, some memory, something crucial that made her the Reva we all knew and loved.

"I can't just leave her like this!" Gray shouted, but I saw the resignation in her eyes, and tried not to show the relief in mine.

Reva was going to die. We both knew it. All that we had left was a precious moment in which to say goodbye.

I knew from my long tenure as Death that even a single moment was more than most people got, and my heart swelled, grateful for the gift that it was. Grateful for the gift that Reva *herself* had been, shining her light into our lives, however briefly.

"We're not leaving you," Gray told her, stroking her cheek. "We'll be right here the whole time."

Reva shook her head. "I want... I need to be alone with Liam. Please, Gray."

Gray bit her lip, shaking her head, but again I saw the resignation in her eyes. She would grant Reva this last wish, despite her own wishes on the matter.

"Are you sure?" she finally asked.

Reva nodded.

Tears spilled down Gray's face, and she bent down and pressed a kiss to Reva's forehead, her shoulders shaking. I placed my hand on her back, wishing I had the power to take her pain, that I could carry it for eternity.

But I also knew that I *wouldn't* take it, even if I'd had that magic. The pain itself was a blessing; it meant that she'd truly loved Reva, and from the depths of that ache, her love would continue to bloom, blossoming anew with every shared memory, every gentle reminder.

"Find Trinity," Reva whispered. "End her."

Gray kissed her once more, sealing the promise. Then, reluctantly, she released Reva's hands and got to her feet.

Her pain fell away, leaving only a steely determination in its place.

"I need to find Trinity," she said.

"I know, Little Witch."

"Look after her," she whispered. And then she was gone, blurring around the corner in the direction Darius had gone only moments before.

The instant we were alone, Reva's brave mask evaporated, and she began to cry in earnest.

"I'm scared," she said, her eyes wide and child-like.

"Me too," I admitted. It wasn't a lie. I was terrified—terrified to lose her. Terrified Gray would never survive the pain of this death. Terrified that I'd caused so much irreparable damage to the people I'd come to love—that I should've been able to find some way to prevent this tragedy.

Terrified that when we woke up tomorrow after all the dust had settled, we'd realize what fools we'd been—how hopeless our cause really was.

But in the end, my fear was no match for my faith, and as Reva took a deep, shuddering breath, steadying herself once again, I knew she would find her path in the Shadowrealm, despite the brokenness of the natural order.

Like Gray, this one was a fighter.

"Liam, I need to tell…" She coughed once, her body going still, even as the light shone bright in her eyes. "I know. I already *know*."

In that single moment, she'd aged a lifetime, and I knew immediately what she was referring to.

"How?" I asked.

"Being Shadowborn… It explains so much. It just… Everything makes sense."

I smiled, knowing she was holding back. "That's all? You just did the math, sketched it out on a napkin, and figured it all out?"

Her eyes glinted with mischief. "Well I... I heard you talking to Gray about it." A smile touched her lips, then faded, her gaze turning serious and ancient once again.

"Yes, Reva," I said. "You are indeed Shadowborn."

There was no point in denying it, though I wished now that I'd spoken with her about it sooner. Would it have changed this outcome? Given her some other advantage, some other path?

"Then you have to do it," she said, her voice faint, but totally clear. Her body was no longer struggling, leaving her mind to focus on this last request. "You have to sac—"

"*No.*" I was resolute. Reva may have surprised me with this new direction, but my instinct to protect her was as sharp as ever.

She wanted to take on the Death mantle. To allow me to sacrifice her to that end, just as the Old One had instructed. A Shadowborn witch, they'd said. That was the only way to undo the chaos of my banishment. The curse.

"It's the only way to fix this." She blinked the snowflakes from her dark lashes, even as more continued to gather. Her eyes were bright blue in the night. Half-wild now.

"I've already accepted the terms of my punishment," I said, "and I will deal with the consequences, however terrible they are. It's not your burden to carry, little one." I touched my hand to her cheek. "I can't ask you to make such a sacrifice."

"Hello?" She rolled her eyes, her playful spark undimmed. "I'm dying. It's not much of a sacrifice."

I shook my head. She was so, so wrong. Taking on the mantle of Death was a greater burden than she could ever imagine, a fate many would find worse than experiencing death itself.

But she was undeterred. And just as she'd been able to convince Gray to leave her, now, she was already slipping in past my defenses.

"Please, Liam," she said, her voice so soft now I had to lean in close to hear it. "I had a dream about this a long time ago, before I ever met you. You appeared as a black raven, and you showed me this moment, right here. I saw the snow falling on my face from above. You said I would know what to do when the time came."

I could only stare, open-mouthed. Reva had never mentioned this to me, not in all our lessons and conversations.

"When I woke up the next morning," she continued, "it was like this great sense of purpose and belonging fell over me, and I knew. I just knew." She closed her eyes, her skin so pale she was nearly translucent. "Let me do this. For Gray. For Haley. For all of the witches who came here today. It's truly what I want. What I was meant for."

Tears rolled down her cheeks, and my own eyes blurred.

Reva sounded so much like Gray in that moment, I could only smile.

304

She was nearly gone now, but in these final moments, she had won me over.

"Are you certain?" I asked.

Reva smiled, and my heart melted, knowing it would be the last I would ever see it.

Gently I placed my hand over her eyes and bowed my head, whispering the incantation given to me by the Old One, the last and only power I'd been left with. The one I'd sworn I'd never use.

When she opened her eyes again, they were electric, holding the wisdom of a thousand stars, the depths of the ancient oceans, the timelessness of the entire universe.

She opened her mouth to speak, but I would never know her final thoughts. Her body convulsed, then shifted before my eyes, the sight as awesome as it was beautiful.

A sleek, white raven flapped its great wings, hovering before me for a single heartbeat.

Fresh tears glazed my eyes, and I blinked them away.

All at once, the snow ceased.

Reva disappeared.

And there, in the place where she'd lain dying, was a single white feather.

THIRTY-THREE

GRAY

There were no comforting words, no promises, nothing anyone could say to make this right.

Reva had been stolen from us by the very woman who'd attempted to snuff out my life when I was a baby. The woman who'd attempted to kill us all. The woman who thought she could take over *our* home, *our* country, *our* world, bending it to her will.

And now, for me, there was only darkness, powerful and all-consuming. Only hatred.

It fused with my magic, black and powerful, pushing me through the crowds of fighters in search of my sisters.

I found Haley first, and she took one look at my face and knew some serious shit was about to go down. Without a word, she followed me, and in a matter of minutes, we found Addie.

"Trinity is here," I said, sparing them the news about

Reva. They'd hear about it soon enough, but right now, I needed them to be strong. Focused.

"Where?" Addie asked, and Haley double-checked her weapons. Where seconds ago they'd been exhausted and battle-weary, my words had infused them with new life. New purpose.

Trinity was the head of the snake. And that bitch needed to go down.

I picked up on Darius's scent, and led my sisters in the direction he'd gone, hoping that he'd already found her. Hoping that he'd kept her alive.

Minutes later, we crossed the abandoned railroad yard, and found ourselves standing in front of a small cathedral, one of the few structures that seemed to have escaped the riots and battles unscathed.

"In there?" Addie asked, narrowing her eyes. "Are you sure?"

"Darius tracked her here. Come on." I led them up a set of stone steps and into the cathedral proper. The scent faded under the heavy smell of incense and candle wax, but I picked it up again quickly, following it down the aisle between rows of pews, to a small set of stairs at the back. Ronan and I had taken a historical tour here once, and now I remembered that the stairs led down to a long, underground chamber that was once used by the town's founders to hide alcohol during prohibition.

Silently, we crept down the stairs into the cold, dank tunnel below. It was deep underground, with high vaulted ceilings and pillars that stretched up to the darkness above.

Of the three of us, I was the only one who could see clearly. But there was nothing but empty darkness, a sense of gloom weighing heavier with each step.

Suddenly, I caught a fresh whiff of Darius's scent, and I darted ahead, turning down another corridor that branched off the end, my sisters close behind.

The moment I reached the end, torchlight illuminated the space, throwing eerie shadows on the wall.

No, not shadows, I realized. A vampire. *My* vampire.

"Darius!" I gasped, taking in the sight of him. He was chained to the wall, blood dripping from his mouth. Four hawthorn stakes protruded from his body. In his eyes I could read a thousand thoughts—*I'm sorry, I love you, run...*

"Gray, we need to get help," Addie said, but I knew it was already too late.

"Oh, I'm sorry," a cruel voice cooed, and I spun on my heel, coming face to face with Trinity.

"Is he yours?" she asked, stepping into the light. "You really should housebreak him, Morgan. Vampires can be rather dangerous."

Fear threatened to overwhelm me, but just as I'd had to do with Ronan, I shoved that fear into a box and locked it away inside. Darius would survive this. All of us would survive this, but only if I kept my wits.

"What do you want, Trinity?" I asked, keeping my sisters close behind me. Of the three of us, I had the most active power, so if Trinity was going to blow, I wanted her to make me the primary target.

"There's no need for hostilities, Morgan. We're all family

here. Isn't that right, Georgina?" Her eyes shifted behind me, and I glanced over my shoulder just as Georgie stumbled into the light.

Her face was pale, her eyes bloodshot. One of them was bruised. Blood crusted over a gash in her forehead, a matching wound slicing across her chin.

"What have you done to her?" I demanded.

"Oh, that? Just a little fall." She waved off my concerns. Then, to Georgie, "Georgie! Don't be rude. Come say hello to your sisters."

Inside, my magic roiled, but I kept it in check, not wanting to show my hand just yet. I needed to know Trinity's endgame.

"Trinity," I said, softer now, hoping to catch her off guard. "Really. What is it that you want? We're all here now. Just tell us."

She looked at me as if I were the dumbest person on the planet.

"*That* is what I want. For us all to be here. Together. A real family again."

I couldn't believe my ears. It was just like the shit we'd overheard in the meeting during the blood spell. She was completely delusional.

"If you wanted a family so bad," Addie piped up, "why did you try to kill us?"

Trinity pressed her lips together, hands on her hips, her eyes blazing with new fire.

Behind me, Georgie trembled.

"Why?" Addie pressed.

Why. For so long, I thought I'd wanted the answer to that question, too. I thought I'd wanted to hear her excuses. Hear her tell me why she'd tried to murder her own babies. Why she thought magic and power were more important than her children. More important than the so-called "real family" she kept espousing.

But staring into her eyes now, I saw only emptiness. Madness. Whatever my birthmother had endured in her life, it had broken her beyond redemption.

There was nothing she could say to me to convince me otherwise. No answer would eradicate the pain of what she'd done.

Raising my staff, I pointed it at her and ordered her to step back against the wall.

"What is the meaning of this aggression?" she asked, still feigning innocence, even now. When I continued to glare at her, staff raised, she rolled her eyes and said, "Oh, for the love of all that is wicked."

She snapped her fingers, and Georgie let out a small yelp.

Seconds later, shapes emerged from the darkness behind Trinity.

Shifters. Hybrids. The same awful monsters we'd fought in the crypts.

"Georgie!" I shouted. "Get back!" I had no idea whether she could fight, but something told me Trinity hadn't trained her to defend herself.

Haley, Addie, and I sprang into action, meeting the monsters in the center of the chamber. I blurred out of their reach, drawing upon my magic and the power of my staff to take down two in a single shot.

"Gray! Help!" Haley shouted, and I was by her side in an instant, launching myself at the beast, knocking him to the floor just before he sank his fangs into her throat. I dropped my staff and grabbed the sword at my back, taking his head clean off before he could even get to his feet.

There were about a dozen of them, but there was no way they were touching my sisters. No way they were touching Darius again. Clearly, my mother preferred not to fight her own battles; she'd much rather use her vampire power on teenaged girls.

The thought of Reva brought tears to my eyes, but no. I wouldn't go down that road. Not yet.

Fueled by rage and adrenaline and magic and hatred, I whirled through the chamber, decimating my birthmother's army in a bloody, chaotic battle that left me exhausted, but ultimately, victorious.

When the last hybrid dropped to his knees, I cut off his head, sending an arc of blood splattering across my mother's face.

"I gave birth to you!" she shouted, as if that had any meaning to me now. I raised my staff, ready for whatever she decided to throw at me next.

Movement in the shadow of the first chamber, and from the corner of my eye, I saw four figures charge forth out of the darkness.

Not hybrids. Not rogue vamps. Not fae soldiers.

Just rebels.

Liam.

Emilio.

Asher.

Sunshine and Sparkle.

And then, bringing up the rear, with demon-black eyes and a seriously pissed off scowl, Ronan.

He was alive. He was okay.

And they were all here.

Hope surged anew.

I glared at Trinity, the magic inside me so desperate for a target, it singed my fingertips. "In case you haven't noticed, *bitch*, I've been reborn."

Without another thought, I unleashed my magic through the staff, slamming a bolt of energy into the column closest to her, bringing down a pile of blasted concrete. It barely missed her head, but her lower body was completely pinned.

"Georgie!" she shouted. "Do something!"

But Georgie was looking at me. At Addie. At Haley. After a beat, she finally smiled, her eyes glazing with tears. She knew us. She *felt* us.

Cutting her gaze back to Trinity, she shook her head, finding her voice. "You're on your own now, you crazy bitch."

"You can't mean that!" Trinity shouted.

Saying nothing, Georgie came and stood beside me, her arms folded over her chest. As far as Trinity was concerned, Georgie wasn't budging.

Relief washed over me in waves. "Sunshine," I called,

gesturing at the pile of rubble. "Sparkle."

The hounds charged forward, taking point on each side of Trinity, growling in warning. Vampire strength or not, that woman wasn't going *anywhere*.

I raised my staff, pointing it at her face. "You've caused enough damage in your lifetime to last a thousand eternities. You're done now. It's over."

"Kill me, then!" Trinity shouted, completely unraveling. "If I can't be with my babies, then just kill me!"

Her eyes filled with fear, with hatred, with a self-loathing so endless it nearly sucked me down with her. Trinity truly wanted to die.

But I wouldn't kill her. Wouldn't give her that gift.

She had wronged us. She had robbed us of our childhood, of each other, of our chance to grow together and come into our powers. She had ushered in the destruction of the home I loved. She had killed and harmed people I cared about. She had masterminded a plot to eradicate most of the world's witches and supernaturals and humans alike.

She was pure evil. A monster in the truest sense.

When I looked into her eyes, I felt nothing now. Not even a vague recognition, not even a flicker of compassion or regret.

She deserved to die.

But I could not—*would* not give her that escape.

I set down my staff. Stripped off my sword and my daggers.

After all the blood I'd spilled tonight, I was done killing.

It was time to stand with my sisters. It was time for the four to rise.

Instinctively, we all joined hands, with Georgie on my right, her grip warm and solid inside mine, her smile broad, her eyes determined.

Sisters.

Reunited.

Rejoined.

All of us had so much catching up to do, so much to reflect on and plan for, to laugh and cry, to learn and get to know each other. But that would come later. I knew it now with a certainty that wouldn't be broken.

For now, we had other business to finish.

As the guys helped Darius down and removed the hawthorn stakes, my sisters and I flowed into a seamless chant, our unique magics combining into a powerful spell.

"Bane of Silver, blood of fae
We call upon your aid today
The powers she's stolen, the powers she's schemed
Reveal what is real, and not what is seemed
Above and below, by stars, moon, and sun
We bind her eternally, as four become one."

"What are you doing?" Trinity seethed, her eyes wide with fear and revulsion. "I'll kill you! I'll kill each and every last one of you! The legacy is mine. It was always mine!"

Her eyes bulged from her face, blood pooling in the corners of her mouth, but my sisters and I were undeterred.

We repeated the spell, chanting until our voices were hoarse, and soon other voices chimed in. The witches we'd fought with in the streets had followed the guys here, and now they all gathered behind us, lending their voices to our chorus.

Deirdre was at the front of the group, her eyes shining with pride. With love.

I looked to her and nodded, making the tiniest space in my heart for forgiveness. Not today, but someday.

Every witch in the room was chanting the spell, slowly leaching the stolen power from Trinity's body, binding her so that she could never again hurt another soul.

And in that moment of complete solidarity, I realized that this was it. What it was always supposed to be.

It wasn't our weapons or our fighting skills or even our magic. It was our loyalty. Our love. Our friendship. The bond of sisterhood that would never again be broken—not by a twisted hunter, not by minions driven mad by someone else's cause. Not by words or fire or blade.

I felt it in my fucking heart, my bones, all of me. *This* was the fruition of the Silversbane Prophecy, the four swords rising as one, uniting the others to overcome our enemies.

It wasn't about dominating or saving or asserting our will through sheer force.

It was about coming together.

It was, I realized now, about forging a new path forward —many new paths, in whichever direction each witch chose for herself.

When the spell was completed, when we'd tapped almost all of our magic, my sisters and I finally unclasped hands.

It was done.

Trinity sat motionless, bloody tears tracking through the makeup and grime on her face.

The witch was all out of words. All out of power. All out of hope.

Turning to Ronan, I placed my hand against his chest, grateful to feel the steady beat of his heart once more.

Then I nodded, steeling myself for what came next.

"It's time," I said. "Summon him."

THIRTY-FOUR

GRAY

"Where is she?" Sebastian's voice slithered into my ears, and this time, I didn't bother to hide my disgust.

Moonlight filtered in through the stained glass windows on the main level of the cathedral. I stepped into the colored light, showing myself.

Standing on the altar fifteen feet in front of me, the Prince of Hell spread his arms and smiled wide, a greeting that normally would've sent chills skittering down my spine.

But tonight, everything had changed. Tonight, I was in charge.

"Ah, Silversbane," he said. "For a moment there, I thought you were going to stand me up."

"I've told you a hundred times, Sebastian. I don't back out of my promises." I took a few steps closer. "But you? You're not exactly a model business partner, are you?"

At this, he narrowed his beady eyes.

"You've made us bow," I said. "You've made us beg. And for centuries, my friends and I have done just that."

His faux-friendly demeanor was all but gone, and when he spoke again, there was ice in his voice. "As you should, witch. I am the Prince of Hell—a fact you seem to keep forgetting."

"Oh, I remember that fact, Sebastian. But now that you mention it, there is something I *had* forgotten until just this very minute."

He coughed out a laugh. "What's that?"

"At the end of the day, you're still a demon, *Prince*." I raised the gun and pulled the trigger, hitting him in the shoulder. His greasy smile evaporated as he stumbled back-ward, crashing against the wall at the back of the alter, sliding down to the floor.

I looked at the gun in my hand and smiled. It was nothing if not efficient. Before Sebastian could even find the words to sputter at me, the devil's trap was already working its way into his bloodstream.

I took aim again, fired off another round. It hit his other shoulder.

"No wonder the hunters love this thing so much," I said. "Effective, right? You don't even have to be a good shot. You just... Oops!" I squeezed off another round, hitting him square in the chest. "Sorry! Sensitive trigger, I guess. Who knew?"

His eyes glowed demon red, but Sebastian could barely hold up his own head.

For the first time in our long and twisted relationship, it seemed the Prince of Hell finally knew the score.

"So that's it, then?" he raged, his words beginning to slur. "You're just going to smoke me like a stuck pig?"

"You deserve it."

"Maybe I do, maybe I don't, but are you prepared to deal with the demon who takes my place?"

I shrugged, letting him stew in the silence for a bit. Then, quickly bored of the game, I rolled my eyes and said, "Who said I wanted to kill you?"

"Kill, obliterate, what's the difference?"

"Are you always this dramatic? God, how did you get so far up the ranks with an attitude like that?" I stepped up onto the altar and crouched down in front of him, enjoying the view of his pathetic body crumpling in a heap. Meeting his gaze, I said, "I don't need to obliterate you, Sebastian. I just need you to know that I *could* have. I need you to remember it. To think about it every day for the rest of your wretched existence. For all your machinations, your tortures, your power games—at the end of the day, it was a witch who put your balls in a jar. A witch whose soul you once thought you could buy."

Sebastian lowered his eyes. He had nothing to say to that. There was nothing he *could* say.

"I'm officially taking myself off the market," I announced, getting back to my feet. "As of right now, I'm no longer for sale—for you or anyone else."

Reluctantly, painfully, he nodded.

"Say it," I ordered.

"You're… You're not for sale, Silversbane."

"Neither is Ronan."

His eyes blazed with fresh anger, but before he got another word out, I pointed the gun at his balls.

"Say it. Ronan is not for sale."

"But his parents bargained away his soul in a fair—"

"There is nothing fair about someone trading the eternal life of a child to further their own greedy ends, and you fucking know it, asshole."

Sebastian unleashed a scream of frustration, but he'd lost, and he knew it. Resigned, he could only glare at me now. "What are you asking me, witch? Be specific. You know I relish in the fine print."

"Release Ronan from his contract," I said. "From all connection to you. And just so we're clear, I'm *not* asking you." I pressed the toe of my boot against his balls, making him squirm. "I'm telling you."

Sebastian's face turned purple with anger, but eventually, he nodded. "You and Ronan are both released from your agreements. My claim on your souls is hereby relinquished."

"That wasn't so hard, was it?" I took a step backward and lowered the gun. "Hey, don't look so glum. Lucky for you, I *do* honor my own agreements."

"Trinity?" he asked, perking up.

I nodded. "But before I release her to you, and release *you* back to hell, there's one thing I need to know."

"What's that?"

"Why her?" I asked, genuinely curious. "What was so

special about Trinity's deal that you spent all these decades trying to find her?"

For a long while, I didn't think he was going to answer. But then he finally sighed, and said, "It was never about her deal, Silversbane. Trinity O'Leary murdered your father. Do you have any idea what that did to your grandmother? To know that her daughter-in-law murdered her only son? Her only child?"

My mouth hung open, my eyes wide with shock. "You wanted to bring her to justice for what she'd done to my family?"

"No. I wanted to bring her to justice to give your grandmother the peace she deserved. Sadly, I was never able to do that for her."

His voice was so human in that moment, so broken, I almost forgot he was the Prince of Hell.

"You can do that for her now," I said, allowing him a one-time moment of my compassion. "But Trinity won't do you much good if you don't survive the night."

"Speak plainly, Silversbane. I may not have that much longer to stay and chat."

"I have the power to save your life," I said, folding my arms across my chest. "But I've got some terms of my own. And no, Sebastian—I won't be negotiating."

He nodded for me to continue, helpless to do anything but.

"I expect Ronan to be fully released from his contract, as I've already mentioned. He will never again be subject to your demands. Trinity will be handed over to you to do with as you please, so long as she is never released, and never returned to the earthly realm, in any form. You will also relocate your primary place of business back to hell, also never to operate from our realm again."

"But I love Las Vegas!" he whined. "That's where—"

"Furthermore," I continued, "At a minimum of twice per year, or more if I deem necessary, you and I will meet on neutral territory to review the current conditions in both the supernatural communities as well as the demonic realms as part of an ongoing effort to maintain balance and ensure no one faction grows too strong again."

"That is a *big* ask," he said, nearly panting now. "I can't just—"

I held up my hand, cutting him off. "The hounds stay with me as well. They're no longer your possessions, but my companions."

Sebastian seethed, but he knew he had no choice. Not if he wanted to walk out of here tonight.

"And in return?" he asked. "How do you propose to spare my life, now that you've shot me full of poison?"

I saw the resignation in his eyes, and in that moment, I knew I'd finally won.

Sebastian would agree to every last one of my demands.

I was finally free of him.

I retrieved a vial of Asher's blood and a syringe from my jacket pocket, holding it before his eyes.

"What is this?" he asked.

"It's the only possible antidote for what ails you."

Hope flickered in his eyes, but then dimmed. "Possible?

You're asking me to wager my life and business and future on a mere *possibility*?"

"Nothing is guaranteed, Sebastian. In this life or the next, above or below. But you know what I've learned?" I set the vial and needle before him, then turned and walked away, leaving him with one last thought to ponder. "Some things are worth taking a chance on, aren't they?"

THIRTY-FIVE

GRAY

After the snow stopped falling, after the blood stopped running in the streets, after the wounded had been treated, after the fires stopped burning, after the final clash of swords faded into the night, I stood in the middle of the warehouse district and took stock of my people. My home.

Blackmoon Bay was ours again. Everything we'd fought for. Everything we'd finally reclaimed.

But as we'd learned time and again, nothing came without a cost.

The city we loved, the city we'd saved... It had been gutted. Rebuilding would take months. Years. Not just the physical construction, but the slow, painstaking resurrection of trust among neighbors, supernatural and human alike.

We'd lost Reva. Two witches from the Bay had been killed by hunters. A fae soldier had taken down one of

Elena's shifters—a rookie cop I'd just met last week. Bex, one of Verona's witches, was mauled to death by a hybrid shifter. And McKenna, perhaps most tragically of all, was wounded in a magical explosion caused by the Bay witches. None of them had known she was in the vicinity. By the time anyone realized she was missing, it was too late.

Every one of those souls had fought for me. For their sisters. For freedom. For all of us.

Every one of those souls was gone.

And still, the fight wasn't truly over. We'd taken out the leadership, the base, but there were still sleeper cells in other cities that would need to be eradicated.

It was so much to consider. So much to mourn.

I hadn't even begun to process these losses. To allow myself to truly feel them.

Yet now I stood before Sheyah, the Queen of the Summer Court, guardian of my soul, wondering what news would befall us next.

"Queen Sheyah," I said reverently, forcing myself to stay strong for just a little longer. Later, back in the arms of my rebels, I could fall apart. But not now. Not yet.

"You and your people have fought bravely," she said. "As I told Mr. Alvarez, I am deeply sorry that it had to come to this at all. I am especially sorry for the losses you have personally suffered."

I choked back a sob and lowered my eyes. "As am I, your Highness. Thank you for your kindness."

"I wanted you to know that I have disbanded the Fae Council. Talia and Fenlos were captured trying to leave the city. They will be escorted back to my realm as prisoners, where they will be dealt with according to our laws. The Council shall be replaced with a new group comprised of representatives from each of the supernatural races, as well as three witches. As guardians of earth's magic, we thought your people should be better represented." She paused to let it sink in, then asked the question I knew was coming next. "Would you consider serving on such a council?"

I was honored by the Queen's faith, but in truth, I had no interest in a government job. My place was here in the Bay, rebuilding my home, however long that took.

As diplomatically as I could manage, I said, "Regretfully, I must pass on the opportunity, though it is quite an honor. I'm wondering if you might consider my sister, Addie." Addie was a natural peacemaker. I knew she'd be perfect for the role, and she'd enjoy it, too.

The Queen gave a small bow of her head. "If she is willing, then it shall be our honor to have her serve."

"Thank you," I said.

At this, the queen took my hands, surprising me with her touch. "There is one more matter I wish to discuss with you, and it is one of great importance."

I nodded, my stomach fizzing. It could only be about one thing.

My soul. My eternal fate.

"I have come with a blessing from the Old One," she said, her voice taking on an official tone that was as intimidating as it was regal. In that moment, I was grateful we were on the same side.

"You, heir of Silversbane," she continued, "daughter of Darkwinter, daughter of the first witches, daughter of the night, shall not be damned."

Before I could even ask what she'd meant, she released my hands and retrieved a glowing sphere from her cloak.

I gasped. The moonglass.

Without warning, she smashed the glass on the ground, and I watched with tears in my eyes as my soul swirled before me, floating back home, filling me completely.

"Thank you," I whispered, feeling whole and right for the first time in years. In decades. "I don't know what to say. I'm…"

I trailed off, but when I looked up to meet her eyes, the Queen was already gone, leaving nothing but mist and memory in her wake.

* * *

Goodbye was the most painful word in the English language, and I'd already had to say it way too many times in this life.

Calla, the mother I loved and missed every single day.

My life in Phoenicia, the home she and I had shared there.

Sophie.

Reva.

McKenna.

All the others I had only just begun to know, their

names still fresh on my lips from the very first time I'd ever uttered them.

The accounting made my heart ache.

After everything we had endured, I thought the universe might hit the pause button, give me a chance to catch my breath. To heal my heart.

But it turns out there was one final goodbye on my horizon.

And no matter how many times she tried to explain it, my brain refused to accept her words.

"We've all made deals to keep each other safe," Haley said. We were back by the vans now, taking stock of what was left, trying to figure out accommodations for the next few nights, and she leaned against the side of the one with the tinted windows, her eyes imploring me to understand. "There was no other way."

"What are you talking about?" I asked.

"By her grace, I was able to stay and fight, Gray. To see this through with you—to fight by your side as my sister and as my best friend. And I've never felt more proud or honored. But now it's over. We did what we set out to do. And I have to pay the price for that grace."

Her grace…

Realization suddenly dawned, and I remembered Haley in the crypts, performing the blood spell that would ultimately save us from the hybrids.

The spell echoed in my memory.

Blood of hell, blood of night

I call on the darkness to show us the light
May evil and malice and violence intended
Return to its hosts uprooted, upended
Dark Goddess I bend, Dark Goddess I bow
Hear my petition, and thusly I vow
My service is yours, by blood and by blade
Until my last breath shall deem it unmade.

"You pledged her your service," I said, remembering. I closed my eyes as the word hung between us, burning through my heart.

Pledged…

"I have been called to her court to meet with her elite guard. She has an assignment for me, possibly training. I don't know the details."

"So you're just, what?" I asked. "At her beck and call?"

"That's kind of how it works. She's a goddess. I invoked her, and she heeded my call. We… We would have died otherwise."

A shadow darkened her eyes, and for the first time since I'd met her, Haley seemed to have lost her sparkle.

"I love you, Gray," she said now. "I just need you to know that."

"Then why does this feel like a permanent goodbye?"

"It's not—I promise you that. But it might be a while before I can see you again. Take care of Addie and Georgie for me, okay?"

"You aren't going to tell them?"

At this, her face crumpled, her voice dropping to a whisper. "I can't."

I hugged her close, feeling the tremble of her sobs in my arms. I tried as hard as I could to hold on tight, to make her stay, to undo the spell that had bound her to this fate.

But in the end, like so many others who'd come before her, I just had to let her go.

THIRTY-SIX

GRAY

After more time and broken hearts than we could count, my rebels and I finally returned to the place we'd once called home. The place we'd decided, somewhere between the end of the Battle for Blackmoon Bay and the showers and naps at the Kingston hotel and the long drive into these woods on the outskirts of town, to call home for good.

The safe house was neglected from our long absence and partially damaged from the storms, but it was still standing, untouched by the violence that had decimated the city.

Inside, we wandered in silence, the only sounds the click-clack of the hounds' nails against the hardwood floors as we tried to get our bearings again, each of us coping with our own pain, our own losses.

Back in one of the bedrooms, I found my old book of shadows. It was cold to the touch, no magic sparking.

I closed my eyes, a feeling of loneliness threatening to suck me out to sea.

But then a familiar scent—leather and whiskey—followed a firm touch on my shoulders.

"Don't suffer in silence, love," Darius whispered from behind, his lips brushing my ear.

Seconds later, his scent mingled with Asher's spicy cinnamon, followed by Ronan's cloves and campfire, and the woodsy vanilla that could only belong to Emilio. Liam came last, bringing with him the ocean and the memories of our first kiss.

Slowly, they coaxed me back into the living room, where Asher started a fire in the fireplace and Ronan put on some mellow music. Emilio rummaged through the kitchen, finding enough non-perishables to put together a small feast. From his old room in the basement, Darius retrieved a few bottles of fancy French wine he'd been saving for a special occasion, knowing that this moment of togetherness, of aliveness, of love was more special than any occasion we could possibly celebrate.

Tonight, there were no battles to fight. No plans to make. No enemies to track. No blood to spill. And as we sat together to enjoy our makeshift dinner, I looked around the table and knew that in that moment, all of us were grateful for this peace.

Finishing our meal, the last bottle of wine empty, we all seemed to sense the shift in energy. Wordlessly, we rose from the table and made our way to the living room, the demons moving aside the furniture, making room in front of the fireplace for the mattresses and blankets Darius and Emilio were dragging out of the bedrooms.

Until we got a proper ginormous bed, it was the only way we could all fit together comfortably. The only way we could do all the things we wanted to do.

To feel.

To love.

To be.

It was the first time I'd ever been with all of them at the same time, and though I was nervous, I was excited, too. Happy. It felt right, all of us like this. It felt like home—a reminder of everything we'd fought for.

The fire crackled and popped, bathing the room in a soft orange glow, and I looked at my men and smiled, slowly stripping out of my clothes and kneeling before the flames.

I was about to invite them to join me when Liam cleared his throat, raising his hand in an adorably awkward gesture. "I just wanted to say that I've completed my research and feel much more prepared."

"What research?" I asked, and poor Liam's cheeks turned the color of apples.

"There were some… films…" he stammered, scratching the back of his head. "It was suggested that I might watch and take notes…"

He trailed off, and I looked at the rest of the guys, trying not to laugh.

"You made him watch *porn*?" I asked.

"Made him?" Ronan said. "That's not exactly how I'd describe it."

"I can't believe you guys!"

"To be fair," Emilio said, "he did ask for our help."

I looked to Liam for confirmation.

He gave me a sheepish smile, the tips of his ears turning bright red to match his cheeks. "I thought perhaps they could direct me toward learning different... different skills."

"By watching porn?"

He ducked his head, clearly mortified. "My under-standing was that watching such... films... I thought it was tradition for males on the earthly plane to prepare for events such as these."

I glared at Asher, knowing full well he was the ring-leader in all of this. The incubus was covering his mouth, his shoulders shaking with the laugh he could barely contain. He refused to meet my eyes.

"Liam," I called, gesturing for him to disrobe and join me by the fireplace. He did as I asked, more nervous about admitting to watching porn than stripping naked in front of four other dudes. As he knelt beside me, I pulled him in for a kiss, then glanced up at Asher. "Since you boys like watching so much, that's exactly what you're going to do."

They unleashed a chorus of groans, but I was unfazed. Gazing into Liam's ancient blue eyes, I took his face between my hands, tracing the line of his jaw with my fingertips, making him shiver.

"Liam, you are amazing," I said. "The way you touched me that night... I've been fantasizing about it ever since."

"You... You have?"

I bit my lower lip, nodding.

"Thinking about you now, knowing you want to touch me again…" I grabbed his hand and guided it between my legs, letting him feel how wet I was. How turned on. How incredibly powerful his touch really was.

He let out a low moan, his fingers sliding into a perfect rhythm. It didn't matter that he was inexperienced, or that he didn't remember doing this before he became Death. He was in tune with my body on a level that went far beyond the physical, and he knew instinctively how to touch me, how to bring us both to the very brink of insanity.

"I still feel sparks when you touch me," I whispered, and he increased the pressure, hitting me just right. "So the next time you want to prepare or practice," I breathed, stealing a kiss, then pulling back, "come find me, because no matter how many so-called films you watch, there's no substitute for the real thing."

Without warning, Liam thrust deeper, his thumb brushing my clit, and I lost it, gasping as the orgasm grabbed hold of me.

Unable to stay on the sidelines another moment, the rest of the guys stripped out of their clothes in record time, joining us on our giant mattress by the fire.

I pushed Liam onto his back, sliding down to take him into my mouth, sucking him slowly, wanting him to feel every sensation. Behind me, I felt Ronan shift into position, his hands wrapping around my hips as he guided himself inside me.

It wasn't long before we all switched positions, and I

straddled Asher, taking him in deep, reaching for Emilio and Darius, stroking them as I had that night in Elena's closet.

There were so many possibilities, so many positions, so many kisses and touches and tender caresses, so many sensitive spots to explore. But this was our first night back, the first of many, and right now, I was just happy to be with them, no matter how long it took us to find our rhythm, to chase our beautiful finish.

I was on my back again, Darius's face between my thighs, Ronan teasing my nipples with his hot, wet mouth. Darius grazed my tender flesh with his fangs, and then he shifted, Liam settling in his place, sliding inside me in a deep, perfect stroke that pushed me right over the edge.

I came with a shuddering cry, a gasp, a moan of pleasure so intense and so deep, it felt like I'd traveled to another realm.

When my legs finally stopped trembling and I came back to myself, tears slid down my cheeks unbidden, but the smile on my face was big and bright, all-consuming.

This was what we'd fought for. What we'd *keep* fighting for. Love and passion and life and laughter and family—the family we chose, the family we made.

I took Emilio next, then Asher, then Darius, all of them taking turns. We carried on for hours, well into the night, until we were certain every last one of us had been satisfied multiple times and exhaustion finally set in completely.

We collapsed in a pile at the center of the mattresses, still touching each other, still sharing stories and dreams, making plans for the rest of the evening, the rest of the week, the rest of our lives.

By the glow of the fire, I closed my eyes, letting myself drift along on the warm current of their voices, their heartbeats, their laughter. A sense of pure contentment and peace washed over me, and I sent a silent prayer of thanks to the universe, to my friends, to my sisters, to my ancestors.

I was here with my rebels. I was safe. I was alive. I was loved.

And for the first time in my life, I was truly home.

THIRTY-SEVEN

GRAY

Four Months Later...

I'd never climbed a mountain at night before.

Come to think of it, I'd never climbed a mountain, period. But it was something Sophie and I had talked about doing.

Some day.

One day.

Another day.

And that day had never come.

But now, I could give her this gift, taking the Colorado trip I knew she'd always wanted to do.

Thanks to Reva's sacrifice, winter had finally released her icy grip, and spring had emerged with renewed ferocity across the United States. Here in Colorado, wildflowers had exploded across the landscape, the aspen leaves so bright green they nearly hurt to look at.

Sophie would've loved it.

Excited to reach the summit, I pushed ahead, forcing myself not to run up the mountain at vampire speed. I wanted to enjoy the view, the sights and sounds of Colorado at night.

"How is everyone holding up?" I called back, pausing at a large boulder to wait for them to catch up.

"Just... give me a moment." Liam slumped against the boulder when he reached me, one hand pressed to his chest as he tried in vain to catch his breath. "It's like... breathing through... a cocktail straw."

"Oh, it's not that bad," I teased.

"Easy for you to say, Little Witch. You don't require oxygen, of which there is precious little at this altitude." He pulled a water bottle from the pack on his back, then took a swig. "Things were so much easier when I could take avian forms."

"Do you want to turn back?" I asked.

"And take a nap," Ash said, patting Liam's back, "maybe get a little room service, have someone rub your delicate feet and—"

"Not on your life, incubus."

"That's the spirit, Spooky." Asher laughed and elbowed him in the ribs, but when we got moving again, Ash hung back, keeping Liam company the rest of the trek up.

An hour later, we were at the top, just me and the guys.

The summit of Mt. Elbert was Colorado's highest peak. At over 14,000 feet above sea level, we were standing three miles up into the sky, each of us taking a moment to ourselves to take in the vast beauty glittering before us.

It was breathtaking.

I waited until the moment felt right, and then I removed the pack from my back, retrieving the items I'd brought with me.

A letter from Haley to Sophie, that I now tucked beneath a large rock on the eastern side of the summit.

Several palm-sized stones, each one painted with Sophie's mandala designs and written with messages of love and the names of each of the witches who'd given their lives in Blackmoon Bay. Addie had helped me paint them, and now I placed them together on the southern side of the summit, whispering a few words for the ones we'd lost.

In some ways, I felt like I should be saying a few words for Reva, too. Losing her had been hard on all of us, and remembering her now sent a fresh bolt of pain through my heart. But Liam had assured us that we hadn't seen the last of her. That she'd be back in one form or another as soon as she completed her training.

Apparently, she'd given the Old One a real piece of her mind, and they were—to quote Liam—"implementing some changes for the betterment of all" in their recruiting and training process. Liam hadn't been privy to the details, but I smiled now, knowing that Reva had come into her own, trusting that she'd find a way to carve out her path, just as we all had.

Then, it was finally time.

I looked across the summit and gestured for Ronan to

join me. The other guys gathered behind us, silent and respectful.

Sophie had been Ronan's friend as much as she'd been mine, and though we still hadn't been ready to talk about her, to share the good memories, we were getting there.

And I was so, so grateful he was here with me now, helping me to finally set her free.

"Thank you," I whispered to him, and he nodded, reaching for the urn that held Sophie's remains. With each of us taking one side, we tipped the urn and scattered her ashes, watching them spin and dance in the night sky, shimmering like the stars above until they finally winked out and disappeared.

Ronan stepped back with the others to give me some space, and I let out a soft breath, but I didn't cry for her. This wasn't a goodbye. Sophie had been with me through all of it, and even if I couldn't see or hold her again, I knew she'd be with me through all the days and nights to come.

"I thought you should know," I told her, "we re-formed Bay Coven. We've got a lot more members now, including Verona, who makes the trip out every new moon for the meetings." I laughed, knowing what Sophie would say. "Yeah," I replied, as if she'd said it out loud. "I said *we*. I'm a founding member, so you finally got your wish. Crazy, right? My sisters are members, too. Addie and Georgie... You would've loved them."

I closed my eyes, reaching out for her once more, knowing I didn't need to say the words out loud anymore.

Of course she was there. She'd always be there.

Even now, I could feel her presence, her smile, her light. She lived in my heart. She lived in the ocean at Raven's Cape, as wild as it had ever been. She lived in the sky. She lived on this mountain. She lived anywhere love and light were found.

Behind me, I felt the strong, calming presence of my men washing over me, soothing me.

Asher, my fiery incubus, who'd never stop making me laugh, even as he set my insides on fire. Darius, my commanding, intense vampire, who still didn't know how to turn on his cell phone, but never failed to make me feel safe and desired. Emilio, my sweet, brownie-baking, swoon-worthy wolf shifter, strong and powerful, gentle and kind, who'd made it his mission to know and care for the softest parts of my heart. Liam, the man who'd already taught me so much, my intrepid explorer, my passionate lover, a man I couldn't wait to see the world with, to know each place through his eyes.

And Ronan, my crossroads demon finally freed, the first real man I'd ever loved. My best friend, my rock, my love, now and forever and always.

I took a deep breath of mountain air, memorizing this moment. This feeling. This peace.

With the bright moonlight soft on my face, my heart full of love and gratitude and wonder, I dashed the tears from my eyes and turned to them with a smile as broad as the horizon stretching out before us.

"Take me home, boys. I'm ready."

* * *

Thank you so much for reading the final book in the Witch's Rebels series, *Rebel Reborn*!

If you loved reading this story as much as I loved writing it, please help a girl out and **leave a review on Amazon!** Even a quick sentence or two about your favorite part can help other readers discover the book, and that makes me super happy!

If you really, *really* loved it, come hang out at our Facebook group, Sarah Piper's Sassy Witches. I'd love to see you there.

But Wait! What About Haley?

You didn't think I'd leave our girl hanging after all that crazy Dark Goddess stuff, right? No way! Haley's got her own series, The Witch's Monsters, starting with book one: Blood and Midnight.

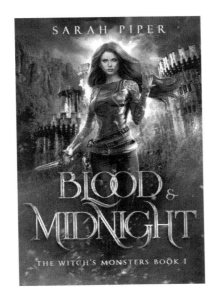

Three sexy-but-psycho monsters. One fiery, determined witch. And a high-stakes heist about to go *very* wrong...

I've made some pretty questionable choices in the name of my witchcraft—dabbling in necromancy, double-crossing vampires—but summoning the dark goddess? *That* was just plain stupid.

Now I'm in her debt, and goddesses don't exactly do payment plans. She wants the blood of the dark fae warlord of Midnight, a realm of exiles where the sun never rises and torture is a competitive sport. It's a death trap only three men have ever escaped—my newly appointed escorts.

Jax, a terrifying demon whose icy touch leaves me trem-

bling in more ways than one. Hudson, a hulking, fiercely loyal shifter hiding secrets so painful he barely speaks. And Elian, a cocky fae prick with eyes like molten silver and a heart full of vengeance—a heart that once belonged to me.

I'll do anything to settle my debts and get back home, even if it means teaming up with my infuriating ex and the other sinfully hot psychos for the most dangerous blood heist in history.

But when it comes to the cruel fae warlord, not even my monster squad can protect me…

Especially when we discover why the dark goddess *really* sent us to Midnight.

Grab your copy of Blood and Midnight now!

ORIGINS OF THE WITCH'S REBELS

I was primarily inspired to write this series by three things: my fascination with Tarot, my love of all things witchy, and my desire to see more kickass women telling stories for and about other kickass women.

I've always enjoyed books, movies, and TV shows about witches, monsters, and magic, but I never found exactly the right mix. I wanted a darker, grittier Charmed, an older Buffy, and most of all—as much as I love the brothers Winchester (who doesn't?)—I *really* wanted a Supernatural with badass bitches at the helm, hunting monsters, battling their inner demons, and of course, sexytimes. Lots and lots of sexytimes.

(Side note: there's not enough romance on Supernatural. Why is that? Give me five minutes in that writers' studio…)

Anyway, back to The Witch's Rebels. We were talking about badass bitches getting the sexytimes they deserve.

Right.

So I started plotting my own story and fleshing out the character who would eventually become our girl Gray, thinking I had it all figured out. But as I dove deeper into the writing, and I really got to know Gray, Darius, Ronan, Asher, Emilio, and Liam, I discovered a problem. A big one.

With so many strong, sexy guys in the mix, I couldn't decide which one would be the hero to win Gray's heart. I loved them all as much as she did!

I agonized over this.

It felt like the worst kind of love triangle. Er, love rhombus? Love—wait. What's the word for five of them? Pentagon! Yes, a love pentagon.

Pure torture!

But then I had my lightbulb moment. In the face of so much tragedy and danger, Gray fights hard to open herself up to love, to trust people, to earn those hard-won friendships. Her capacity for giving and receiving love expands infinitely throughout the story, so why the hell *shouldn't* she be able to share that with more than one man?

There was no reason to force her to choose.

So, she doesn't. And her story will continue!

You, dear reader, don't have to choose either—that's part of the fun of reverse harem stories like this. But if you happen to have a soft spot for a particular guy, I'd love to hear about it!

Drop me a line anytime at sarah@sarahpiperbooks.com and tell me who's winning your heart! I'll tell you mine if you tell me yours! *wink wink*

MORE BOOKS FROM SARAH PIPER!

Paranormal romance fans, I've got even more sexy books ready to heat up your bookshelf!

VAMPIRE ROYALS OF NEW YORK is a scorching paranormal romance series featuring a commanding, dirty-talking vampire king and the seductive thief who might just bring him to ruin... or become his eternal salvation. Sizzling romance, dark secrets, and hot vampires with British accents abound!

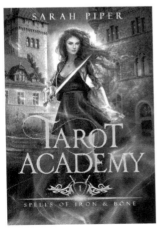

TAROT ACADEMY is a paranormal, university-aged reverse harem academy romance starring four seriously hot mages and one badass witch. Dark prophecies, unique mythology, steamy romance, strong female friendships, and plenty of supernatural thrills make this series a must-read!

ABOUT SARAH PIPER

Sarah Piper is a Kindle All-Star winning urban fantasy and paranormal romance author. Through her signature brew of dark magic, heart-pounding suspense, and steamy romance, Sarah promises a sexy, supernatural escape into a world where the magic is real, the monsters are sinfully hot, and the witches always get their magically-ever-afters.

Her works include the newly released Vampire Royals of New York series, the Tarot Academy series, and The Witch's Rebels, a fan-favorite reverse harem urban fantasy series readers have dubbed "super sexy," "imaginative and original," "off-the-walls good," and "delightfully wicked in the best ways," a quote Sarah hopes will appear on her tombstone.

Originally from New York, Sarah now makes her home in northern Colorado with her husband (though changes frequently) (the location, not the husband), where she spends her days sleeping like a vampire and her nights writing books, casting spells, gazing at the moon, playing with her ever-expanding collection of Tarot cards, binge-watching Supernatural (Team Dean!), and obsessing over the best way to brew a cup of tea.

You can find her online at SarahPiperBooks.com and in her Facebook readers group, Sarah Piper's Sassy Witches! If you're sassy, or if you need a little *more* sass in your life, or if you need more Dean Winchester gifs in your life (who doesn't?), come hang out!

Manufactured by Amazon.ca
Bolton, ON